W9-APF-694

M

This book is on loan from the
Mid York Library System

When you are finished reading, please return the book so that others may enjoy it.

The Mid York Library System is pleased to partner with **CABVI** in assisting those with special vision needs.

If you found the size of print in this book helpful, there may be other ways **CABVI** can help. Please call today toll free at **1-877-719-9996** or **(315) 797-2233.**

MID-YORK Library System
1600 Lincoln Avenue Utica, New York 13502

THE GILDED CAGE

Denise Robins

Chivers Press
Bath, England

G.K. Hall & Co.
Thorndike, Maine USA

This Large Print edition is published by Chivers Press, England, and by G.K. Hall & Co., USA.

Published in 1999 in the U.K. by arrangement with Severn House Publishers Ltd.

Published in 1999 in the U.S. by arrangement with Chivers Press Ltd.

U.K. Hardcover ISBN 0–7540–3533–6 (Chivers Large Print)
U.K. Softcover ISBN 0–7540–3534–4 (Camden Large Print)
U.S. Softcover ISBN 0–7838–0362–1 (Nightingale Series Edition)

Copyright ©. All rights reserved.

The moral right of the author has been asserted.

Originally published in different format in 1927 under the title *Love's Triumph*.

All rights reserved.

All situations in this publication are fictitious and any resemblance to living persons is purely coincidental.

The text of this Large Print edition is unabridged.
Other aspects of the book may vary from the original edition.

Set in 16 pt. New Times Roman.

Printed in Great Britain on acid-free paper.

British Library Cataloguing in Publication Data available

Library of Congress Cataloging-in-Publication Data

Robins, Denise, 1897–
The gilded cage / Denise Robins.
p. cm.
ISBN 0–7838–0362–1 (lg. print : sc : alk. paper)
1. Large type books. I. Title.
[PR6035.O554G55 1999]
823'.912—dc21 98–33781

CHAPTER ONE

Leaving behind the mean alleys, reeking slums and crowded taverns of Montmartre, passing through the commercial centre of the city of Paris, you will come to the Champs-Élysées—a great wide road that leads to a star—The Étoile. But it's a hard thing for a man to hitch his waggon to a star, as this story sets out to tell.

The Bois on this calm summer's day was the usual scene of activity. Long streams of cars passed each other; little cars, sombre cars, long, luxurious cars with bonnets that glittered in the sun. On the lake numbers of boats glided up and down, and against the blue of the water the bright frocks of the women, the gay scarlet or green of a parasol, the white flannels of the men, were like vivid splashes of colour from a painter's brush.

The Pré Catalan Café was full of fashionable people at this hour of half-past twelve. Here and there sat a group of Americans, conspicuous by their loud voices and nasal twang. Here and there an English couple sat more quietly, watching the vivid, busy scene with interest.

The little tables outside the café, overlooking the drive, were not vacant for long. Cars drove up to the main door by the dozen; couples strolled in; waiters hurried hither and thither. The hum and buzz of voices, the gay laugh of a girl mingled with the clatter of plates; the popping of corks. Here and there a stout, bearded Frenchman spreads out his legs and regards the scene with contentment, noisily gulping a great glass of iced beer. Here and there a love-sick young man drinks to his lady's eyes, with a goblet of frothing champagne.

From the interior of the café came the strains of music, and through the glass windows could be seen a few couples, dancing feverishly in spite of the hot weather.

At one table, overlooking the drive, a group of young men and two pretty girls, exquisitely dressed, were drinking champagne and listening to their host, who was holding their attention and causing a good deal of merriment by reading them his latest poem.

This young man, the perfect dude in his check suit, wide bow tie, and white spats, was René Duval—just one of those things that happen even in the best regulated family. Many long moments had Monsieur Duval spent in brushing, oiling, fixing that smooth and glossy head of hair; that upcurled moustache which did not conceal a weak, girlish mouth. With languorous grace he leaned his elbow on the table. One white, manicured hand supported his forehead, the other held up his manuscript.

'My latest poem is entitled "Purple Passion",' he was lisping. And repeated, seriously: '"Purple Passion".'

A burst of laughter greeted this. One of the other men slapped him on the back.

'Bravo, Duval! But why not purple with pink spots?'

'Oh, René, do tell us what purple passion is like? Is passion more alluring in purple than in any other colour?' giggled one of the girls.

René looked at his audience with a hurt expression on his vapid face.

'I assure you this is not a joke,' he said. 'It is very serious. I write only when I am inspired . . . Please do not laugh.'

Fresh laughter greeted this remark. René sighed and passed a silk handkerchief across his lips.

'It is lamentable, this lack of recognition of my talents,' he said. 'You choose to be ribald, my friends, but let us not forget that many geniuses go at first unrecognised by the swinish public, and—'

'Come on, René—cast your pearls before us,' interrupted the young man who had slapped him.

The girl on Duval's right took his arm and brought a pretty powdered face close to his.

'Ah, *chéri*, what a shame,' she murmured, 'to mock your genius! Come—read us your poem.'

Instantly mollified, he spread out his manuscript and squeezed the pretty arm tenderly.

'You are more beautiful than a spring morning, Camille,' he said, raising his eyes heavenwards; 'and more kind.'

Camille gave the rest of the party a wicked look from her laughing eyes, and continued to interest herself in the stupid young man. After all, he had money; gave extravagant presents. One can put up with stupidity for the sake of diamonds.

Duval began to read his poem.

'*I cry to thee from the sick aching of my wounded heart . . .*'

'"Sick aching",' interrupted Camille. '*Mon Dieu*! But how passionate.'

Such laughter now issued from the throats of the others that people at the neighbouring tables turned to stare at them curiously. Duval continued with the poem, however, waving his hand in the air, putting full dramatic force into his voice.

'Oh, come to me, fly to me,
Press thy lips against my mouth
Until I swoon with ecstasy . . .'

He paused, gulping, looked up, and saw that Camille had turned her back to him. Nobody was listening. Indignantly he stuck his monocle into his eye and was about to demand attention when he saw what had distracted his audience.

Three horses, two white and one black, had pulled up outside the Pré Catalan, and their riders were dismounting, attracting much interest from the groups at the various tables. The rider of the black horse was a young man; the other two were girls; one a vivacious brunette, the other a charming blonde—both dressed in well-fitting habits and smart felt hats.

But it was the young man who was the cynosure of all eyes as he strolled along the terrace outside the café. The moment René Duval saw him he sprang from his chair and, began to walk towards him, waving excitedly.

'Boucheron! By gad! It's Boucheron!'

The young man, who was tall and handsome, elegantly dressed in white breeches, black leather boots and a black coat, smiled and acknowledged greetings as he passed each table. It was obvious that he knew a great many people and that the whole world knew him. He walked with unconscious grace, swinging his riding-crop, his hat under his arm. The two girls with whom he had been riding had disappeared, and he was making his way to the café to secure a table.

He walked towards the main entrance and was at once surrounded by attendants, clamouring for his hat.

'Monsieur!'

'*Bonjour*, Monsieur!'

The young man disposed of his hat, said a

few words to the maître d'hôtel, who fawned upon him, rubbing both hands together, then with an indifferent glance at the couples outside, dancing on the open dance-floor, he passed through the swinging doors into the café.

Duval made his way towards him.

'Hi, Boucheron!' he called. 'Boucheron! Come and join us!'

Boucheron waved back, half-bored, half-amused, then moved towards the table by the window at which Duval's party were sitting. On his way he paused by the side of a lovely woman, who was drinking iced coffee, with a younger girl opposite her.

'Pierre!' she said, her eyes devouring him.

'Ah! How do, Yvonne?' he said, took the hand she held out to him and very gracefully kissed it. Her companion, the younger girl, also held out her hand, with a pretty blush. Boucheron pressed a light kiss upon her fingers, then moved on.

A stout, rather weather-beaten female at an adjoining table, observing this, hunched her shoulders and leaned across the table to the old woman opposite her.

'Pierre Boucheron,' she sniffed. 'I've no use for that young man at all. He's spoiled. The way the girls run after him is disgraceful. Did you see how that Yvonne Lelausseur made eyes?'

'Who is he, my dear?' demanded the older

cat, following Boucheron's graceful figure with a secret yearning she dared not express to her friend.

'Under-secretary at the Foreign Office and the idol of Paris. But I've heard shocking scandals. They say he was nobody before Comte Henri Mercereau launched him . . . however Mercereau is very distinguished and important, so one accepts his protégé . . .'

The object of discussion, meanwhile, had reached Duval's table. Room for him was at once made between the two women of the party. The pretty Camille hastily dived into her vanity bag for powder and lip-stick.

Pierre Boucheron chatted to them for a few moments, drank down a glass of champagne, then looked round the room, with dark, restless eyes.

Pierre Boucheron—under-secretary! Since he had captured the heart of the Smart Set, he had almost forgotten that he once was The Rat—an apache of 'The White Coffin' in Montmartre.

He had been called spoiled. Yes—he was spoiled and bored. Too many beautiful women sought for his favour; too many sweets had been poured into his lap, and he was sick of too much sweetness. It came naturally to him to flatter a pretty girl, to kiss a proffered hand; but he both kissed and flattered women mechanically. Every woman he met thrilled under his magnetic smile, and not one of them could thrill him. Pierre Boucheron was suffering from that very sad complaint—satiety.

René Duval, having rescued his manuscript from the party who were threatening to read it aloud in the café, dragged Boucheron a little away from the rest.

'Boucheron, my dear fellow, come and talk to me. I need your advice.'

Immediately came a chorus from the girls.

'René, you beast—you shan't take him away from us.'

Duval stuck his monocle into his eye.

'Now, now, you girls!' he lisped. 'Don't be naughty. I want Pierre to myself for a moment.'

Boucheron felt suddenly sick of the whole crowd. He rose and followed the delighted Duval to a corner table.

'What is it, Duval?' he asked wearily. 'Hurry up. I'm hungry and I want to order my lunch.'

'Be kind to me, Pierre,' said Duval in a dismal voice. 'I've been watching you come into the café. All the ladies rush for your smiles and kisses. Pierre, be a good fellow and tell me the secret of your success with the fair sex! They only laugh at me.'

Pierre shrugged his shoulders. His beautiful, clean-cut mouth, with its rather cynical curve, relaxed into a smile. He knew René Duval well, and the utter idiocy of the man could not fail to amuse, even while it irritated him.

'You run after 'em too much, my dear Duval,' he said. 'I'm fast coming to the conclusion that it's a mistake to imagine that women like men to be hunters. I am of the belief that they are born huntresses. You never give them a chance to hunt. Have you still to learn that love is a game without rules? Often a cold shoulder will carry you farther than a warm embrace.'

'What astonishing philosophy,' said Duval. 'But you must be right. They all fall for you, Pierre. I've tried everything—presents—pleading—threats to commit suicide—swoons—even a week in bed. But they only laugh at me.'

'You poor fish,' said Boucheron, smiling more broadly.

'And look—now I've sunk to this,' said Duval, thrusting his manuscript into Boucheron's hands. 'Tell me, oughtn't that to melt any woman's heart?'

Pierre began to read the poem 'Purple Passion'.

'Sick aching of my wounded heart,' . . . he quoted. Then he thrust the manuscript away, shaking his head. '*Mon Dieu*! I shall be sick if I read any more. No wonder the girls laugh at you, Duval.'

René did not answer, but stuck his monocle forlornly into his eye. The expression on his face became so pathetically puzzled and disappointed that Boucheron stopped laughing and patted him on the back.

'Cheer up, my dear fellow. Try the cold shoulder. The more I show it, the warmer they become. They're queer creatures, women, but when you know how to treat 'em, they are very simple.'

'You're the first man I've ever met who has called a woman "simple",' groaned Duval. 'To me they are more complex than a crossword puzzle.'

He turned to the interior of the café, then clutched Boucheron's arm.

'Hello, here comes a friend of yours, Pierre.'

Boucheron followed the direction he indicated, and gave a little start and frown.

'Zélie!' he muttered.

'Adorable . . . beautiful!' sighed Duval.

Zélie de Chaumet, who had just stepped out of a splendid Hispano, with a dapper man of some fifty years, dressed in grey, and carrying a grey top hat, swept through the Pré Catalan, conscious of the admiring glances thrown at her by men from all sides, and not quite so bored by them as Pierre Boucheron. For what woman ever ceases to extract pleasure from the world's approval? It is for that she tries to preserve her beauty even when she approaches old age; for that she spends hours choosing her gowns and hats and shoes.

Boucheron watched her coming without a single thrill of pleasure. She was lovely. But he was used to her loveliness. It had belonged to him; was still his for the taking. He was tired of her. He was slightly contemptuous of her. To his mind, had Zélie been a man she might have been a Receiving Officer—as a woman she took all she could get and tried for more.

She was faultlessly dressed in a gown of pale rose pleated georgette; a silk coat of the same hue, with collar and cuffs of chinchilla—thrown back from her beautiful shoulders. A black lace hat, with a daring pink ostrich feather curling down to her neck, was pulled low over her golden head. Very bright, very proud, she walked down the centre of the room, her lips, pencilled with carmine, curved in a slight, disdainful smile.

'She is superb,' Duval whispered to Boucheron. 'Look—Mercereau follows—are they going to join us, do you think?'

'I hope not,' said Pierre.

But at that moment Zélie's blue eyes, glistening between lashes which were skilfully blackened, focussed upon him. Her whole face lit up.

'Pierre—what an unexpected pleasure!' she said, advancing and holding out her hand.

Boucheron rose politely; barely touched the white fingers with his lips.

'As beautiful as ever, Zélie,' he murmured.

But his voice was cold, his whole bearing indifferent and bored, and the light vanished from Zélie de Chaumet's eyes.

CHAPTER TWO

Zélie de Chaumet loved Pierre Boucheron madly; had never ceased to love him from the day that little Odile, his sweetheart and saviour in the underworld, had died and she, Zélie, had comforted him. She had known the ecstasy of his passion even if she had never won his love. At least he had simulated love then, had been thrilled by her beauty and graces. He owed his present position to her. He had risen to the brilliant job at the Foreign Office through Comte Mercereau, whose jewels she wore and at whose expense she now lived.

'These chairs are unoccupied?' she said authoritatively, nodding towards the empty chairs by Pierre and Duval. Pierre bowed. A waiter hurried up to Zélie. She sat down at the table, and Pierre and Duval sat with her, Pierre at her side.

Comte Henri Mercereau joined the party, and with a swift, frowning glance at Boucheron sat down on the other side of Zélie. It was easy to see that he was not pleased to be done out of his tête-à-tête luncheon with Zélie. She turned to him instantly and laid a hand on his.

'You do not mind, *mon cher*? The café is so full—and this is a quiet table.'

He shrugged his shoulders and gave her a cynical smile. He was a man of more cash than consequence, who kept his soul in his trouser pocket along with his other small change. He had spent half a fortune upon Zélie and was still anxious to spend. He knew the value of money with women like Zélie de Chaumet, and he also knew that their notorious 'friendship' was one of those give and take 'affairs' in which milady reserved the entire receiving rights. He did precisely what she wanted—always. He was enormously rich and important in Paris, and he could afford to satisfy her whims. He was satisfied to buy an extravagant jewel just for the pleasure of seeing it against the whiteness of her throat or her arms. But the one thing he refused to countenance was infidelity, and he had always been jealous of Pierre Boucheron.

The head-waiter thrust a menu into the Comte's hand. He began to study it, ignoring Duval, who was trying to interest him in 'Purple Passion'.

Zélie moved her golden head near Pierre's.

'Why haven't you been to see me yet?' she asked in an undertone. 'You've neglected me shamefully.'

'I've been busy,' he said, with a look of disinterestedness which conveyed to her only too plainly his indifference.

'Too busy—to visit me, Pierre?' she asked, an angry little flush staining her cheeks.

'My dear Zélie, I have a job at the Quai d'Orsay,' he said.

'That does not say you are occupied in the evenings,' she said. 'Oh, Pierre, Pierre, you are breaking my heart.'

'Hearts do not break, my dearest Zélie,' he said, stifling a yawn.

Her hand clenched and unclenched.

'Brute . . . brute,' she muttered.

'Heaven be praised! Here is an exhibition of the cold shoulder,' Duval muttered to himself, having overheard the little scene. 'How he has the heart, I don't know. I couldn't bear to speak to a pretty woman like that.'

Pierre was not even looking at Zélie now. He was staring, for the first time with a suggestion of eagerness in his gaze, at a little group just entering the Pré Catalan.

Zélie studied his profile for a moment, bitter yearning in her eyes. He was incredibly handsome, with his pale skin, his perfect, chiselled features; straight dark brows over brown, brilliant eyes; fine head; smooth dark hair brushed straight back from the broad forehead. Nobody knew better than Zélie how charming, how utterly adorable Pierre could be when he chose to act the lover. She had seen those dark eyes melt, swim with ecstasy; had felt the passion of that beautiful, boyish mouth on hers. She was burnt up with her desire for him. Oh, the cruelty, the heart-breaking elusiveness of him!

She followed his gaze and suddenly she stiffened. Her eyes narrowed. She saw what was holding his attention. A girl! A girl surrounded by a crowd of admiring men. She was very simply dressed in white; a dainty white hat on her head. But her very simplicity singled her out from the other women in the café who indulged in more vivid and outré creations.

Boucheron regarded her intently for a moment, then turned to Duval.

'Who is that?' he asked.

'That girl in white? Ah, that is the ravishing, exquisite Madeleine, Comtesse de l'Orme,' said René in a soulful voice. 'Pardon me, my dear fellow. I must go and say a word to her. An angel, I assure you—an angel!'

'An angel,' echoed Boucheron. 'Yes, she might well be one. She has a face, an air that sets her apart from other women.'

Madeleine, Comtesse de l'Orme was very young, and not so tall, so superbly built as Zélie de Chaumet. She was of medium height, and slender; like an immature child in her white gown. But her throat and arms were exquisite, giving promise of lovely womanhood. She was very fair; not with the bright metallic fairness of Zélie's golden hair and blue eyes, but with the soft colouring of an old miniature. As she drew nearer the main entrance, Pierre, eagerly watching through the glass windows, noticed that she had a pale, camellia-like skin, fair brown hair with golden threads of light, waving under the white hat, and the most beautiful eyes he had ever seen: hazel, luminous, long-lashed, with an expression of extreme innocence. There was a complete absence of cynicism, of world-weariness about Madeleine de l'Orme which attracted Boucheron. She was like a flower—fresh—sparkling—pure. As she drew yet nearer his gaze rested on her mouth, and a look of sensuous desire came into his eyes. What a mouth . . . small, red, curving with just a hint of wistful passion to belie those innocent eyes.

Zélie watched Boucheron for a moment in silence, then, with heaving breast and clenched hands, she addressed him:

'The Comtesse de l'Orme! Which puts you out of the running, Pierre.'

He swung round and faced her, his face hard, smiling.

'And why?'

'Has my Pierre forgotten how, not long since, he was The Rat of the underworld?' she said.

Just for an instant her words cut him like a knife, as they had meant to do. He did not wish to be reminded of his life as The Rat . . . of those old, wild days in 'The White Coffin' when he had slunk about, a ready knife in his hip-pocket, scarce a sou in his pockets . . . The Rat . . . an apache, brilliant amongst his kind, but still—a Rat!

Since Odile's death, with Zélie's help and

Mercereau's money and influence, he had buried that life completely. Poor little Odile . . . he did not forget her! She had died of pneumonia, the cruel winter following his release from prison, and he adored her memory as that of a saint. But now, with the passing of years, he had put away The Rat. He was under-secretary at the Foreign Office. He was Pierre Boucheron; popular idol of Society. Nobody, nobody except Zélie and Mercereau knew from whence he had sprung.

Just for an instant he looked at Zélie as though he could kill her. Then he turned and stared through the window at Madeleine, who was coming down the terrace with a lady-chaperone, and René Duval, now at her side.

Zélie pushed away her wine and sprang to her feet.

Boucheron looked up at her half contemptuously.

'Winning hearts is just the matter of playing your cards right,' he said. 'I could win Madeleine de l'Orme if I wished, my dear Zélie.'

'Oh, I hate you, I hate you, Pierre,' she said in a sobbing breath.

He rose and took her hand. As he was about to raise it to his lips, he smiled down at her with his dark, handsome eyes.

'Just to prove to you what even a Rat can do, I wager you Madeleine de l'Orme shall be in my arms within a month from today,' he said.

Zélie snatched her hand away, her whole body shaking with rage. Boucheron bowed to her and the Comte, who bowed coldly back, then strolled to the entrance to meet Madeleine, who was just entering the café.

Zélie sat down again, her eyes full of passionate tears. The Comte glanced at her, his lips twisted.

'*Tiens*! You are easily distressed by your ex-apache lover,' he remarked.

Zélie made a gesture of exasperation.

'Don't forget, *chérie*,' continued the Comte in a sarcastic voice, 'that I took him from the gutter and made him what he is today. But I'll send him back if I have much more trouble with him.'

Zélie looked at him with an expression of supreme contempt.

'On the contrary,' she said, 'you will use your influence to get our brilliant and popular under-secretary a much higher position.'

Mercereau fell back with an expression of amazement.

This proud, cold woman, with all her beauty and charm, could accept a snub from Pierre Boucheron, and still desire his good? It was more than Henri could understand. And what cheek, what nerve to say this to *him*.

Zélie was thinking:

'I need not worry about the de l'Orme girl. Her mother would not permit her to speak to Boucheron. He will lose his wager and return to me, crestfallen . . .'

She laughed suddenly, the derisive little laugh of a woman who is confident of herself, then leaned forward and looked into Mercereau's withered face (which resembled cracked porcelain), and pressed his hand under the table.

'*Chéri*,' she whispered. 'You are jealous. I adore you for it.'

Instantly he thawed. A look of passionate devotion entered his eyes. She could twist him round her little finger, and she knew it.

CHAPTER THREE

Pierre Boucheron on that day following his first glimpse of Madeleine de l'Orme walked into the boudoir of René Duval's apartment, where he knew the fashionable young man was to be found, just before noon, attiring himself for the pleasures of the day.

Duval was standing before a three-fold mirror, partially dressed in trousers and fancy waistcoat of very exaggerated cut, shaped into the waist. He also wore a high wide-winged collar and cravat, and patent leather boots with white uppers. The whole room was in disorder, clothes thrown over the bed, over the chairs, the carpet strewn with articles of apparel. The atmosphere was hot and scented, and Pierre, fresh from a morning's ride, grimaced and sniffed as he entered.

'Good morning, Duval,' he said. 'I wonder you are not choked in here.'

Duval's valet was in the act of tightening the laces of his corset. With purple face and bulging eye, the fop held on to the back of a chair. When he saw Pierre's tall figure reflected in the looking-glass, he gasped out an order to the valet to let him go, sank painfully into the chair, then greeted his friend.

'My dear Boucheron ... *mon cher ami* ... welcome, ever welcome. I need your advice.'

'What—again? Don't ask me how to make the ladies love you, Duval—it's too difficult a problem,' smiled Pierre.

'No, no—it is about my moustache,' said René gravely. He leaned forward and examined the little, fair moustache over his silly mouth. The valet was about to approach him with heated tongs. 'See, this must be curled properly, Boucheron. Shall I have it curled down for a change, instead of upwards?'

'Oh, *mon Dieu*, don't ask me,' said Boucheron, lighting a cigarette. 'But why wear your moustache upside down?'

Duval fingered the moustache lovingly.

'Because it tickles the girls,' said Duval, then went off into a paroxysm of laughter at his own joke. Instantly his expression changed to one of agony. His hand had accidentally knocked the tongs out of his valet's fingers and they had touched his mouth. Tears began to gush from his eyes. He hopped out of the chair, caressing the burnt lip. '*Mon Dieu* . . . *Mon Dieu* . . . *my lip* . . . *quelle horreur*!'

The valet offered profuse apologies. Pierre roared with laughter. Duval wiped the tears from his eyes and cast a reproachful look at his friend.

'How can you be so unfeeling, Boucheron? I have got to go to Madeleine de l'Orme's garden party . . . and with a grilled lip . . . it is the most dreadful thing that has ever happened to me!'

Boucheron's smile faded. The mention of that name, Madeleine de l'Orme, reminded him of his wager with Zélie, and of the girl . . . the slender girl in her white gown, with her luminous hazel eyes, her exquisite mouth.

'Duval,' said Boucheron, 'I wish you would take me along with you.'

'Why, my dear Boucheron, I would be charmed!' Duval exclaimed. 'It is so rarely you wish to go anywhere with me. I am honoured. And you will be ravished when you see the charm, the adorable sweetness of the Comtesse.'

Pierre twisted his lips. René's superlatives, the whole attitude of the fop sickened him. But poor Duval meant well . . . and he knew Madeleine de l'Orme. It was, at the moment, the ambition of Boucheron's life to meet Madeleine. To obtain an introduction to her, he suffered a fool gladly.

'*Eh bien*,' he said lightly. 'I'll just slip back to my flat and change my clothes, then I'll join you, Duval.'

Later that day—a fair afternoon of mid-summer, when the sky was a flawless blue and Paris a city of shimmering gold in the sunlight—Pierre Boucheron drove with René Duval in the latter's car to Madeleine de l'Orme's home in Versailles—the Château Lernac.

Never had the fine old pile of that historic château looked lovelier than today silhouetted against the bright blue sky, surrounded by glorious gardens, fringed with woodlands which offered cool green shade from the heat of the sun.

Boucheron, bored though he was by parties of this kind, was forced to admit that the de l'Ormes' garden-party made a charming panorama. The white terraces were relieved by borders of flowers—blazing with vivid and varied colour. Every pathway was bordered with flowers, blue, crimson, violet, yellow. At the bottom of the garden stood a fountain, spraying cool water into the air, where the sunlight caught and dazzled it into a shower of diamonds ere it splashed back into the great stone basin.

Moving to and fro through the spacious grounds were groups of people; the lovely dresses and jewels of the women as vivid and colourful as the flowers.

'It is a heavenly sight, Boucheron,' said Duval with a sentimental sigh. 'Women and flowers . . . as delicate, as fragrant as each other.'

'Oh, dry up, you idiot,' laughed Boucheron. 'Now, whom do we know amongst all these people?'

'The girls all seem to know you,' said Duval with a touch of envy. 'Look at them—nodding and waving.'

Pierre's dark, handsome eyes roved over the scene, as he stepped out of the car and, followed by Duval, walked towards the main entrance of the château, where Madeleine's mother stood receiving her guests. Most of the women who, beside their escorts, shielded themselves from the sunlight with gay, silken parasols, turned to nod and smile at Boucheron as he passed by. It was a recognition to which he was well accustomed. He smiled and bowed with that slightly indifferent manner which added to his charm. He was extremely good to look at, in his smart grey morning suit, with a red flower in the button-hole; top hat, yellow gloves and gold-headed cane in his hands. He was a head taller than Duval, who swaggered just behind him, simpering and smiling, in the endeavour to be reflected in Boucheron's glory and receive a few of the charming smiles directed at the idol of the hour.

Boucheron bowed over the hand of the Comtesse de l'Orme. Madeleine was not to be seen. But the old Comtesse received Pierre very graciously. The foolish René was distantly related to the de l'Ormes and had known them all his life; hence any friend brought to this château by René was accepted by the family, added to which the Comtesse had heard that Boucheron was a protégé of Mercereau, that very distinguished diplomat.

Boucheron regarded Madeleine's mother with genuine approbation. That was the type of woman which never failed to please him; a gentle, exquisitely bred old lady of a bygone age, with her Dresden china face, lovely white hair; beautiful laces and jewels. A pity, thought Pierre, that that age had given place to the modern. He despised the old women who dyed their hair, painted their faces, wore short skirts and low necks. A curiously romantic streak ran through this man who had once been The Rat of the underworld. For all his apparent hardness and cynicism, he was sensitive and imaginative. In his fancy, he saw Madeleine's white-haired, gracious mother in the old court of Versailles with brocaded gown and powder and patch ... entertaining for the hapless Marie Antoinette whose glory had passed with the glory of a thousand aristocrats—victims of the blood thirsty mob.

'I am of that mob, really,' Boucheron told himself with cold irony. 'And yet I love these aristocrats . . . I try to forget that I have ever been any thing but Boucheron—their equal . . . their idol . . . their guest.'

The memory of Zélie's stinging words was reiterated in his mind.

'You are out of the running . . . you are only a Rat . . .'

But no . . . he would show her that she was wrong; that he could make any woman in France eager for his kisses . . . even Madeleine de l'Orme, who was of the first-water, whose blood was blue, whose ancestors had been royal.

'Madeleine is down at the bottom of the rosary, René,' said the old Comtesse with a gracious smile at both the young men. 'Take M. Boucheron there and introduce him to her.'

René put an arm through Boucheron's and led him through the gardens towards the rosary. Just before they reached that perfumed spot, Boucheron paused. He had caught sight of Madeleine. She was standing in the centre of a little group—all of them men who were obviously very interested in their young hostess. Pierre watched her for a moment intently. She was laughing and shaking her head, as thought the chatter of the crowd was too much for her. She was charming; but aloof. She made the men keep their distance. That pleased Pierre. She was one of the few girls he knew who could be charming without the least suggestion of coquetry.

Once again, she was distinctive by the simplicity of her dress. She wore no jewels except a necklace of pearls. But she was a lovely, slender figure in her white cloth gown, little white cape with white fox collar; a big white hat on her fair brown head.

'Well, come along, Boucheron,' said Duval impatiently.

To his amazement, Boucheron deliberately turned on his heel.

'No—I'm going to speak to Yvonne Lelasseur,' he said calmly. 'I see her over there with Madame de Giraud and her daughter.'

'But—but Madeleine,' stammered Duval.

'Later; later,' said Pierre, shrugging his shoulders. 'I am in no hurry.'

Duval raised his eyes heavenwards. The spoiled fellow! However, let him do as he wished. Duval hurried off to Madeleine.

At this moment Madeleine de l'Orme had ceased laughing and chatting and was looking across the lawn at the tall, distinguished figure of the young man in grey who was talking to the Girauds and Mlle. Lelasseur. How handsome he was, she thought frankly . . . what a head, with that jet-black hair; what a face . . . so pale, so classic . . . How gracefully he moved.

Who was he? Why had he not come to pay court to her? Madeleine was truly feminine, and she was piqued. She greeted Duval, her gaze still centred upon Boucheron.

'Who is that man, René?' she asked. 'He

came in with you.'

'Ah, that is Pierre Boucheron, under-secretary,' said Duval. 'He is a marvellous fellow, Madeleine—all the women are crazy about him.'

Madeleine's fine brows drew together in a little frown.

'Who has not heard of Pierre?' sighed Duval. 'He is as handsome as a Greek god, and so fascinating! *Mon Dieu!*'

'H'm,' said Madeleine. 'Well, why do you not bring him here and present him to me?'

'Oh, but he is *dying* to meet you!' Duval assured her. 'Literally dying to meet you. He begged to come here—just to catch a glimpse of you.'

'Oh, get along with you, René,' said Madeleine laughing. 'Go and tell him to come here.'

Duval walked with his mincing little steps to Pierre, who was now smiling down into Yvonne Lelasseur's eyes in a manner calculated to make any woman's heart beat the faster.

'Come at once, Boucheron,' he said. 'The Comtesse de l'Orme wishes you to be presented to her.'

Pierre's heart inwardly leaped. But he turned his handsome head lazily, cast a look at Madeleine, who was watching, then shrugged his shoulders.

'In a moment, Duval . . . I am engaged . . .'

René's eyes bulged. Such nerve . . . such conduct towards the most beautiful and sought-after girl in France! Was the man mad?

Madeleine saw Pierre glance at her, then turn back to Yvonne. The blood rushed to her cheeks. Her eyes gleamed with anger. His effrontery was not to be borne. She did not care how handsome or fascinating the fellow was. She would refuse to know him. All the same, her heart sank a little. She was a spoiled child . . . used to the admiration of men. Pierre Boucheron, having ignored her charms, seemed the most desirable of all men, now.

Duval pulled at Boucheron's arm.

'*Mon Dieu, mon ami*, you must really come. You cannot be so outrageous.'

Pierre turned his head again.

'Oh—ah! Of course—sorry,' he drawled. Then, with a bow to Yvonne, he accompanied Duval to the young Comtesse. Madeleine's charming mouth grew set and her big hazel eyes hardened as he came towards her. She determined to make him suffer for his indifference. As he greeted her, she tilted her head very haughtily.

'I am sorry to have dragged you from your admirers,' she said.

Boucheron bent over the small hand which she held high in the air, and answered in a bored voice:

'The admiration was all on my side, Comtesse.'

Then, with a deep bow, he turned and left her and rejoined the group of women to whom he had been chattering.

Madeleine's eyes glittered with fresh anger. How dared he! Well, she would make him suffer, somehow.

'You may take me indoors, René,' she said curtly, and went off with her small, gloved hand on Duval's arm; her thoughts full of the man who had dared show her such indifference.

Pierre saw her sweep into the château and his cynical mouth curved into a smile.

'You're rather a darling,' he reflected with amusement. 'Really, rather a darling. I've made you think, haven't I? My wager with Zélie is already half won.'

Tea was brought by the footman on to the lawn. René Duval rushed about, trying to make himself useful and to win a smile from every girl to whom he handed cakes. Pierre strolled to the chair in which Madeleine's lovely old mother was sitting.

The Comtesse looked up at the handsome young man with a kindly smile. No woman, however old or haughty, can resist masculine beauty when it is coupled with charm, and Pierre addressed her with just the suggestion of admiration, of humble courtesy in his manner which an old lady appreciated. She was charmed.

'Come and talk to me, M. Boucheron,' she

said. ‘Have you met my daughter yet?’

‘Yes, I have had the pleasure,’ said Pierre, stirring his tea. Then he added in a thoughtful voice: ‘She is very beautiful.’

‘Many think her so,’ said the mother, pleased.

‘And if I may say so, how like her mother she is!’ added Pierre.

The old lady flushed to the roots of her white hair. He was really a delightful boy.

‘That’s very charming of you, M. Boucheron,’ she said.

Boucheron began to talk politics, which he had heard was her pet subject. By the end of a quarter of an hour he had made himself very popular with her, and he knew it. It was very satisfactory and all part of his scheme. A few minutes later Madeleine appeared, between two men, and her mother beckoned to her. Madeleine answered with a smile. Then, seeing Boucheron at her mother’s side, the smile faded and a look of cold displeasure crossed her charming face.

‘Oh, the darling,’ thought Pierre. ‘I’ve piqued her vanity horribly.’

Madeleine turned her back on him. He sat forward in his chair, smiling broadly.

‘I am surprised at Madeleine—she is not usually rude,’ said the old Comtesse, who was annoyed. She beckoned to her daughter again. ‘Madeleine—come here.’

Madeleine turned and walked towards

them.

'If you want me to come, I must obey, *maman*,' she said.

Pierre met her gaze and rose, offering her his seat. She took it, without thanks. He gave a significant little bow and shrug, then moved away from mother and daughter.

'Madeleine—my dear!' protested the Comtesse. 'What has come over you? M. Boucheron has been so delightful to me—he is such a clever, entertaining young man. Why are you behaving like this?'

'I don't care for him,' said the girl.

'But he is so very handsome and charming.'

'And very conceited,' added Madeleine.

'Nonsense,' said her mother. 'I thought him very modest and nice. And he has done nothing but rave about you.'

'Rave about me!' repeated Madeleine. 'Oh, no, you must be wrong. He has scarcely spoken to me.'

'All the same, he thinks you the most beautiful girl he has ever met—he expressed warmest admiration of you.'

Madeleine's hazel eyes widened. She was mystified. Why should Boucheron have raved about her to her mother and so palpably ignored her, indeed snubbed her? He was incomprehensible. She looked across the lawn and saw him, in the midst of a crowd of women, laughing and chatting gaily. Certainly he was handsome . . . and when he smiled like that . . .

Thoroughly nettled and bewildered, she excused herself from her mother's side and walked off alone down to the rosary. There she seated herself in a favourite hiding-place . . . a little carved, stone seat surrounded by a tall hedge, and facing the fountain.

She sat there, pondering, trying to fathom Boucheron's extraordinary behaviour.

At that moment Pierre and Duval strolled down the rosary. Pierre stopped as he saw Madeleine, and quickly before she noticed them drew Duval behind the hedge. He then began to speak to Duval in a loud voice, confident that she could hear it:

'Ah, my dear Duval, have you ever wanted anything so madly that you wish you'd never seen it? Madeleine is the loveliest, most wonderful and unattainable girl I have ever seen.'

Then he peeped through the hedge like a mischievous boy; saw the look of astonishment and mystification cross Madeleine's face. He laughed softly and walked away with Duval.

CHAPTER FOUR

In Montmartre there are many café's and underground dancing haunts which are run for the pleasure of any rich American or Englishman who cares to enter them. Most of them offer sensational apache dances, very sweet champagne and a number of little cocottes with dead white faces, scarlet lips and close-cropped heads, waiting to partner any and every man who may want them—at a price.

But there is one underground café in the Quarter, well known to the apaches, to the genuine *gamins* of the slums; the haunt and hiding-place of the law-breakers. It is 'The White Coffin'.

There is one big room in that café with seven doors, coffin-shaped ... confusing to those who do not know the place intimately. There is also a sewer which runs underneath the café. All very intriguing; very useful to those who would escape from the police; very annoying to the detective hot on the track of his criminal.

'The White Coffin' is a permanent institution—like Mère Colline, the little stout, sharp-voiced woman behind the counter, with her beady, shrewd black eyes and her tolerance of much noise, much dirt, much defiance of the laws of France.

Who does not know Mère Colline? ... Who does not remember Odile, poor little Odile, who was like a white flower in all that squalor and dirt and sin, and who was the beloved of The Rat? Who does not remember Rose, America, Mou-Mou? ... They are still there, laughing, dancing, drinking, with their moments of triumph and success to balance the starvation, the heart-break and the tears.

Tonight, Mou-Mou crouched up in the coffin-opening above the dance-floor, poring over an illustrated journal which Rose had just handed to her. Mou-Mou was a little older . . . yet unchanged with her wild black eyes, her small, lithe body, her untidy mop of curls. Just at this moment there was a half pathetic, half-bitter look in her eyes. She stared at the photograph which was of a handsome young man standing beside a dainty, beautiful girl, perfectly dressed. Underneath were the words:

> 'At Longchamps. Comtesse Madeleine de l'Orme and M. Pierre Boucheron.'

Mou-Mou fingered the face of the young man tenderly, then put her lips against it. A hot tear splashed on to that photographed face, raising a blister on the smooth paper.

'Rat . . . *mon* Rat!' she murmured. 'When shall we see you again?'

Down on the dancing-floor, Rose, with a cigarette between her reddened lips, tossed her head and shouted up at Mou-Mou.

'Don't be a fool, Mou-Mou . . . to weep over that picture. I shouldn't like to admit that that dolled-up poodle-faker was once one of us.'

'Poodle-faker yourself!' retorted Mou-Mou. 'He's still The Rat at heart or he wouldn't come here as he does.'

A little group on Mou-Mou's side cheered vigorously. Rose gave a sneering laugh and placed herself on the knee of an apache who immediately put an arm around her and dropped a kiss on her plump, fair neck. She was just a little fatter, a little coarser than she had been in the days when The Rat had frequented 'The White Coffin' and she had kept herself for him. She had forgotten her old passion for him, but Mou-Mou, strange, fierce little creature, had missed The Rat intolerably and grown more fond of him with the passing of the years.

A red-haired girl joined Mou-Mou in the coffin-opening and began to laugh at Pierre Boucheron's photograph. Mou-Mou defended him with passion. The apache who was embracing Rose put her down; got up, strolled to the coffin-opening, and looked up at Mou-Mou through half-shut eyes.

'What's all this row about?' he asked.

Mou-Mou glowered down at him. She had no love for Otto, the apache, who was a Polish-Jew of the lowest type . . . a great hulking fellow with unclean, straggling hair framing a coarse, sensual face . . . a man with vice and crime written in his shifty eyes . . . a cunning, foul-mouthed bully. Not like The Rat had been . . . ah, no! For all his faults, his selfishness, The Rat had been beautiful and clean!

'Go to hell, Otto!' she said.

The red-haired girl pointed to the journal in

Mou-Mou's hand.

'See the photo of the "White Rat in the Gilded Cage",' she sneered.

Mou-Mou tried to hide the journal under her blouse, but with a sly, swift gesture, the apache reached up a hand and pulled at her arm.

'Let me go, you filthy beast,' she said, her eyes glittering.

He laughed derisively and began to pull her down from her perch. She made a sudden leap, executed a somersault, and landed on her feet, facing him. He snatched at the journal, but she clung to it fiercely.

'It is mine . . . mine . . . what do you want with it, you white-livered Jew?'

His smile faded. His eyes became slits.

'I want that photo and I'm going to have it, you little toad . . . come on, give it to me . . . or I'll break every bone in your body.'

He lunged at her. She bent her head with a lightning movement and bit at his hand, drawing blood. The others in the café regarded the scene with idle curiosity. It was one to which they were used. Mère Colline, at her desk, shook her head and said to Rose, with a shrug of the shoulders:

'Mou-Mou fighting with Otto again . . . one day he will slit her throat, the foolish girl. He has an ugly temper.'

The struggle ended in victory for the apache. He tore the journal out of Mou-Mou's hand, stared down at the face of Pierre Boucheron. Then he flung it back at the girl, bellowing with cruel laughter.

She crouched on the floor, sobbing over her prize, and nursed her bruised wrists.

Otto slouched over to the bar and ordered beer. A young man in check suit, with a hat well on the back of his oily head, called to Mou-Mou:

'*Ici, petite* . . . come and drink with me and dry your tears.'

Mou-Mou drew a hand across her eyes, walked sullenly to his table and sat down by him. She allowed him to order her a bottle of wine. But she kept the photograph of The Rat on her lap, and while she drank, chin cupped on her hand, she stared through the smoke of 'The White Coffin' at the door which led into the street as though expecting that graceful, familiar figure of Pierre to enter at any moment and turn this little hell into heaven for her. Such is the heart of woman who loves man.

Mou-Mou loathed 'The White Coffin' these days, without her Rat. She stared with black, sullen eyes around the room. Otto, the apache, with some of his evil-faced friends, hung over the soapy marble slab, chatting with Mère Colline. One or two little grisettes, cocottes of the underworld, sat at their respective tables, drinking with their unsavoury companions. The carmine lay heavily on their mouths, and their hollow cheek-bones whitened with cheap powder suggested a nervous poverty of intelligence which did not succeed in throwing a lustre over their vices.

Fragments of many languages mingled with the *argot* commonly spoken in this type of café. Now and then, when a man grew too familiar, his companion sprang at him with clawing hands shouting her fury. Now and then, to the tune of a violin, an apache swung his companion into the centre of the dusty floor and performed an agile dance, an open knife in his hand.

A little crippled boy moved painfully on his crutch up to Mou-Mou's table, and searching amongst the monkey-nut shells on the marble surface found a nut and put it into his mouth with a happy smile. He was hungry.

The young man in the check suit gave the cripple a brutal push which sent him sprawling on the ground. Instantly Mou-Mou sprang to her feet and landed a stinging blow on the young man's cheek.

'Coward, to hit a cripple child . . .' she spat at him.

Tenderly she raised the crippled boy on to his feet, gave him his crutch, and marched up to Mère Colline, her black brows drawn together in a fierce scowl.

'Mère, I am sick of this life,' she said.

'Many are sick of it, *ma gosse*,' said the woman, shrugging her plump shoulders. 'But you are growing bad-tempered, which does not help you to make the best of a bad job.'

Mou-Mou produced the crumpled, half-torn photograph of Boucheron.

'See! They sneer and jeer at him . . . at our Rat,' she said through clenched teeth. 'But not one of them is fit to lick his boots.'

'You are right,' said Mère Colline. She leaned over her desk and put her lips to Mou-Mou's ear. 'They would not abuse him as they do if they knew that the money I give them came out of his pocket,' she added.

Mou-Mou's frown deepened.

'I don't know so much, Mère,' she said. 'They are always asking where the money comes from. You tell them from a rich uncle, but one day they will discover that The Rat is the uncle—then there'll be hell to pay!'

Mère Colline raised her hands and her eyes.

'Ah, well—sufficient unto the day is the evil thereof, *mon enfant*.'

The cripple whom Mou-Mou had defended limped up to the two women.

'I am hungry,' he whined. 'Have you a centime for me, Mère?'

'Not a centime,' said Mère Colline. 'But I am expecting money from my lawyers tonight.' She added, in Mou-Mou's ear: 'When the money is short, The Rat never fails.'

Mou-Mou glanced at the main entrance to the café.

'Ah . . . if only he would come,' she said.

Otto, the apache, elbowed his way through the crowd at the bar and came face to face with Mère Colline.

'I want some money,' he said roughly.

She looked at him with her shrewd little eyes.

'Many want it, Otto. But I have none. I am expecting some from my lawyers tonight. You must wait.'

'Come, you old hag,' said Otto. 'You are hiding the money from us. Give me a few francs or . . .' he brought his brutal face close to hers, threateningly.

Mère Colline slapped him across the face.

'*Sale fourche*! I will not be bullied,' she cried.

The apache sprang at her. His fingers closed round her throat. Mou-Mou gave a little cry of fear. But almost as soon as Otto's fingers grasped Mère Colline, steel-like fingers closed about his own throat, and he released the old woman, his eyes bulging with surprise. The fingers tightened . . . tightened . . . Otto's cheeks grew purple, his tongue protruded. Then he was flung like a sack of bones on to the floor. He stared up into the cool, mocking eyes of—The Rat.

'I have caused you some inconvenience, my friend,' said The Rat, dusting his hands. 'But the next time I find your filthy fingers on Mère Colline, I will cause you even greater discomfort. In fact—I will kill you.'

The apache got up, shaking with anger and

tried to speak. But The Rat looked at him with such piercing gaze that the bully held his tongue and slunk off, muttering to himself:

'We shall see . . . I will get even with you . . . you white Rat in a gilded cage,' he snarled under his breath.

The Rat was quickly surrounded by his old friends, who were delighted to see him. His smart clothes did not embarrass them. He was the same . . . the same Rat, with his brilliant, handsome face, his friendly voice, inviting them to drink at his expense.

Rose hung on to his arm, forgetting that she had sneered at him an hour ago.

'Ah, *mon Rat*, I live again now that you are here,' she sighed.

He pinched her cheek playfully . . . dropped a light kiss on the head of another girl . . . grinned at Mère Colline, who was beaming, and who returned his grin with a significant wink. As he passed her desk, a roll of notes found their way from his fingers into her lap. The little cripple limped eagerly up, and Mère Colline passed him twenty francs. With a look of heavenly contentment, the child rubbed his stomach, and hastened to buy food and a bottle of wine. He leaned up against the wall, drinking, eating, ecstatic—no longer hungry.

The Rat watched him. His eyes met the gaze of Mère Colline, and again a significant smile passed between them. The Rat's dark eyes were contented. Never was he happier than on these few occasions when he stole down to his old haunt, drank with his old friends, and without their knowing financed half their enterprises through Mère Colline.

But Mou-Mou, who had longed for this moment, whose loyal little heart had ached for a sight of her Rat, and who had defended him through thick and thin, sat up in her coffin-opening, unnoticed by him . . . the tears streaming down her cheeks.

CHAPTER FIVE

One calm summer's night, about a week after Pierre Boucheron had visited his old friends in Montmartre, he lay on the couch in the sitting-room of his handsome apartment in the Avenue du Bois (which is just past the Arc de Triomphe at the top of the Champs-Élysées), reading a book by Marcel Proust.

It was one of Pierre's boasts that he could now read and enjoy the literature of France . . . There were two bookcases in this room, containing both classics and the best modern works. There were also volumes of philosophy; books dealing with commerce; with politics. Pierre Boucheron had not wasted his time. Here were evidences of hard study and application.

The sofa on which he lay was piled with

great satin cushions; the floor was thickly carpeted; the curtains framing the tall windows were of a rich dull gold satin. It was a luxurious room. Pierre was a sybarite. But while he indulged his body he improved his mind.

One of the tall windows was open, letting in the soft, warm air of the night. The sky blazed with stars, and down the Élysées the traffic of Paris passed to and fro with twinkling lights that moved and circled ceaselessly.

Above the roar and hum of the traffic came the sound of a gramophone from the suite below... But Pierre read on calmly, undisturbed by the music or the hundred and one sounds of the night-life which was just beginning in Paris at this hour of twelve.

Suddenly Pierre yawned, laid down the book and began to toy with the silk tassel of the mauve satin dressing-gown which he was wearing and which suited his dark, classic beauty admirably.

A woman who had been pacing up and down the room at the back of the couch came to his side, picked up the book and examined it.

The woman was Zélie de Chaumet. She wore full evening dress and had just come from the opera. She looked very beautiful, diamonds sparkling in her golden hair and on her white neck. Her sequin gown flashed and scintillated with every movement. A black velvet cloak with a huge collar of sable was fastened by a jewelled clasp about her shoulders.

Boucheron looked at her out of the corners of his eyes and yawned again.

Zélie turned over the leaves of '*Du Côté de Chez Swann*' rapidly, then put it down. Her brows were knit, her lips quivering. It was evident that she was labouring under some strong emotion.

'You find this novel much more entertaining—than you find me,' she remarked, breaking the long silence between them.

'My dear Zélie,' he said, 'I was engrossed in the book when you swept in just now. I did not expect you, and—'

'No—but I had to come,' she interrupted. 'You never come to see me.'

'There is the very excellent Henri to consider, my dear,' said Pierre, putting his hands behind his dark, smooth head. 'He would be annoyed to find you here, now, would he not?'

'That's all rubbish,' said Zélie. 'You would not consider Mercereau if you really loved me. There was a time when he did not count . . . when only I and my love mattered to you.'

Boucheron frowned. What a pity it was, he thought, that women do not realise that a man finds it objectionable to be reminded of what he has once done or said. He had been Zélie de Chaumet's lover—for a time. But that was passed and gone. She now left him unmoved. During his process of self-education he had taught himself sufficient English to read Kipling. Kipling said: 'When a man is tired, naught will bind him.' But, of course, Zélie did not read that kind of verse.

She looked down at him in silence for a moment. She was trying to retain her self-control and finding it very difficult. She was half mad with her longing for Pierre Boucheron . . . burnt up by the flame of her passion . . . and he lay there, with his hands behind his head, like a cold statue. It was a very bitter pill for Zélie de Chaumet to swallow; for she had made this man what he was today, and he was the only lover she had taken and honestly loved for love's sake alone; the only man of whom she had never grown weary. For weeks, months now, he had not been to visit her, had not given her one word, one glance to show that he remembered the wonderful days and nights they had spent together as lovers.

'Pierre,' she said, swallowing hard, 'you are taking me to the Fancy Dress Ball at the Château Lisbon on Friday, aren't you?'

Boucheron shook his head.

'But you must—you must,' said Zélie, breathing very fast.

For answer he handed her a letter which he had been using as a book-mark. She took and read it.

'My dear Pierre,

I should be very pleased if you would take Madeleine to the Fancy Dress Ball at the Château Lisbon.

Yours sincerely,
HENRIETTE DE L'ORME.'

Zélie's heart gave a twist of fear. The old Comtesse de l'Orme . . . writing in this friendly fashion to Pierre. Heavens! What progress he had made . . . how intimate he must have become with her, with Madeleine, since his introduction to the family. With hands shaking, Zélie returned the note to Boucheron.

'Pierre,' she said, trying to speak calmly, 'this farce has gone far enough. It's obvious you've won your silly bet. I'm sorry I called you a Rat at the Pré Catalan that day. Darling . . . take me to the ball . . . you will . . . you must!'

She had thrown off her cloak and was on her knees beside the couch now, dragging both his hands down from his head, and clasping them with her own. 'Pierre, you must take me,' she repeated, her voice thick with passion and jealousy. 'You *must*.'

Boucheron lay rigid, his hands lying in hers without response. A cruel expression came into his eyes.

'My dear,' he said, 'I don't allow that word "must" in any vocabulary but my own. I am taking Madeleine to the ball.'

'Madeleine . . . that stupid girl!'

'Oh, you women, you make me sick with your jealousy,' said Pierre. 'Nobody but a jealous woman would call Madeleine stupid. She is beautiful and cultured. She has infinitely more knowledge in her head than you could ever acquire.'

Zélie's eyes filled with tears.

'You intimate that I am an ill-educated fool?'

'Not at all. But you spend most of your life before your looking-glass, and Madeleine de l'Orme is interested in other subjects than her complexion or her hair, which, by the way, need no artificialities—since they are naturally beautiful. She gives quite a lot of time to intelligent reading and conversation.'

Zélie stared at him, dazed with misery. Every word he said proved to her that he was in earnest about this girl, Madeleine de l'Orme. He was in love with her. What had commenced as a silly wager had ended in a serious affair. For Zélie it was disastrous. She was almost stunned by the knowledge that the affair had gone so far.

'Pierre,' she said in a heart-rending voice, 'do you mean that you—have fallen in love with the Comtesse?'

'That,' said Pierre, 'is my business.'

'Tell me—tell me—you must tell me.'

'You are far too fond of that word "must",' he said, trying to withdraw his fingers from hers. But she held on to them desperately, and, bending her head, pressed a passionate kiss on both his wrists.

'Oh, *mon Dieu, mon Dieu*! You are killing me,' she said, her face white under its rouge, her eyes streaming with tears. 'Answer me, Pierre—do you love this girl?'

'If I do, what concern is it of yours, Zélie?'

'A great deal my concern. You were my lover before you were hers, and you belong to me.'

'Pardon me. I belong to nobody . . . save myself.'

'You belong to me,' she repeated wildly. 'You owe everything to me.'

'I owe you many things,' he said. 'But I have paid you back . . . I returned the money you loaned me the moment I began to make money of my own; I—'

'It isn't a question of money,' she broke in with a look of despair. 'I would willingly have spent all my money on you and had no return. It is you . . . your love I demand.'

'Love is a thing you cannot demand. It can only be given voluntarily.'

The cold, logical voice nearly drove her mad. Nothing is more galling to a beautiful woman than to know that her day is over . . . that the man she adores no longer cares for her, that although she might attract a hundred other men, this one man remains unstirred by her beauty or her pleading. But Zélie could not yet grasp the fact that Pierre Boucheron had entirely ceased to love her. She was too vain, and the thing seemed incredible. She used every woman's wile to cajole him; tonight she was Eve herself, tempting, offering, but, unfortunately for her, she found no yielding Adam in Pierre Boucheron who was bored by her tears and her sighs and to whom her beauty was no longer a temptation.

'For God's sake, leave me alone,' he said brutally, pushing her back from him.

'You can't stop loving me, wanting me,' she gasped. 'Pierre, you used to say I had the loveliest body in Paris . . . look . . . it is yours, still yours . . . oh, *mon Dieu, mon Dieu*, be kind to me, kiss me, love me again, Pierre.'

She threw herself across him, her arms clasping his throat convulsively. She covered his face with passionate kisses. But that handsome face was like stone; the lips she pressed were set and unresponsive; the deep, dark eyes looked back at her with a half-pitying, half-scornful expression that cut her like a whip.

'Pierre, Pierre,' she said, choking with sobs, 'don't lie there like that . . . I can't bear it . . . it will kill me. Put your arms around me, beloved, kiss me as you used to in those days when we were so happy together.'

He put his arms around her, but the gesture was mechanical and it broke her heart. She laid her flushed cheek, wet with tears, against his face.

'Pierre, forget this girl and your foolish wager. You don't really love her—it is only to win the bet—to show that you can win a Comtesse. I give in . . . I admit you can win any woman you wish, on earth. I will do anything you ask to show how sorry I am for insulting you in the Pré Catalan. What more can I say? Only forgive me . . . love me again.'

Boucheron moved restlessly and gave a weary sigh. A hysterical woman irritated him. He had been through scenes like this before. The more Zélie wept and pleaded, the colder he became. He hated a woman to make herself cheap. When Zélie de Chaumet had been proud, haughty, miles above him and he had been The Rat of the underworld he had desired her and triumphed in his wooing, his victory. But now, when he was sated, and she had become the wooer, she the humble suppliant, he no longer wanted her.

It was of Madeleine de l'Orme whom he dreamed. He had seen her many times since the garden party at the Château Lernac. Each time he had played his game skilfully . . . each time treated her with a little more eager courtesy, a little more attention. And she, at first piqued and mystified by his conduct, had become interested, more gracious in her treatment of him. It was an absorbing game and occupied most of Boucheron's time and thought. Madeleine was so exquisitely aloof and delicate . . . so exquisitely bred . . . so infinitely above him, although he had become the equal of her friends. To win the love of this pure girl seemed the one and only thing in life worth doing. He did not merely desire to win the wager with Zélie. His feelings were more honourable, more worthy than that. He wanted to kneel at Madeleine's feet and kiss her shoes, scarce presume to touch her innocent lips.

Passion without love is like the butterfly of a summer . . . brilliant, fascinating for a day . . . and then no more. Once such passion is dead, it is very dead . . . like the cold ashes of a fire which can never grow warm again. The passion Boucheron had felt for Zélie was utterly dead.

He unclasped her arms and put them gently away from him. In a vague way he was sorry for her, but he was also irritated. When pity and irritation run side by side the latter invariably wins.

'My dear Zélie, for heaven's sake calm yourself and go home,' he said. 'You are ruining that perfect face of yours with all this crying.'

She sat up, her eyes wild, her golden hair disordered. Piteously she looked down at him and read her doom in his face.

'Oh . . . *Mon Dieu* . . . *Mon Dieu*!' she said.

He sat up, his straight brows knit.

'*Mon Dieu*!' repeated Zélie in a strangled voice.

'What do you want me to do, my dear

Zélie—kiss you?' he said brutally, tired of the whole scene, and wanting to go to bed. 'I'll kiss you if you like.'

He put an arm around her, but she suddenly sprang to her feet. That he should speak to her like that . . . insult her . . . humiliate her.

She snatched her velvet cloak from the chair over which she had placed it, and, without speaking to him, ran from the room.

Pierre gained his feet.

'*Mon Dieu*!' he said, with a yawn. 'How very tiring women are when they lose their heads. Poor Zélie!'

Then he picked up the letter which Madeleine's mother had written him, and the boredom in his eyes was replaced by a look of eager passion which gave him a boyish and altogether charming expression.

'Madeleine,' he whispered. '*Mon ange*! *Mon coeur*!'

CHAPTER SIX

The fancy dress ball given by the Duchesse de Quintreville in her beautiful château on the outskirts of Paris was in aid of a new hospital for the blind. Everybody of consequence, and many people of no consequence, came to the ball. Tickets had been sold liberally to those of the public generous enough to pay a considerable sum for the pleasure of the ball. The personal guests of the Duchesse included M. Boucheron and his companion, Madeleine, Comtesse de l'Orme. But amongst those who flitted on the fringe of Society, and were admitted only because they were rich enough to buy their tickets, came Zélie de Chaumet.

Since that night when Boucheron had given her her *congé* Zélie had lived through days and nights of sheer hell . . . that little hell reserved for women in love whose passion is unrequited. White hot rage and resentment gave place to a piteous belief that she could yet win Boucheron back to her arms. He was taking Madeleine de l'Orme to the ball. She, Zélie, must also be there. She would go, looking her loveliest and best. She would make him realise the folly of this wager about Madeleine de l'Orme, force him to admit that there was no woman who would ever count in his life except herself.

Heavy-hearted, but buoyed by that one pathetic hope, Zélie prepared herself for the ball, and went to it. Hope is like a drug which temporarily deadens pain, and deceives the sufferer into the belief that when the effect of the drug has worn off the pain will have vanished.

But for Zélie de Chaumet's heart-ache there was no cure, and although hope was her narcotic tonight, she was conscious of that dull, gnawing pain which threatened to drive her mad.

Mercereau followed her into the salon, slightly bored by the idea of a carnival. He was too old to enjoy dancing. He had only brought Zélie here because she had wanted to come and he was proud of her beauty. There were few women in the room to touch her. She eclipsed them all in her magnificence. She was attired as Mrs. Siddons . . . with a powdered wig, the hair curled and dressed to great height, and the big black picture hat of the Gainsborough period. The style suited her cold, beautiful face, which was exquisitely made up; the lashes darkened; the mouth pencilled with vermilion; rouge skilfully applied to hide the pallor of her face. She was tall enough to carry off the voluminous gown of heavy gold and mauve brocade, and on her white bosom glittered jewels which Mercereau had given her and which might well be the envy of the Duchesse de Quintreville herself.

'You are superb, *ma mie*,' Mercereau whispered to her as they entered the ballroom. 'You have no need to fear any rival here.'

Zélie answered with a mechanical smile, but his flattery did not move her. Under her mask of hauteur, of defiant beauty, that intolerable pain agonised her. Her restless eyes searched the crowded room for Pierre Boucheron and for the Comtesse de l'Orme, in whose place she would have given half her fortune—if not all of it—to be tonight.

The crowd was dense, however, and it was impossible to pick out Pierre or his companion amongst all these men and women who were wearing fancy-dress. A Hungarian band, half-hidden by a bank of flowers, had commenced a popular waltz, and the shining floor became quickly covered with dancers. Pierrots, harlequins, knights and chevaliers whirled past with their ladies in their arms; gipsy-girls; ladies of the old French courts; Isolde, in search of a Tristan; Juliet awaiting her Romeo . . . two by two they flashed by. The frocks and jewels revolving thus made a veritable kaleidoscope of colour.

'Your programme, *chérie*,' said Mercereau in Zélie's ear.

She handed it to him and allowed him to scribble his initials where he would. Some other men whom she knew, a withered old millionaire (dressed like Mark Antony and unlikely ever to inspire a Cleopatra), a decadent young Duc attired as a girl; one after another they crowded around the magnificent Mrs. Siddons and begged for a dance. But although her card became covered with initials she rewarded her suitors with a bare nod and smile. She continued to search the salon with terrible intensity for Pierre and Madeleine.

The salon presented a wonderful aspect . . . a relic of the bygone magnificence of French noblemen long since in their graves. The ceiling, painted by Lemoyne, was a work of art;

illuminated by great crystal chandeliers which hung like colossal diamonds, glittering and sparkling over the crowd. The light was reflected in the round, gilt-framed mirrors between rare old Gobelin tapestries. Tonight Zélie found no enjoyment in the splendour, which at other times might have thrilled her. She drew back into the little ante-chamber through which the guests passed before reaching the ballroom, and thus escaped from the libidinous old men who were clamouring for her favours, and left a somewhat disconsolate Mercereau to deal with them. She stood silently staring through the *oeils de boeuf* (oval bull's-eye windows) through which she could see the dancers without being seen.

Pierre . . . where was Pierre?

A comic Bacchus, with enormous, padded stomach; a chaplet of roses awry over his brow, danced into the ante-chamber accompanied by a very fat Mephistopheles.

Zélie turned to them. The Bacchus greeted her with cries of joy.

'The beautiful, the ravishing Zélie!' he said, one hand over his heart, the other wiping beads of sweat from his forehead. 'Greetings!'

'Heavens!' said Zélie with a short laugh. 'It is René Duval.'

'At your service,' said Duval, and made a deep bow which nearly pitched him on his head. With his bare, knock-kneed legs and short tunic he presented a spectacle at which even Zélie in her despairing mood was forced to laugh.

'Bacchus is always welcome,' she said, returning the bow.

'A dance . . . I crave a dance,' said Duval, mincing towards her and grasping her card.

'I too,' said Mephistopheles. 'But hark!'

'Hark!' squeaked Duval, who was the echo of his friend.

There was a distant popping of corks. Mephistopheles licked his painted lips.

'Methinks I heard a sound as of some sweet bubbling brook,' said he.

Duval stared vacantly around him, pushing his wreath yet further over one eye.

'Did you?' he said.

'Bacchus, old friend, what about having one?' inquired Mephistopheles.

'One what?' asked Duval vacantly.

Mephistopheles glanced at Zélie, touched his forehead significantly, shook his head, then danced away.

René turned to Zélie.

'What did he mean, most fair and kind lady?' he asked.

'Drink . . . champagne, you idiot,' said Zélie.

Duval's eyes glistened. He returned Zélie's programme to her.

'Ah . . . then I follow, I follow,' he lisped, patting his padded stomach.

'Wait,' said Zélie, swallowing hard. 'I . . . have you seen Boucheron?'

'Boucheron? Ah, yes, with that ravishing, exquisite, perfect Madeleine de—'

'Well, well,' interrupted Zélie, clenching one jewelled hand. 'Go on—where are they, fool?'

'They were in the garden a moment ago . . . I heard Boucheron asking her to dance . . . they must be dancing.'

Zélie waited to hear no more. She turned and walked from the ante-room up a staircase that led on to a balcony overlooking the ballroom. From there she could command a perfect view of the entire salon.

The dancers were in more carnival mood now, and a thousand balloons twisted and rolled in the air, suspended from the women's wrists or tied round their partners' necks. That cloud of irridescent balls, red, blue, orange, green, obscured the dancers for a few moments from Zélie's eyes. But gradually, one after the other, the bubbles burst or drifted up to the ceiling, and she could see the faces of the dancers more clearly.

Suddenly she stiffened, and, leaning over the balcony railing, stared down with painful intensity at a couple who were now immediately below her. Pierre . . . at last. That handsome, boyish face was unmistakable. She would have known it amongst a thousand others. He was attired as Monsieur Beaucaire . . . and never had she seen him look more attractive. The close-fitting white wig; the rich white satin of his suit; the delicate lace ruffles at the wrists, the knee-breeches and black silk hose, set off the dark, graceful beauty of the man to perfection. At this moment when Zélie concentrated her attention on him, he was gazing down into Madeleine's face with a rapt, adoring expression which Zélie had never seen from him and which made her flinch as though she had been struck. He could not look at any woman like that unless he loved her.

He was waltzing, slowly, with that unconscious grace which marked him out from most other men. Zélie remembered only too well the pure pleasure of dancing with Pierre . . . just as she remembered that first night in 'The White Coffin' when she had watched him do the apache dance with one of the girls down there, and had been entranced by the sight.

And now Madeleine de l'Orme was tasting the joys of the dance in his arms . . . Madeleine was receiving the burning ardour of his gaze.

Zélie's fingers clenched so hard that the long nails pierced the soft flesh of her palm and drew blood. But she did not feel the physical pain, the mental anguish she endured was so much more acute.

She dragged her gaze from Boucheron's attractive figure to the girl with whom he danced. She was bound to admit that Madeleine was exquisite . . . Madame Pompadour, tonight . . . soft white wig framing her pale, pure face . . . dress of white and silver brocade, drawn in at the slender waist; very voluminous and long, just revealing the small silver-shod feet. The historic gown drooped off the shoulders . . . which were like 'rose-misted marble'; the slender throat and girlish arms were beautiful enough to intoxicate any man.

Zélie concentrated on the couple, fascinated yet seething with jealousy. Never before in her life had she felt so old, so haggard, so artificial as now, when she saw that immature yet exquisite young girl in Boucheron's arms. She realised how Madeleine's purity and freshness must appeal to the man who was jaded, sick of the women who flung themselves at his feet.

Zélie could not tear her gaze from them, although when she saw Madeleine smile up at Boucheron, a shy, yet radiant smile indicative of the fact that she was thrilled and happy to be with him, Zélie could have taken a revolver and shot Madeleine dead, while she danced there in the arms of Pierre.

It seemed that they could not take their eyes off each other.

Heavens! how far the affair must have gone, Zélie reflected . . . what headway Boucheron must have made. Anybody could see that the child was in love with him.

They came round below the balcony once more. Madeleine was laughing now, blushing at something which Pierre had just whispered in her ear.

Consumed by the fiercest jealousy and passion she had ever known, Zélie moved away from the balcony. She cast one anguished look over her shoulder, just in time to see Pierre guide Madeleine away from the revolving crowd, through French windows out on to the terrace. With a sob tearing her throat, the unfortunate woman followed them.

CHAPTER SEVEN

Moonlight flooded the grounds of the Château Lisbon.

The windows of the great building were like oblongs of rose-coloured light in the velvet darkness of the summer night. But out in the gardens everything was white . . . the pure cold white of moonshine. The sky throbbed with stars.

Down in the woods on the fringe of the grounds, a few nightingales burst their little brown throats with singing, and incongruously, the gay lilt of a fox-trot accompanied the song.

Pierre Boucheron, with his charming Pompadour on his arm, walked out of the hot, crowded ballroom and drew a sigh of relief as he breathed the cool air.

'*Mon Dieu*—that's better,' he said.

'Yet it was wonderful—dancing,' said Madeleine.

He looked down at her, quickly, ardently.

'You enjoyed dancing with me . . .'

'I—I—am fond of waltzing,' she said

'But with me . . . did you enjoy that dance with me?'

The pretty face blushed. He had wanted her to blush. He was never tired of seeing the shy colour flood her cheeks. He was so bored by women whose painted cheeks the coarsest joke or allusion could make no redder.

'Why—oh—yes, indeed. Monsieur,' she stammered.

'No dance for me has ever meant so much as the one we have just finished,' he said.

He meant what he said. Pierre Boucheron had flirted with women all his life; had loved one or two; had been sated almost as soon as he had been thrilled. But tonight he was not flirting. He had done with artifice, with hypocrisy, with all those unworthy factors which go to make up an *affaire pour passer le temps*. He had danced lightly on the fringe of love like a thousand others who only play at it; think of it as the game which has no rules. He had even deceived himself into thinking he loved . . . Zélie de Chaumet for instance. But with the exception of his affection for little Odile which had been real and lasting, he had never known the meaning of love until he had met Madeleine de l'Orme.

With Madeleine, he had begun badly . . . entered into his friendship with her just to win an idle wager . . . the result of an unworthy boast. But, as Robert Browning wrote, 'It is a dangerous matter to play with souls', which is a truth many learn too late. Pierre had played with Madeleine's soul and with his own, and the time was to come when he would realise the danger of it, and pay the penalty of the risk he had run. Just at the moment, however, he knew neither fear nor remorse. He was in love—madly in love for the first time in his life—and everything was forgotten except the glorious thrill of the chase . . . a chase which he intended to pursue until Madeleine was in his arms . . . as his wife.

His wife! The very thought intoxicated the man to whom matrimony had once seemed a most formidable business to be avoided by the wise bachelor. He, who had been free, independent, exulting in his freedom, laughing at his friends who wore the shackles of marriage, now sought most arduously to imprison himself in the fetters of a young girl's pure love.

For a month now he had followed her everywhere; haunted the *hôtel de l'Orme*; won the confidence of the old Comtesse; bridged the gulf of coldness and indifference which at the beginning he had thrown so cunningly between Madeleine and himself in order to waken her interest. That gulf had been forgotten by them both. What woman could resist Pierre when he chose to be charming? He had soon made Madeleine care for him; soon made her forget that he had ever appeared rude or bored. He had taken her to dances, to parties; accompanied her to the races; sent her gorgeous flowers, great boxes of chocolates; in fact, done all the things which a man does when he is in love with a woman. And she, a little dazed and a good deal thrilled by the fashion in which this idol of Paris stormed her, put up only a weak defence which soon collapsed before the strength of the invasion.

Before the end of that month Madeleine knew herself to be in love with Boucheron. But she did not let him know it. One of the very things which most bewitched Boucheron was her shyness . . . her aloofness . . . the purity of her. He stormed the citadel noisily, to begin with, but when he stood face to face with her . . . when a little of her astonishing innocence was revealed to him he fell back, abashed. For the first time in his career he was ashamed of things he had done . . . of other things left undone. He felt unworthy to touch Madeleine de l'Orme, and like most men of his experience and cynicism, wished he had kept himself for The One Woman. Nevertheless, he was too much in love to abandon his chase. What man, no matter how much in awe of a young girl's innocence, turns from her because of his past? That must be wiped out and a new, more worthy life commence. For Madeleine he would do great things, achieve honours and distinctions to lay at her feet; to prove his worship.

It never entered his head that he could fail. He was the happy philosopher which he had always been as The Rat.

He was confident of success and in his ability to keep what he had won and make himself fit to possess it. Combined with his physical passion for Madeleine was a mental adoration which brought out the more chivalrous side of his nature. Her youth, her purity, roused his protective instincts. He must take care of her. No other man's rude hands must touch her . . . for she was to Pierre like rare and delicate procelain, easily broken. And it was all part of the natural arrogance of any male being that he should imagine himself more fit to take and protect her than any other man on earth.

The impulse that moved him to Madeleine de l'Orme, however, was the finest he had known, and tonight at the Duchesse de Quintreville's ball he was determined to give himself utterly into her hands and become her lover, her slave, whatever she would make of him.

To fail, to be refused seemed inconceivable.

'Come,' he said, 'let us find a seat somewhere and talk. The night is so beautiful . . . and in the salon it is difficult for me to speak to you.'

Madeleine's heart raced. What did this mean but that Pierre Boucheron meant to tell her that he loved her? She was half-frightened, half-enraptured by the thought. She wanted to go with him; she wanted to fly from him. She would say 'Yes'. She would say 'No'. She did not know what she would say or do. But she was in the meshes of some strange enchantment on this night of moonlight and stars beside a Beaucaire whose good looks and charm would have rivalled the dead idol of France and fashion himself; and she went with him, whither he led her.

They strolled down the broad steps leading from the terrace. On either side stood six flunkeys carrying lamps of old, artistic design on long poles. The soft yellow light of the lamps was reflected in the hazel eyes of Madeleine, who leaned on the arm of Pierre. And he, gazing down into those luminous eyes, drowned in them and was happier than any human being has any right to be.

Before the terrace stood a fountain. The pale marble body of a nude, glistening nymph stretched her arms above her head in an attitude of ecstasy, face lifted to the moon. The silver water glistening in the moonlight drenched her from head to foot and fell, tangled with moonbeams, into the marble basin. The sight drew a cry of admiration from Madeleine.

'Ah! How beautiful.'

Boucheron nodded and stood still a moment, watching the fountain play. Then he looked beyond, down an avenue of green yoke-elms; of box-hedges, cunningly clipped into fantastic shapes, one a peacock, one a lady and gentleman dancing the *pavane*, one a rider on horseback with a spear. And beyond the flagged paths and the hedges tall cypress trees pointed their heads to the starry sky.

He drew a deep breath. The beauty of the château, the grounds, the night, excited and pleased him. And the warm, moving presence of the lovely girl on his arm seemed the most wonderful thing that life had to offer him. The breeze blew a fragrant curl of her hair towards him, just touching his chin, and it sent the blood rushing madly through his veins. He shut his eyes, then opened them again and smiled, a queer, secretive little smile.

'Come,' he said. 'Walk with me through the gardens . . . please!'

They began to stroll down a flagged path, illuminated by coloured, fairy-like lamps. The jewels in Pompadour's hair and on her snowy breast scintillated as she moved. Every now and then a couple passed them, arms entwined; or a stream of merry-makers, in fantastic dress, dancing, blowing their horns, laughing, shouting to each other. It was carnival! . . . Life, love, laughter, were here tonight and there was no tomorrow!

'How happy the world is,' said Madeleine.

'I did not know it could be so happy,' said Boucheron. 'Yet how long does the happiness last? How many promises will be made, how many vows taken this night . . . only to be broken . . . forgotten.'

She shivered a little, then smiled up at him.

'You are a cynic, Monsieur.'

'No. Not really. But I know the world.'

'I prefer to live in one of my own,' she said. 'It is foolish, yet it is better, for you conduct things to please yourself and shut sorrow out of it.'

'You have lived a very sheltered life,' said Pierre. 'And may you continue to live it . . . if I had my way, no sorrow, no pain, should ever come to you.'

'That is very kind, Monsieur,' she said.

They came to a slab forming a stone seat, which was sheltered by a clipped box-hedge. Boucheron drew Madeleine down upon it. Before them lay a bed of crimson roses which threw out a strong perfume. In the centre of this flower-bed stood an old faun, chipped, discoloured with age, nevertheless very attractive with his grinning, mischievous face, a reed held to his lips.

'Look how he laughs at us,' said Madeleine.

But Pierre was looking at her.

She stole a glance at him, then looked away again very quickly, frightened by the intensity of his gaze. Those dark eyes of Pierre were burning . . . on fire with his passion for her, and it made her shrink back, even while it fascinated her.

'Madeleine . . .' he said.

She did not move . . . she could not speak.

'Madeleine,' he said again.

'Monsieur . . .' she said in a half-suffocated voice.

He took one of her hands, his own hot and shaking. Her fingers were long, slender, cool, with pink polished nails; like the waxen stems of a flower against his hard brownish palm. He concentrated on those fingers. She, with heart beating fast and eyes half-closed, drew her hand away and put it up to her throat. But he seized it again, and this time spoke her name in a voice that pleaded.

'Ah, Madeleine . . .'

'Monsieur . . .' she said. 'I . . . I . . .'

'I love you,' he broke in. '*Mon Dieu*, how I love you.'

Once more she was speechless with her agitation; but she felt all the thrill of the elusive nymph who, after the delicious fear of the chase, is caught and held, a panting, willing prisoner.

Pierre crushed the soft palm of her hand against his lips. A little shiver ran through her, and she gave a soft cry.

'Oh, Monsieur . . .'

'Call me Pierre, Madeleine, for I love you,' he said. 'I implore you to love me.'

He took her other hand, and with swift, unconscious grace, knelt before her and leaned against both her hands, which were like cool white buds cupping his face. His cheeks were flushed and hot with the shame of his thoughts. Miracle of miracles! . . . that Pierre Boucheron . . . The Rat should know shame. But now that he was on his knees to this girl and yearning for her lips; now that the game which had commenced in jest had become such deadly earnest he wished to God he were more worthy to tell her of his love.

Madeleine looked down at his bent head . . . such a dark, boyish head; and she seemed to be in a state of transition . . . passing from thrilling fear to much more thrilling pride and a yearning to match with his. Behind her reserve lay the passionate woman waiting to be set free . . . and the sensation caused by Boucheron's warm face against her hands unlocked the gate of that reserve. She breathed very quickly, and her whole body trembled.

'Madeleine,' he said in a muffled voice. 'I am not worthy to love you, but I do, my darling, my most dear. Madeleine, for God's sake, tell me that you will not send me away.'

Now he looked up at her and she met his gaze. His face was beautiful in the white heat of his ardour and humility. She tried to withdraw her hands.

'I do not know . . . Monsieur . . . I do not know . . .'

'Yes, yes, you must know . . . you must tell me. Call me Pierre. I am yours . . . I am at your feet. I worship you. Take me, Madeleine . . .

break me . . . make of me what you will . . . only take my love and give me your pity, if you cannot love me in return.'

He did not wait for her answer. He went on pouring out his worship and his longing. He covered her hands with kisses, alternately pleading with her, adoring her. He seized one of her small feet . . . kissed the little silver shoe . . . the instep . . . then her hands again.

'*Je t'aime . . . je t'aime . . .*' he kept on saying. 'Oh, Madeleine . . . beloved . . . give me your pity . . . only do not send me away!'

He was torn with his love, burnt up with the intensity of it. His eyes were burnt up in his white, young face. He was anguished in case she should refuse him, find him distasteful to her. He was more terrified than he had believed it possible to be, in case he had learned this wonderful thing called Love—too late.

What woman, older, more experienced than Madeleine de l'Orme could have resisted such a passionate appeal, such adoration . . . and from an extremely handsome man, with such a reputation as Boucheron possessed? He was supposed to be tired of women . . . bored with beauty . . . it was said that he never knelt to any woman, but that they knelt willingly to him. Madeleine had heard all these things from René Duval, from her girlfriends who were acquainted with Boucheron. It was a great wonder and glory to her that he should kneel at her feet and worship her in this way. His humility gave her confidence, even while his eager kisses on her hands—such kisses as no man had ever dared lay on those hands—roused her curiosity. She was so modest; she had lived so sheltered an existence . . . but she had read . . . she had thought . . . she had dreamed. How could she possibly resist Boucheron's pleading? She could not. She looked down at that upturned face, beautiful in the white moonlight, and her heart shook within her. Her own cheeks were marble-pale; the rich laces fluttering, the jewels sparkling on her breast as it rose and fell with her agitated breathing.

'Madeleine, speak . . . put me out of my agony,' he said in a very intense voice.

He rose from his knees, sat beside her again and dared to put an arm about her waist. The thrill of his embrace penetrated the last veils of her reserve. She leaned towards him, half-fainting.

'Ah, Pierre . . . Pierre,' she said.

He was answered. He gave a cry of joy and with the other arm encircled her shoulders, and drew her, unresisting, towards him. And then adoration was coupled with the most ardent passion he had ever known in his life. Madeleine, lying so lightly against his heart, thrilled him to the pitch of agony. This pure creature, this gentle, tender girl loved him. From her feet he could rise . . . to her lips. His arms tightened. His eyes held hers, rapt and smiling.

'Je t'adore,' he said.

Then his lips closed over her mouth ... clung in a kiss that was an intoxication to them both ... a kiss unending, of mutual passion and yearning ... a kiss of such white fire as some young and splendid god might have laid upon the lips of his goddess in such a garden as this under such a moon.

Madeleine rested in his arms, unmoving, eyes sealed, arms clasping his neck. There was no time, no space ... no world save their own ... while that first unforgettable kiss endured.

At last when Boucheron raised his head he was like one drugged with the magic of it, and she gave a little soft sigh and unclosed her eyes. He read love and surrender in those hazel eyes.

'Madeleine, beloved ... best-beloved,' he said. 'Is it true? Can it be possible that you care for me?'

Her lids drooped again under the ardour of his gaze, and she leaned her head on his breast, hiding her face.

'Yes, it is true, I love you, Pierre.'

'I can't understand why,' he said, 'but oh, my dear, my darling, I'll be good to you ... I'll worship you for ever ... if only you will give yourself into my keeping ... if I might dare ask you to marry me.'

This the haughty, blasé Boucheron! How

true love does make a man humble and bring him down from the pedestal upon which all the other women in his life have placed him.

'Marriage,' she said, her face still hidden. Her voice was trembling a little. 'Ah . . . we must ask my mother . . . it is impossible for me to marry without her consent. But I . . . I do love you, Pierre.'

He covered her hands with kisses.

'Ah, *ma mie* . . . to hear you say that . . . it is more wonderful than I can tell you . . . it is a greater honour you confer upon me than if I were crowned king of France.'

She raised her charming head and smiled at him.

'You say such lovely things, *mon* Pierre.'

Mon Pierre . . . he was hers, now. The shy yet possessive words '*Mon* Pierre' enraptured him.

'Nothing I could think of or that poets could write or songsters sing would be lovely enough for you, beloved,' he said. 'But of course you must ask your mother. And somehow I think she will say "yes". She has accepted me as a friend of yours and of hers . . . she will consent.'

'I believe she will . . . unless she thinks me too young for an engagement.'

'Too young? How young are you, heart's dearest?'

'Not yet twenty, Pierre.'

'Not yet twenty!' he repeated, staring at the

face which was so pure, so exquisite in the glamour of the moon. There was starlight in her eyes . . . She seemed to him as fair, as chaste as a young moon . . . yet no longer remote . . . no more the unattainable, for she loved him—had confessed her love. And she was not yet twenty . . . and he was thirty-five, man of the world . . . Rat . . . adventurer . . . gentleman . . . everything in one. Even though the shy passion of Madeleine's kisses had thrilled and amazed him, he was still conscious of his unworthiness to take or touch her.

He leaned his head on her shoulder.

'My dearest,' he said, 'you are indeed very young, but I will take care of you, and if your mother will give you into my keeping, God forgive me if I fail you.'

'I am not afraid,' she said, her eyes shining.

To her it was the most stupendous thing of her life . . . this discovery of such a love . . . such a marvellous lover.

Boucheron rose to his feet and helped her on to hers.

'Come, *ma mie*,' he said. 'Walk with me through the gardens. I can't take you back to the ballroom—yet. I must have you to myself a little longer.'

She leaned on his arm and walked with him down the flagged path which led from the statue of the faun towards the moonlit terraces of the château. As she went, she smoothed the ruffled laces on her bosom and the crushed folds of her brocaded gown; patted one snowy curl of her powdered hair into order.

'Am I presentable?' she said with a low laugh.

'You are ravishing,' he answered with a downward glance at the flushed little face lifted for his inspection.

A sudden shout of boisterous laughter broke the witchery, the silence of the night. Through the gardens a crowd of revellers danced madly towards Boucheron and his companion. Madeleine clung to his arm.

'Oh, who are they . . .?' she breathed.

Beaucaire pressed the arm of Madame Pompadour close to his side.

'You are safe with me, dearest,' he said.

The crowd reached them and was revealed as a group of scantily-clad Bacchanalian nymphs, dancing with clasped hands around the figure of Bacchus, whose padded stomach had slipped to one side and whose wreath of roses hung over one eye.

'Heavens!' laughed Boucheron. 'It is that fool, Duval. He is grotesque.'

René, panting, dishevelled, but inordinately pleased with his charming escort, spied the Beaucaire and Pompadour and kissed his hands to them.

'This is heaven itself,' he simpered. 'I am a god indeed . . . and behold my enchanting playfellows!'

The nymphs, their short chiffon skirts

blowing about their slender limbs, broke into peals of laughter again and began to pelt their Bacchus with flowers and confetti.

'On, Bacchus!' screamed one of the girls.

'On Bacchus . . . on!' chorused the others.

He tried to break through the ring and reach Boucheron who, with Madeleine, stood watching him in amusement, but the mischievous nymphs bore Duval onward and they disappeared into the night, their merry voices echoing:

'On . . . on, Bacchus . . . on . . .'

Boucheron laughed.

'Poor Duval—it is a night of nights for him,' he said.

'And for me,' said Madeleine.

He turned to her, enraptured by the spontaneity of her remark. He caught her hands and kissed them.

'Oh, Madeleine . . beloved,' he said.

The pretty, powdered head dropped shyly. Then she was in his arms again and their lips met in another breathless kiss.

CHAPTER EIGHT

In one portion of the gardens a swing had been erected for the Duchesse de Quintreville's children. The merry-making nymphs of Bacchus rushed him along to this swing, forced him into it, then pushed him until he grew dizzy and clung to the ropes, screaming for mercy, at which they laughed and tossed him all the higher.

Finally he fell out of it and was borne away by the encircling arms of his escort to fresh mischief . . . pleading for mercy without in the least desiring it.

To this swing came Boucheron and Madeleine, slowly, dreamily, their rapt young faces upturned to the moon while they exchanged all the vows, the promises that lovers have exchanged since the world began.

The ropes of the swing were festooned with roses and twining fern, and swung there in the night-breeze, inviting the lovers.

'Let us share the seat, Madeleine,' murmured Pierre. 'You one side . . . I the other . . . see . . .'

They sat back to back on the swing, then turned to each other, his arm encircling her waist, her charming head resting against his dark one . . . their warm cheeks pressed together. He rocked the swing gently, to and fro. With half-closed eyes, exquisitely at peace they swung . . . a little higher . . . a little higher . . . until Pompadour's feet left the ground and her white brocade gown billowed in the breeze.

Through their half-closed eyes they looked on an enchanted garden . . . high . . . at the moon-silvered leaves of the trees and the walls of the château which seemed a fairy castle through the green lace of the leaves . . . low, at the silvered lawn, the sleeping flowers . . . the glistening body of the nymph in the fountain drenched in the ceaseless play of the water.

Swing high . . . up towards the magic of the stars and the sky . . . Swing low . . . back to the gardens, the flowers, the dew . . . Swing high up to heaven itself . . . swing low down to earth, grown so heavenly.

Pierre pressed his cheek closer to that of Madeleine.

'I love you . . . I love you . . .' he said.

'I love you, Pierre,' she whispered, her heartbeats shaking her body.

He turned his head slowly, and, still swinging, found her lips with his mouth and rested thus in an ecstatic kiss.

Gradually the swing died down . . . there was scarce a movement now . . . and the lovers stayed lip to lip, enchanted; trembling; drinking in the intoxicating sweetness of an hour that might never come again.

On the lowest terrace of the château the magnificent figure of Zélie de Chaumet appeared with her ribboned stick. She was weary to death of the libidinous old men who besought her to dance; of Mercereau, who bored her . . . of everything. She wanted to find Pierre. She had been seeking him for an hour, her heart sick within her.

She caught sight of two figures on the flower-festooned swing. A flash of

Pompadour's white and silver gown in the moonlight first caught her eye. She looked more sharply. From her elevated position she could now see the pair quite plainly, in that close and tender embrace.

For a moment she stood rigid; face haggard under the powder and rouge, eyes stricken.

Pierre and Madeleine were lovers. She could no longer deceive herself. And with every drop of blood in her body she loved Boucheron and wanted him.

Anguish gave place to terrible resentment. She put a hand up to her burning forehead.

'She shall not take him from me—she shall not!' was her inward cry. 'I won't let him go. I cannot. It will kill me!'

She caught her hooped skirts up in one hand and began to walk from the terrace towards the swing, impelled by the strongest passion in the world—primitive jealousy.

But before Zélie reached the swing Madeleine disengaged herself from her lover's embrace. René Duval, freed from his Bacchanalian revellers, had bounced up to her and reminded her that it was his dance. Pierre tried to send the fool away, but Madeleine, laughing at the expression of comic dismay on the features of Bacchus, condescended to go with him.

'I had better, dearest,' she whispered to Boucheron. 'I have other duty-dances to fulfil. Later, we will meet again . . . later . . .'

Pierre kissed her hand fervently and watched her walk away with the delighted Duval. Then he sat down on the swing which she had just vacated, and, with a sigh of happiness, pulled a case from his pocket and drew out a cigarette.

Zélie saw him light the cigarette, throw away the match, then lean his head against the garlanded rope of the swing and rock himself to and fro. He was obviously in a dreamy, contented state of mind. It infuriated the wretched woman who knew him so well. Pierre was by nature a restless creature, craving fresh excitement and conquest. If he could sit thus in the swing and dream of Madeleine who had just left him he must love her dearly.

Zélie moved closer to him. Pierre heard the swish of her skirts and glanced over his shoulder. When he saw Zélie he frowned. Her white face and gleaming eyes heralded a 'scene', and he was not in the mood for scenes. He was in love with Madeleine, and his cup of happiness was full to the brim. He did not want Zélie de Chaumet to come and remind him of what had been . . . of all that he was trying to forget, now that he had found Madeleine.

'Pierre,' said Zélie.

'Oh, hello, Zélie,' he said indifferently. 'Is it our dance or something?'

'Our dance!' She repeated the words with a bitter laugh. 'You have not asked me for one, so far as I know.'

He flicked the ash from his cigarette.

'Oh—sorry. Well, shall we have this?'

'No, thank you.'

He shrugged his shoulders and went on rocking himself in a way maddening to the unfortunate woman who was torn with her passionate jealousy. Suddenly she came round to the other side of the swing and faced him, hands clasped together, great tears gushing into her eyes. She was fast losing all control.

'Pierre, Pierre, stop before it is too late,' she said. 'You've won your bet. All this folly is breaking my heart.'

'Folly?' He looked at her with a frown. 'What exactly do you mean, Zélie?'

'I saw you—just now,' she said. 'I saw Madeleine de l'Orme in your arms. You have won your wager. I admit it. Now for God's sake stop . . . and come back to me.'

He made no answer for an instant. He looked at her, his tongue in his cheek. Then he threw his cigarette away into the bushes.

'My dear Zélie,' he said, clearing his throat. 'Don't let us mistake one another. There is no "folly" connected with this. I am quite serious.'

'Serious . . . you mean that . . .?'

'That I love Madeleine de l'Orme and that I hope to marry her, if she will do me that honour,' he said.

Zélie drew a quick breath . . . with the tip of her tongue she moistened lips that were cracked and dry. She felt physically as well as mentally ill in this moment . . . beaten . . . crushed by this man who was more to her than any other man on earth had ever been.

'Pierre,' she said hoarsely, 'you can't mean that. You—marry the Comtesse de l'Orme? . . . You, who have hated the very word marriage?'

'I believe all men do hate the word until they find the right woman,' said Pierre.

She stared at him blindly. The awful truth that this man loved Madeleine so much that he meant to marry her crushed her more and more as she realised it.

'Pierre,' she said, 'for God's sake say it isn't true.'

'It is true. I love her and I hope to marry her,' he repeated a trifle irritably.

Zélie swayed and put up her hands to her face.

'Oh, *mon Dieu . . . mon Dieu!*' she moaned.

He eyed her sharply. He saw that she was not acting . . . that her grief, her amazement were genuine, and he was worried. He was not fundamentally cruel. Women who make themselves cheap ask for cruelty from men . . . rouse it. But Pierre Boucheron at heart was a kindly man and a generous one. He remembered the many days and nights which he had spent with Zélie de Chaumet . . . the many times when he had been thankful to lay his head on her breast and accept her caresses. It seemed to him that it was all rather brutal . . . this blow he was directing at her, if she really loved him. He had never once offered to marry her, never wanted her for his wife.

He was inclined to be soft, more sympathetic than usual, following so closely upon his hour with Madeleine. Her influence was still strong upon him, making him more kind, more respectful to womanhood in general than was his habit.

'My dear,' he said, without a trace of irritability now, 'I am more sorry than I can say if this—er—distresses you so much. But I never promised to stay with you for ever, nor did I take any vow that I would never marry when the right girl came my way.'

She uncovered her face and looked at him, the tears pelting down her cheeks, making piteous channels through the coat of powder and rouge.

'But you loved me . . . we were all in all to each other after Odile's death,' she sobbed. 'Pierre, you can't leave me altogether and marry Madeleine de l'Orme . . . oh, you can't! You are labouring under a delusion—you are bewitched—you don't really care for her. You only started out on this affair as a wager with me.'

I would rather you did not remind me of that,' he said.

'But it is true—it is true. You don't really love her or want her. You are infatuated.'

'No, Zélie. I have found my own soul tonight.'

She moved her head to and fro like a creature mad with pain.

'I don't believe it—I won't believe it. You love me.'

Pierre rose from the swing. His face was grave, his eyes compassionate. Zélie's beauty and pleading left him unmoved, but tonight he could afford to give her his pity because he was so utterly happy with Madeleine. He put a hand on her shoulder.

'My dear, you must make yourself believe the truth and face it. I love Madeleine as I have never loved anybody—even poor little Odile. I am sorry if this hurts you so profoundly, but you are still young and beautiful; you will find some better man than I to make you happy.'

'Never, never, never,' she said, choking with sobs. 'It is you I want—you I have always wanted. Pierre, you know that I adore you; that I'd give up Mercereau, the money, the jewels, all that I possess for you.'

Much moved, he put a hand on her other shoulder and looked down at her agonised face.

'Poor Zélie . . . I am sorry.'

His pity, so suggestive of his indifference and the hopelessness of her case, drove Zélie to a state of wild hysteria. She flung herself into his arms, locking her arms about his throat.

'No, no no, Pierre—I can't bear it. Pierre,

have mercy—you loved me once; love me again. Give her up—please give her up. It was only an idle bet.'

'It is not a bet I have won, Zélie, but my heart that I have lost.'

'No, Pierre—please give her up. She could never love you as I do—never love you as I would . . . as I always have . . . as I always will.'

'My poor Zélie, I am sorry—but it is impossible,' he said, trying to unclasp her arms.

She made a last desperate effort to win him. She covered his face with wild, intemperate kisses . . . kisses that bruised his lips and to which he did not respond.

'She is only a chit of a girl . . . only a child . . . she could never give you the passion, the delight I have given you, Pierre,' she kept on sobbing between her caresses. 'You will be bored with her after a week. Pierre, Pierre, kiss me, love me, come back to me.'

Boucheron sighed. He was being very patient—for him! But he could not endure much more of this scene, which rather disgusted him. When he compared Madeleine with Zélie de Chaumet, the comparison was cruel. Zélie was a woman of thirty-five . . . exotic, cloying . . . Madeleine was a young, pure girl, as fresh as a breath of spring. He thought of her, in his arms, quivering like a bird, her lips responding to his kisses with the passion which he was teaching her. Ah, Madeleine! . . . his darling . . . his other soul . . .

he would never grow tired of her . . . never.

He tried to push Zélie from him. Great though his pity, he dared not encourage her with one kiss, one caress.

'Zélie, please pull yourself together,' he said. 'You are ruining your face . . . and what will people think?'

'I don't care. I only want you.'

Pierre began to lose patience. He unclasped her arms and spoke to her sharply.

'Zélie, be sensible, for God's sake.'

'Sensible . . . you say that to me . . . when you have broken my heart,' she moaned. 'Oh, you are cruel, cruel . . .'

'Zélie—please!'

She suddenly dashed the tears from her swollen eyes. The agony of suffering, of thwarted passion, was replaced by a look of intense resentment and fury.

'You can't get off so lightly—you can't abandon me for that chit of a girl and not suffer for it,' she said.

'I am prepared to suffer anything for the sake of Madeleine de l'Orme.'

'But you may never have the chance to marry her,' she said, in a gasping voice, a handkerchief to her lips. 'You are a fool—a fool, Pierre Boucheron, if you think you can make me suffer like this and go unpunished.'

'Oh, come, Zélie,' he said, as he might have spoken to a child in a temper.

She stamped her foot, shuddering with rage.

'No, you men are all the same—you think you can take everything a woman has to give then find a fresh fancy and go off! . . . You think you can go your way, Pierre, and meet with no rebuffs—just sail to glory. But you're wrong. You've broken other women's hearts before mine and this time you will pay for it.'

'In what way?' he asked coldly.

'You shall go back to the gutter again,' she said. 'I pulled you out of it, but I can easily push you back.'

'Indeed?'

'Yes, indeed.' She had ceased sobbing. She was ice-cold with her anger and bitterness. She no longer wanted his kisses. She had got beyond that feeling, She hated him . . . hated him. Passion turns very rapidly into loathing. In this moment if it could have done any good, she would have struck him across his beautiful, cold mask of a face with her clenched hand. '*You* marry the Comtesse de l'Orme . . . *you* . . . you Rat! Pshaw! I'll make it precious hard for you. You shall lose your job at the Quai d'Orsay. Mercereau will see to that, and you will find it difficult to get another.'

He neither moved nor spoke, only stared at her with cold dislike in his eyes. But his heart leaped uncomfortably. He was just beginning to realise that Zélie de Chaumet could make his life a hell for him if she chose.

'Much your love will be worth to Madeleine when she sees you in your true colours . . . sees you as an apache ... a Rat ...' said Zélie between her teeth. 'You'll crawl back to me, soon enough.'

Then Pierre Boucheron spoke.

'Would I?' he said, his voice like a whip. 'Then just make up your mind to the fact that if I were reduced to crawling, it would not be towards you, but in the opposite direction. Now, if you have finished abusing and threatening me, I will say goodbye.'

With a curt bow he turned on his heel and left her. Zélie had broken the spell. The happiness he had found with Madeleine was clouded. He went in search of her, anxious, doubting, wondering what Zélie de Chaumet meant to do.

He found it difficult to get Madeleine to himself again that night. She was surrounded by friends, dutifully dancing with the men who were friends of her family.

Boucheron, for the first time in his whole life, found himself in the throes of jealousy. He stood watching the pretty Pompadour gliding over the floor in the arms of some fellow in fancy-dress. Pierre's dark eyes never left her face. He would like to have knocked her partner down, seized her in his own arms, just as he would have done down in 'The White Coffin' in the old days. Then he hated himself for that feeling.

'I am not The Rat now. I must not give Zélie any foundation for her sneers,' he told himself.

When Madeleine's eyes met his through the crowd he was sublimely happy. Mutual love and understanding flowed between them like a great, strong river. Jealousy shrank before the face of such truth.

When drawn was breaking over the Château Lisbon, Boucheron took Madeleine home.

'Tomorrow I will come to the Château Lernac,' he said. 'I will ask your mother for your hand. Meanwhile, beloved, all my love is yours.'

'And mine is yours,' she said.

She nestled back in his arms, as they drove in his limousine back to Versailles. For a few moments in silence they contemplated the beauty of the morning while the car sped over the roads leading to Madeleine's home.

The dark clouds of the night had broken. Dawn had laid a rosy finger across the sky, leaving a streak of pink and amber and palest green—like a strip of apple-peel across the grey. One or two brave stars shone pallidly, fighting against the stronger light of the rising sun. The moon was a pale, melancholy face, outshone by so much splendour. The pastel tints in the east altered rapidly as the dawn passed into morning, and the sun rose higher and higher. And now a bar of pure gold rimmed the colour-washed horizon. The clouds vanished. Chinks of azure blue broke through the pearl-grey curtain of the dawn.

Boucheron let down the windows of the car.

The air blew in upon their flushed faces, pure and sweet. The last gallant star flickered, then vanished. It was day . . . a new radiant summer's day. From the woods fringing the deserted road rose the morning hymn of a hundred birds, chirping, twittering, calling to each other.

Boucheron turned to Madeleine. She looked very young and fair in the morning-light, with just the suggestion of fatigue in the lilac stains under her eyes. She smiled back at him.

'Isn't it wonderful?' she said in a hushed voice. 'We have seen the dawn break . . . you and I together . . . for the first time.'

He looked into the glory of her eyes and he trembled as he thought of other dawns that they might know and watch together. He drew a deep breath, stooped, and raised the hem of her gown to his lips.

A few minutes later he had handed her safely over to the care of a yawning footman at the door of the Château Lernac and was driving rapidly back to his flat in Paris.

CHAPTER NINE

In the Quartier Wagram—on the ground floor of a handsome building of flats in the Rue Alphonse de Neuville—Zélie de Chaumet lived in extravagant and exotic style as the mistress of Henri de Mercereau.

On that morning following the Duchesse de Quintreville's ball, in her marble-floored bathroom, Zélie took her bath at half-past ten; an unusually early hour for the woman who like so many Parisians turned her night into day and was rarely up before midday.

But this morning Zélie had important business to attend to. A message, telephoned through to a certain detective-agency by her maid, Gabrielle, earlier that morning, had fixed an appointment with a certain well-known detective named Jules Benoit for eleven o'clock. That was why Zélie had arisen before her usual hour.

She lay in the steaming, greenish waters, cloudy with bath-salts which threw out a strong perfume of carnation, and contemplated her toes. The nails were as exquisitely kept as her fingernails. Then she looked at her hands, her arms, her legs, that statuesque body which Pierre Boucheron had once described as the 'loveliest in all Paris,' and which gleamed like the body of a white water-nymph in that perfumed bath. But the expression on Zélie de Chaumet's face was far from contented with her personal beauty. It was bitter and hard. There was a terrible look in her eyes.

She had not slept until long after dawn, and then she had fallen into an uneasy slumber brought on through sheer physical exhaustion following a prolonged fit of sobbing. But she was done with crying now. Dark purple shadows underlined her eyes, and her lips were a thin pale line, sucked in with the repression of her emotions.

Zélie de Chaumet had reached a very great and bitter crisis in her life. She was face to face with hard facts. She no longer deceived herself. She had lost hope. The man she adored belonged to another woman. But she was not the type to sit down and suffer the indignity of being 'shelved'; of letting all the world see her humiliation, and submitting to it meekly. There was a strong vein of malice in her; she was more vindictive by nature than most women. And she was determined to ruin Pierre Boucheron—ruin him body and soul—before he reached the altar with Madeleine de l'Orme.

Her bath finished, she called for Gabrielle, her clever little French-Swiss maid.

'Rub me down,' she commanded. 'Then get out my rose-chiffon rest-gown with the sable trimming. And Gabrielle—I am not at home to anybody who calls to see me this morning—except the Comte, of course, and M. Benoit.'

'*Oui*, Madame,' said Gabrielle, wrapping a huge, warm towel about her mistress and rubbing that beautiful white back briskly.

Five minutes later Zélie sat before her mirror, in a loose rest-gown of pale pink chiffon, edged with sable; long wide sleeves with broad bands of the soft, rich fur falling back from her arms. She leaned forward and stared at her ravaged face; shuddered when she saw what havoc her emotions had played with her. Such pale lips . . . such shadowed eyes . . . such hollow cheeks! And all for a man who had treated her like a toy; played with her while she amused him, discarded her when he was tired.

'I must be mad to suffer so . . . to hurt my beauty so . . . for him,' she said aloud in a vicious voice.

Gabrielle, her confidante, brushed the bright gold hair into shining waves with a soothing movement.

'No man is worth a woman's tears, Madame,' she murmured. 'And Madame is so lovely . . . men become her slaves . . . why should she weep?'

Zélie stared at her reflection and gave a bitter laugh.

'I have done with weeping, Gabrielle,' she said. 'Now I am going to laugh . . . laugh at M. Boucheron when he returns to the gutter from which I lifted him.'

Gabrielle, who, like all other women, had adored Pierre, sighed and shrugged her shoulders.

'Will it make Madame happy to do that?'

'Yes,' said Zélie between her teeth. 'And it shall be done. Give me my lipstick.'

Gabrielle handed her a vermilion pencil. Zélie reddened her mouth . . . then applied cream, powder and rouge to her cheeks. After that with a tiny brush she skilfully blackened the tips of her long lashes . . . while Gabrielle plucked out one or two stray hairs in the pencilled brows. Then Zélie stared at herself again. She was beautiful now; vivid; all traces of exhaustion and despair had been cunningly removed. She clasped a diamond collar about her throat; put two jewelled bracelets above her elbow; one great bizarre ring (a valuable antique) on the forefinger of her right hand. She was ready now to meet any man—even Jules Benoit, a detective.

Suddenly her gaze rivetted on a ring in the jewel-case open before her; a beautiful emerald set in platinum. She took it up in her fingers, eyes narrowed, breath quickening. Pierre had given her that ring on the day when he had become under-secretary at the Foreign Office. For an instant the old cloak of despair wrapped her about. Her brows contracted in the agony of remembrance. How could she forget that day? . . . he had been so grateful to her for her help; so adorable that night as her lover. And when he had given her the ring she had been lying in his arms on the divan in her boudoir; his heart had beaten madly on her own; he had called her the queen of all women and kissed her in that subtle way that no other man she had ever known could kiss.

The blood rushed to her temples . . . then receded. Agony gave place to cold and bitter hatred again. She handed the beautiful ring, which had once been her most treasured possession, to her maid.

'You may have this, Gabrielle,' she said. 'It is worth a great deal of money.'

The maid took it, gasping.

'But, *Madame!* ... your cherished ring which Monsieur Bouch ...'

'Take it and hold your tongue,' interrupted Zélie savagely.

Gabrielle retired, not displeased.

Zélie walked into her drawing-room. She was thinking:

'Now he will be putting a ring on Madeleine de l'Orme's hand ... but not for long ... *mon Dieu!* ... if I have to fight with every drop of blood in my body to prevent it ... that ring shall not remain on her damned finger for long ...'

She made a tour of her room ... a very large and sumptuous salon furnished in Louis Quatorze style ... the ceiling painted; three big windows curtained with heavy rose satin. Rose ... exotic, vivid rose, was Zélie's favourite colour. There were no photographs in the room save one of Mercereau, in a gilt frame on the mantlepiece. It was not that she wanted Mercereau's withered face ever before her, but it flattered him to see it there when he visited her.

She inspected everything in the room and removed three articles from different tables ...

one an expensive gold casket for sweetmeats; one a shagreen cigarette box; one a Lalique glass vase which she had particularly prized. All three were gifts at various times from Boucheron, unknown to Mercereau. Zélie looked at the three things. Then an almost fiendish look of fury and spite came into her eyes. Deliberately she flung the delicate glass vase on the parquet floor. It smashed into fragments. The shagreen box and the gold casket she hammered into shapelessness with a heavy paperweight from the desk.

Panting, she surveyed her work, her cheeks livid under the rouge.

'There . . . that is the end of you, Pierre . . . Rat!'

She rang for Gabrielle to remove the débris.

The maid put up her hands in horror.

'Madame has gone crazy with love for the beautiful young man who does not love her,' she thought. 'Alas, the poor hearts of all poor women!'

This time she made no comment about the actions of her mistress. It was wiser to remain silent. This was too good a post to lose.

Zélie flung herself down on the divan which was piled with luxurious cushions of all shapes and colours. But she could not remain there. Every cushion reminded her of Pierre. His handsome head had rested on them all . . . at some time or another. She bit her lip fiercely and began to pace up and down the room, humming under her breath.

Punctually at eleven o'clock Jules Benoit arrived.

Gabrielle showed him into the salon. Zélie, always a poseuse, was ready for him, standing beside a stuffed panther whose head was raised, showing snarling lips, curled back from sharp white teeth. With one jewelled hand on that tawny head the mistress of the flat received her visitor.

Benoit blinked when he saw her. It was rather too early in the morning for such exotic loveliness. And Jules Benoit was a very hard-headed, hard-bitten man. His quick, cunning brain was masked by a particularly heavy face.

He bowed low to the famous mistress of Comte Mercereau.

'Madame . . .'

'Sit down,' said Zélie.

He thanked her, seated himself gingerly on the edge of a delicate Empire chair, and whipped a note-book and pencil from his pocket. He was a man of few words and of ready action.

'At your service, Madame,' he said.

Zélie's fingers clenched over the rough fur of the panther's head.

'Monsieur Benoit,' she said, 'I understand that you are a detective who can be relied upon to invent a crime even if you fail to discover one.'

Benoit smiled drily and lifted his shoulders.

His little beady eyes, like black pins stuck in his flabby white face, darted round the salon taking in every detail of it.

'You do me an honour to say so, Madame.'

'Well—is it true?'

'I believe that I am an inventor as well as a discoverer,' he said, with a bow.

You are to be relied on, I am told.'

'My discretion is perfect, Madame. No man whom I have followed has ever seen my shadow.'

'You will undertake anything . . . at a price?'

His beady eyes became slits.

'Anything—at a price, Madame,' he said with an obsequious smile which would have nauseated her had she not been in need of this type of slave.

'Do you know Monsieur Pierre Boucheron of the Foreign Office?'

'M. Boucheron?' Benoit put his tongue in his cheek and reflected. 'We-ell—I think so, Madame.'

'Wait,' she said.

She walked to an escritoire, unlocked a drawer and drew from it a photograph of Pierre, taken six months ago. She thrust it into the detective's hand.

'This is he. Keep it.'

'Yes, Madame.'

'Do you know—or remember—a certain apache of the underworld, named The Rat, from 'The White Coffin'?'

Benoit looked at her with interest.

'The Rat? But who does not remember The Rat, Madame? My friend Caillard. God rest his soul . . .'

'Yes,' interrupted Zélie. 'M. Caillard died without realising his main ambition, which was to bring The Rat whining to his knees for mercy. But you, Monsieur Benoit, shall achieve the triumph for your dead friend.'

Benoit's brows contracted. He looked at the photograph of the handsome young man in evening-dress.

'Then this . . .'

'Is The Rat,' she said. 'Pierre Boucheron and The Rat are one and the same.'

'Indeed,' said Benoit.

Another few words from Zélie and he knew exactly why he had been sent for and what Madame de Chaumet wished him to do. She desired the ruin of Pierre Boucheron, *alias* The Rat. He regarded her with a slightly cynical expression on his face. Jealous women were the devil, he thought. The terrible spite and thirst for revenge which gleamed in Madame de Chaumet's blue eyes were not good to see. An old, old story. The lover grown tired . . . the discarded mistress seeking a revenge.

He jotted down notes in his little book while she talked. When he looked up at her again, she was shaking with the force of her anger, her intense desire that he should do what was required of him and do it thoroughly.

'You quite understand, M. Benoit? You are to follow him everywhere—you and your men—you are to see that he gets no work; that every man who offers him a job is told that he is a gutter-snipe, a thief, an apache—The Rat!'

Benoit nodded.

'I understand. But his present job . . .?'

'Terminates tomorrow,' finished Zélie. 'Comte Mercereau has seen to that. The world will very soon know that Pierre Boucheron is The Rat.'

Benoit pursed his lips and looked at the photograph he held. A handsome young man. A fool, too. Had he not realised the power of this woman, Zélie de Chaumet, when he had abandoned her?

'Day and night . . . day and night he must be followed,' continued Zélie in a low, harsh voice. 'He must not be allowed to obtain employment. Step by step we will break him. He will starve . . . do you understand?'

'Yes, Madame,' said Benoit, and glancing quizzically from her to the panther beside her, he reflected that apart from the trees, a lady's boudoir may have much in common with the jungle. The prey is destroyed more politely in these surroundings, but—

'You have your orders now, M. Benoit,' the hard voice broke in upon his reflections. 'If you fail me, it will be so much the worse for you.'

Benoit rose and cringed.

'I shall not fail, Madame. Jules Benoit never

fails.'

'You will be adequately paid,' she said.

He bowed lower, smiling.

'*À votre service, Madame* . . .'

She looked down on him and knew him for the knave he was. No . . . she need not fear. Benoit would not fail her.

He bowed himself out of the salon. She walked to the divan and flung herself down upon it, shuddering from head to foot in spite of the heat of the room, for it was a warm summer's day.

Henri de Mercereau was her next visitor.

Ever dapper, ever courteous, Mercereau bent over the hand Zélie offered and kissed it.

'Up so early? But how delightful. Perhaps you will come with me for a drive, *chérie*. How are you feeling? You look lovelier than ever.'

She swallowed hard. Her throat was dry; her eyes like blue stones. But her painted lips smiled at him.

'I am in splendid health, Henri, I am up early because I have just interviewed M. Jules Benoit.'

'Benoit?'

'The detective.'

'Ah!' said Mercereau, seating himself on the divan beside her, and removing an imaginary speck of dust from the immaculate grey of his coat-sleeve. 'With reference to our friend The Rat?'

'Yes, *The Rat*,' said Zélie. 'He has ceased to

be Pierre Boucheron.'

Mercereau laughed drily. He was very tired of Pierre Boucheron and of his mistress's *penchant* for the conceited fellow. He was ready to spend as much money on Zélie's behalf to achieve Pierre's ruin as he had spent in order to make him the idol of Society in the first place.

'Yes, he has ceased to be Boucheron,' he said. 'At the Foreign Office, when I gave the tip to—' (he mentioned the name of a leading light at the Quai d'Orsay), 'I told him (in horror) of my sudden discovery of the true identity of the fellow, he was not long in sacking him. He has a nephew whom he would like to see in The Rat's place. The news will be in all the papers tomorrow. Then the fun will begin.'

Zélie cupped her chin on one hand and stared with brooding eyes out of the window.

'Yes, the fun will begin,' she repeated. 'And Madeleine de l'Orme will receive the nastiest shock of her life. By the way, I am visiting her this afternoon.'

'To make more mischief, *hein*?'

'Yes,' said Zélie, savagely and frankly.

'Do not look so concerned about it all,' said Mercereau, playfully pinching her cheek. 'Do you not belong to me, my darling, and are you not my queen?'

Queen . . . Zélie's face contracted. That word . . . which Pierre had used so often. But she had her nerves well under control this morning, and with a swift, lithe movement, turned and rested in his arms.

'I am not unhappy . . . merely absorbed in the whole affair. It will be interesting to watch Jules Benoit at work and to see the result upon The Rat.'

Mercereau caressed her hair.

'*Eh bien, ma mie*. And now let us forget The Rat and think of ourselves. What shall we do?'

'Anything . . . anything. Take me out—amuse me.'

'Shall we go south—to Monte-Carlo . . . to Mentone?'

'Later . . . later . . . when I have seen The Rat on his knees and had the pleasure of refusing him mercy.'

'La, la, my little wild cat,' murmured the old Comte, his jaded senses amused by the vicious spite of this beautiful woman who belonged to him. 'Well, then, what shall we do today? Will you drive with me in the park . . . and later we will lunch at the Meurice . . .'

'Very well,' she said, rising. 'I will go and change my dress.'

'One kiss,' he wheedled.

Feeling was dead within her. She was an automaton. She was too numb to care what happened to her today.

She moved towards him, and as she went something made a little scrunching sound under her heel. She looked down and saw that she had trodden on a fragment of the Lalique glass which Gabrielle had omitted to sweep away.

CHAPTER TEN

On the terrace of Château Lernac that golden summer afternoon following the Duchess de Quintreville's ball, Madeleine de l'Orme stood looking down the broad avenue of elms which led to the great wrought iron gateway. At four o'clock Madeleine expected to see that gateway open and Pierre Boucheron's car glide up the drive.

It was now only half-past three. But there was always the hope that he might be early. She watched with that excited quickening of the heart-beats and thrill of anticipation common to lovers who wait. Her cheeks were flushed and her eyes bright. (She had slept soundly until mid-day, and now her face bore no trace of last night's fatigue.) She had been awakened by a telephone call. Her maid had brought the instrument to her bedside. She had answered and found Boucheron at the other end of the line.

A long conversation had followed enchanting to them both. They had said 'I love you!' as though it had never been said before. They had said 'If only I could see you . . . touch you . . . what agony it is to hear . . . to be so far apart . . .!' as though no other lovers on earth had thought of saying such things. They had exchanged a dozen fresh vows . . . Then Pierre had grown serious. He had meant to call at Château Lernac before lunch, but had received an urgent message summoning him to the Foreign Office, and could not come until four this afternoon. Madeleine had assured him that she would wait a thousand years until he came, and he—ridiculously pleased with such exaggeration—had answered that to be apart from her a thousand seconds meant anguish to him, but that he would be with her—at four.

Then Madeleine had suggested that she should warn her mother of what Pierre meant to say . . . plead with her to consent to an announcement of the engagement. To this, Pierre had responded that he would leave her to do just as she wished—that he was certain that whatever she said or did would be correct.

Remembering the telephone conversation now, Madeleine half closed her eyes and drew a long breath of happiness.

She adored Pierre. It was marvellous to be loved as he loved her . . . and to love him so much . . . Not once, but a dozen times since last night she had lived through the whole of that scene in the enchanted garden at Château Lisbon last night; had felt the pressure of his arms and lips . . . thrilled all over again at the memory of his rapt, dark eyes, his ardent face.

There could be no other lover in the world like Pierre.

Madeleine was too young and too innocent to worry her head about Pierre's past. Extreme youth lives for the present and ignores the past and the future. She knew nothing about the somewhat smudged reputation Pierre had earned in connection with many women in Paris. Madeleine was not the type of girl to invite scandal. She was rarely drawn into the circle of women who love to extract thrills from a discussion about other people's sins and follies. If Pierre had been a flirt (the word 'flirt' meant very little to Madeleine) . . . what did it matter? He had told her that she was the first woman in the world he had ever loved. That was sufficient.

The de l'Ormes were good Catholics. Château Lernac possessed its own oratory. In this little oratory, before a statue of the Virgin, Madeleine had knelt this morning and prayed for a blessing upon her love with Pierre.

Just such another girl, with just such a spotless mind, had knelt before her Virgin and prayed for Pierre . . . Odile of the underworld, who had not lived long to know the glory of his love.

Alas! Women who loved Pierre Boucheron were doomed to suffer. But without suffering there can be no great love. Love thrives on anguish and the women who receive the love of a man like Boucheron must pay for his kisses with their tears.

Tears, however, were far from the hazel eyes of Madeleine today. She was radiant with happiness.

She looked down the sunlit avenue for some moments without moving; a charming figure in an apple-green gown of pleated georgette, with turn-down collar, cuffs just above the pretty elbows, and a floppy black bow at the throat which made her look like a schoolgirl of seventeen.

She thought of her extravagant Pompadour gown of last night . . . and how her Beaucaire had admired her . . . she blushed a little . . . then sighed a little when she regarded the simplicity of today's attire.

'Now that I am to be affianced I must ask *Maman* to give me less childish things,' she reflected. 'I am nearly twenty.'

The interview with her mother after luncheon had been very successful. Madeleine had sat on a hassock at the Comtesse's feet and told her of her love for Boucheron.

'I want you to let me announce my engagement to him . . . you must accept him as your future son-in-law when he comes this afternoon, *Maman*,' she had pleaded.

The Comtesse had looked down into her child's face and searched the luminous eyes. She had felt a slight trepidation.

'You are so young, Madeleine, and you have

known M. Boucheron so short a time.'

'But I love him . . . he loves me . . . that is surely enough?' Madeleine had argued.

'Yet once you disliked him.'

'That was my stupidity. Ah, *Maman*, darling, please, please say "yes" when he comes . . . you know you approve of him.'

'I like him immensely. He is a very delightful young man,' the Comtesse had agreed. 'But we don't know very much about him—or his family.'

'That doesn't matter—we love each other. *Maman*, it will kill me if you say no!'

The Comtesse had smiled. Oh, the exaggeration of youth . . . the ecstasies . . . the blind faith and splendid folly of it! Through all the ages youth remained the same . . . the same raptures, follies, hopes, smiles and tears were flung into the melting-pot of life. She, herself, had loved, once . . . she had known the impatience, the ecstasies through which her daughter was now passing. She found it difficult to resist Madeleine's pleading. And she did like Boucheron—very much.

'Very well, my darling,' she had answered. 'I will accept him when he comes. I will let you be engaged.'

Madeleine had flung herself into her mother's arms and kissed her; rapturously thanked her.

'Pierre—*mon* Pierre!' Madeleine's lips framed his name while she stood on the terrace watching and waiting.

Suddenly a hideous noise broke the quiet beauty of the afternoon. Somebody in the salon was strumming the grand piano. A high falsetto voice, just sufficiently out of tune to be maddening, floated through the open windows to Madeleine.

'Come to my garden of roses,
'Come, dearest heart, to me!'

Madeleine put her hands to her ears, laughing.

'René must have arrived,' she thought. 'But I shall not permit him to come to *my* garden of roses unless he refrains from making that noise.'

She walked round the corner of the château to the windows of the salon and stood framed in them, gazing into the big, spacious room. She was a charming figure in her apple-green gown, drenched in sunlight.

'René! René!' she protested.

Duval, who was seated at the piano, singing shrilly, swung round on the stool and faced her.

'The enchanting, the ravishing Madeleine!' he began.

'Stop!' she interrupted. 'I can't bear it.'

'Nor I,' seconded the Comtesse de l'Orme, who was seated in a high-backed chair at the other end of the room, with some embroidery in her hands. 'Although I have tried to put up with it for the last ten minutes. The terrible fellow went straight to the piano as soon as he arrived.'

'I didn't see him arrive,' said Madeleine. 'He must have come up the back drive.'

'I did,' said René in a disconsolate voice. 'I was so afraid of being thrown out if I came to the front.'

'How absurd you are,' said Madeleine, laughing.

'And now I am here—you do not want me,' he said.

'You—but not your singing, *mon cher*,' she said. 'It rends my heart . . . I am too moved . . . too shattered with the emotion you cause me.'

Duval sighed and shook his head.

'You mock me,' he said.

'As Bacchus last night you were a success with the ladies, anyhow,' she consoled him.

His face brightened. He preened himself, smoothed his beautifully creased grey trousers, straightened his tie (the latest pattern in peacock blue), and spread out his black patent leather boots and white spats.

'Ah!' he said. 'Last night. Yes. The girls fairly ran after me.'

'René!' said the old Comtesse in a disapproving voice. 'You grow vulgar.'

Duval caught Madeleine's eye. She tried not to laugh, although she shook with merriment. Duval apologised profusely to the Comtesse of whom he stood in awe. She was the head of his family.

'As for my friend Boucheron—he was, as usual, the idol of the hour,' he added.

Pierre's name brought a deeper pink to Madeleine's cheeks. Suddenly she bit her lip, caught her breath excitedly and walked closer to Duval.

'René, I have such glorious news to tell you . . . guess.'

'Don't make me,' said Duval. 'I'm a perfect fool at arithmetic.'

'Guess.'

'I can't. Tell me, Madeleine. Has the cat had kittens?'

'René!' said the old Comtesse sternly. 'You forget yourself!'

'Your pardon, *ma tante*,' said Duval, completely withered. Then, as the Comtesse rose and marched from the salon: 'Now, Madeleine, don't tease me—tell me your news.'

She clasped her hands together, and very slowly, pausing between each word, began:

'I . . . am . . . engaged to . . . be married . . . to . . .'

'Me!' finished Duval, falling off the piano stool on to his knees.

'Heaven forbid!' she laughed. 'No—'

She got no further. The door of the salon was thrown open and a footman entered.

'Madame de Chaumet to see you, Mam'selle la Comtesse.'

Madeleine advanced further into the room.

'Madame de Chaumet ... to see *me*? ... you are sure?' she asked, amazed.

'*Oui*, Mam'selle. She asked for you.'

René Duval put a hand to his lips and coughed.

'The devil take it,' he thought. 'What mischief is the beautiful Zélie contemplating?'

'Oh, very well,' said Madeleine. 'You had better show her in.'

The footman bowed and retired. Madeleine turned to Duval.

'Madame de Chaumet ... you know her, René?'

'Ahem ... do I not?' said Duval, clearing his throat. 'Damned pretty woman ... jolly temper, too ... bit well known in Paris and—er—'

'You had better go, René,' said Madeleine, as though she had not heard what he was saying.

'Go? Not meet the fair Zélie? It's always so interesting to see what fashion she is adopting ...' began Duval pleadingly.

'Please go, René—I had better see her alone,' broke in Madeleine. 'I really cannot imagine why she has come.'

Duval made his exit through the windows on to the terrace, somewhat disconsolately. He was just in time to see Zélie de Chaumet sweep into the salon, blew a kiss to her and pranced off, smiling.

Madeleine stood very still, watching the other woman advance towards her. She held her young head erect. Her whole bearing was haughty and dignified. But inwardly, all the child-like happiness and glory of the day had departed for her. A strange sense of coming disaster . . . a premonition of evil had seized her . . . she knew not why.

The name of Madame de Chaumet conveyed nothing of much importance, except that she was a rather notorious woman not generally received in salons such as this one. She had also heard her name connected with Comte Mercereau. But to nasty scandal Madeleine paid little heed. She had certainly never heard Zélie's name coupled with that of Boucheron.

Zélie de Chaumet stood face to face with the young Comtesse de l'Orme.

'How do you do,' she said boldly, holding out her hand.

Madeleine did not take the hand. Quite politely, but with that cold dignity which she could muster at will, she motioned Madame de Chaumet to a chair.

'Won't you sit down?' she said.

Zélie put her tongue in her cheek. Madeleine's refusal to shake hands with her was an insult not to be forgiven or forgotten. But she shrugged her shoulders and smilingly accepted the chair Madeleine indicated. She began to unbutton her long white kid gloves and to remark on the heat of the weather. Madeleine did not sit down. She remained standing, gravely regarding her visitor.

'May I ask what has brought you here, Madame?' at length she said.

Zélie gave her a long look—a cruelly critical look such as only one woman can give to another. For the first time she was face to face with the girl Pierre Boucheron had chosen . . . was speaking to her. She took in every detail of the charming young figure; the brown, curly head; the face which might have been that of a saint in some stained glass window, for all its grave purity. And the heart of Zélie de Chaumet beat fast with envy, with jealous hatred. She would like to have seen this girl lying dead at her feet. But instead she would enjoy watching her die a mental death, before she left Château Lernac this afternoon.

This girl was the beloved of Pierre; it was for this baby he had deserted *her*—Zélie—made her suffer more horribly than she had ever suffered in her life. Well, now Madeleine de l'Orme should be made to suffer. It would be some satisfaction to Zélie to know that, although she had for ever lost Pierre, Madeleine would lose him, too.

'As if a child with those eyes, those lips, could love him as I have loved him,' she thought bitterly. 'Oh, it makes me sick . . . sick to think that I have taken second place in his affections to an inexperienced little convent-bred miss!'

She looked round the salon. It was a beautiful room; Empire furniture; satin-panelled walls; floors like polished glass; lovely Persian rugs; graceful curtains of deep petunia-coloured velvet framing the square-paned windows. The pictures and ornaments were all rare, and in exquisite taste. In one corner of the room on an ebony pedestal stood a bust of Marie Antoinette; a very valuable relic of that ill-fated queen from her own palace at Versailles and given by the last King of France to a de l'Orme for services rendered to the crown. It was the salon of a *grande dame* . . . Here was an atmosphere of dignity, of repose. From rooms like this, Zélie de Chaumet was debarred . . . she was not considered fit to touch the hand of girls like Madeleine de l'Orme.

A cruel and vindictive passion submerged all the good in Zélie de Chaumet as these humiliating thoughts passed through her mind. She looked up at Madeleine.

'I am here to speak to you of Pierre Boucheron,' she said.

Madeleine flushed to the roots of her hair.

'Of Monsieur Boucheron? Madame . . .'

'Oh, wait,' interrupted Zélie. 'Don't say that I am making a mistake, or that it does not concern you, Comtesse. Allow me to say what I have come to say.'

'I think it would be better if you said no

more, Madame,' said Madeleine very coldly.

'No,' said Zélie. 'Better for you if I do speak. It is on your behalf—for your good I risk your anger. There are absurd rumours abroad that you care for Pierre.'

Madeleine winced. To hear her lover's name spoken with such light familiarity by such a woman hurt . . .'

'Madame!' she protested. 'Please do not go on.'

'Wait,' said Zélie, with a cold, cruel smile. 'I must hear from you yourself that the rumours are not true . . . that you cannot have been so indiscreet.'

'Indiscreet? I do not understand.'

Zélie shrugged her shoulders. She looked from Madeleine's frock to her own gorgeous Lanvin model . . . thin black chiffon heavily embroidered in eastern design with gold and scarlet threads. She drew her black picture hat with its scarlet ostrich feather lower over her golden head. Even in the midst of the dramatic discussion concerning Pierre she was feminine enough to reflect that she was dressed very much more stylishly than this Madeleine de l'Orme.

'I do not understand,' repeated Madeleine. 'And I think you had better go, Madame de Chaumet.'

Zélie rose. She shook her head, and assumed an expression of pity.

'Alas, poor child, you are naturally angry

with me. But I assure you that I came here prepared to be insulted, because I felt it my duty to warn you.'

'Warn me of what?'

'Of your folly, Comtesse. No—do not speak—listen to me. I am older than you are—a woman of the world. You are a mere child. You have much to learn that I can teach you. You had better know what manner of man Pierre Boucheron is before you go too far.'

'Madame, this is intolerable—!'

Madeleine was trembling now, and her cheeks were pale. She made a movement towards the silken rope of the bell as though to summon her servants. But Zélie laid a hand on her arm.

'Comtesse, for your own sake be advised to listen to me.'

'No, Madame—'

'Comtesse . . .' Zélie's voice was low and pleading now. She even managed to squeeze tears into her eyes . . . tears that Madeleine saw and which made her pause and listen. 'For your own sake. Try to believe I am not here to make mischief . . . only to tell you something that you ought to know. I cannot bear that one so young and so trustful should be the victim of such villainy. Ah, Comtesse, I implore you to listen to me in a kindly spirit . . . for it is in the spirit of kindness that I have come to Château Lernac for the first and last time.'

This speech, spoken in a most moving voice

(for Zélie was an excellent actress), softened Madeleine. Her proud anger evaporated. The poor woman seemed genuine. But she was making a great mistake in coming here, in trying to speak ill of Pierre.

'Madame,' she said more gently, 'I will listen. But I assure of you that nothing you can say will alter my personal opinion of Monsieur Boucheron. I did not know you even knew him.'

Zélie laughed.

'Know him? I knew him when he was The Rat of the underworld . . . a vulgar apache.'

'An apache?' Madeleine repeated the words wonderingly. 'Pierre . . .?'

'Yes, an apache from a dancing-den in which you would not be allowed to set foot, Comtesse.'

Madeleine's heart beat very fast.

'I do not of necessity admit your information to be correct,' at length she said—very bravely and proudly. 'But if it is true—'

'It is indeed. I knew him then. He loved me then,' interrupted Zélie.

'If it is true,' repeated Madeleine, ignoring the last few words, although they cut her like a knife, 'it makes no difference to me. You had better know at once that I am engaged to be married to Monsieur Boucheron, and that if there is anything in his past life he wishes to tell me—he will tell me himself.'

'Bravely spoken, Comtesse,' said Zélie with

a sneer. 'But he does not deserve such loyalty.'

'Neither do I need your warning, Madame,' said Madeleine. 'Goodbye.'

'Wait,' said Zélie. She assumed that soft, sad expression and voice again. 'Poor child . . . my heart bleeds for you . . . but more than ever now that I know how true, how innocent you are, must I tell you the truth about Pierre. You are the victim of a despicable trick.'

'Trick?' Madeleine echoed the word sharply. 'What do you mean?'

'Just this. You may forgive a man for being an apache if you love him and he loves you, but you cannot believe in a man's affection nor forgive him if he has made a wager to win your love—vulgarly boasted of his power to attract you.'

That struck home. The red blood stung Madeleine's cheeks. She said in a trembling voice:

'I do not understand.'

Zélie walked towards the door.

'I have said what I came to say. Now I will go, Comtesse. You will hate me, but I have done you a good turn for which you and your mother may thank me one day. In the Pré Catalan Restaurant, some weeks ago, Boucheron boasted that he would have you in his arms within a month. He was only speaking of it to me at the Château Lisbon last night. I saw you both on the swing. He arranged that I should see his triumph. He may want to marry you—but you can't want to marry him now that you realise how you have been treated.'

'Stop!' said Madeleine. 'You are not speaking the truth, Madame.'

'It is the truth. Ask him if he did not make that bet with me,' said Zélie. 'Ask him yourself. And now, Comtesse, good afternoon.'

She swept out of the salon, red lips smiling . . . eyes triumphant. She believed that she had fulfilled her mission.

Madeleine stood in the salon, staring at the door through which the other woman had passed. Her mind was in chaos. Doubts, fears, indignation, horror . . . a mixture of emotions swept across her, one after the other.

The things Zélie de Chaumet had said were sinking slowly in. Pierre Boucheron was an ex-apache. Well . . . that might have been forgiven . . . but that he had once been the lover of such a woman as the de Chaumet; and that he made a wager with her to hold her, Madeleine, in his arms . . . heavens! That was intolerable.

She put her hands up to her lips with a little cry.

'Pierre . . . Pierre . . . is it true?'

She remembered her first meeting with him . . . how he had snubbed her, ignored her. Had that all been part of his plan?

Suddenly two warm hands were placed over her eyes, and deep, laughing voice whispered:

'Guess who it is . . .'

She tore the hands away and swung round,

breathing hard and fast. It was Pierre ... himself. He had tiptoed through the open windows, and surprised her. He must have been talking to Duval in the garden and not seen Madame de Chaumet depart.

Pierre looked at her with eyes eloquent of his love. He held out his arms.

'*Ma mie!*' he said.

That melting voice . . . that beautiful, boyish face so alight with adoration swept all her doubts, her suspicions away in a flash. She had been disloyal, wicked to let the lies that that scheming, jealous de Chaumet creature had uttered worry her for an instant.

She flung her arms about her lover's neck.

'Pierre!' she said with a sob.

He held her tightly against him and for a moment their lips clung in a kiss that seemed as endless as it was sweet. She lay against his breast ... felt the hard, strong beats of his heart upon hers. She surrendered herself wholly for a few moments to the ecstasy of his embrace. She loved him so much. And he, wholly her lover, raised his lips from her mouth only to cover her cheeks, her hair, her eyelids with passionate kisses.

'My adored Madeleine ... my soul ... my life,' he said while he caressed her. 'I have lived only for this moment.'

Then he noticed the tears on her lashes and instantly grew grave and concerned.

'Madeleine ... *mon ange* ... you cannot be

crying! Dearest of all women, what is it? Who has dared to make you cry?'

'Oh . . . nothing . . . only . . .'

'Only what, *ma mie*?'

'I . . . Zélie de Chaumet has been here.'

Pierre stiffened. Every muscle in his body became taut . . . He pressed Madeleine's soft brown head against his breast and looked over it with eyes grown hard and—afraid.

'Zélie de Chaumet . . . here?'

'Yes, Pierre.'

'For what reason?'

'Some unkind reason of her own. She wanted to make mischief. She dared to say dreadful things of you . . . and of a wager.'

'A wager,' he repeated. And now his very lips were dry. For he knew without questioning her further what Zélie de Chaumet had said.

This was the beginning of her revenge.

Already he had received a curt request from the Foreign Office that he should send in his resignation. That was what had sent him hurrying down to the Quai d'Orsay this morning. He had guessed it to be the work of Zélie, through Mercereau. He had not imagined a woman could be so vile, so vindictive. The loss of his job as under-secretary had been a blow, though not a mortal one. He believed that he could soon secure another position. He did not know that Mercereau meant to publish the truth about his identity throughout Paris.

But this . . . this thing that Zélie had done to Madeleine hit him very hard . . . because it hit at Madeleine's pride, Madeleine's faith. He did not know what to say. He was like one stunned.

Madeleine raised her head. With quivering lips she smiled at him.

'It was a lie, wasn't it, Pierre?' she said.

He remained silent. He was looking down into her eyes. And no man could look into Madeleine's eyes and lie to her—certainly not the man who loved her—who was willing to lay his life under her feet.

Madeleine grew cold in his arms.

'Pierre,' she said . . .' Pierre . . . say it was a lie. You did not—you could not have wagered that you would hold me in your arms within a month . . . made such a vulgar, horrible boast . . . to Zélie de Chaumet.'

His arms fell to his sides. His head drooped forward. Pierre Boucheron was filled with shame. But he could not lie to the woman he loved.

'Pierre,' repeated Madeleine pitifully. 'Answer me. Is it true?'

'Yes,' he said, 'God forgive me—it is. I would give half my life to undo it . . . to unsay what I said to Zélie de Chaumet. I know it was unspeakable—the act of a cad. I have been a cad most of my life, Madeleine. But I have tried to be different since I have cared for you.'

She drew back from him, the tears drying on

her lashes. She looked pinched and grey.

'You made that wager . . . about me . . . to that woman? Then all the other things she said were true . . . that you were once an apache . . . that you were her lover before you were mine . . . that . . .'

She stopped, gasping. She could not go on. He raised his head and looked at her, his face a study in tragic regret.

'Madeleine, for God's sake don't be too hard on me. Everything she said was, no doubt, true. But try to remember that it all happened before I had ever spoken to you. That day in the Pré Catalan she had been taunting me with being a Rat . . . an apache of the underworld. She hurt my pride and I was so furious that I made that wager about you. She had said you would never look at me. Oh, it all sounds disgusting and you have every right to be disgusted. I come not offering any excuses. I only beg you to believe that once I knew you I was ashamed and I wanted to make amends.'

She drew back from him. Her whole body was shivering.

'Make amends! And you let her see us on the swing last night—let her see your triumph. Oh, *mon Dieu*!'

'No, no,' he broke in, shocked. 'That isn't true.'

'I don't believe you. I can't believe a word you say now.'

'Madeleine—' he held out a hand. 'For

heaven's sake listen to me calmly. I swear by all that I hold holy that I was sorry for making that bet once I had met you.'

'But nothing can wipe out the fact that you made it—held me up to ridicule before your—friends.'

'No, Madeleine—never that.'

'You did. You made a public wager to feed your horrid vanity because that woman had laughed at you.'

'Madeleine . . .' Drops of sweat stood out on Pierre's forehead. Every word she uttered was like death to him. 'It looks like that to you, but won't you believe that it was because I didn't know you . . . didn't care for you then? Once I met you I worshipped you—like a saint.'

'Please go,' she said.

'No, Madeleine—beloved . . .'

'Don't call me that. Don't ever dare come near me again.'

'Madeleine . . .' his voice became hoarse with anxiety. 'You can't be so merciless. I implore you to try to understand—to forgive me.'

'I gave you my love,' she said in a hard, toneless voice. 'I gave you my whole heart and you only cheated me . . . insulted me by every kiss you gave me in return. You not only tricked me into giving you my love—you gambled for it—made it a common bet with a woman you had grown tired of. You are the most despicable thing I have ever imagined.'

Boucheron, arms at his sides, stared at her, dumb with despair. Never before in his vain, selfish career had he felt so despicable as she made him feel. He realised that he had earned her scorn. He was all that she called him. He would like to have lain down at her feet and let her see him grovel there . . . prove his remorse, his humble desire for pardon. But he could neither move nor speak. He was too shattered by the agony she inflicted on him.

'Please go,' she said.

Then he moved. He flung himself on his knees; he caught the hem of her gown and covered it with kisses.

'Madeleine, Madeleine, don't send me from you. Oh, my dear, my dear, if you knew how sorry I am for everything . . . if you knew how I loved you—you'd forgive . . .'

She drew her gown from his fingers.

'Don't touch me. And don't behave in this dramatic fashion. It doesn't move me. You do not understand what love is and you are incapable of decent feelings. You have made me loathe men. Please go.'

He stood up. He wondered if she could say or do anything further to him to make the hell of his shame and remorse more unbearable. He looked at her, a terrible expression convulsing his face. How cold she was! . . . How cruel! She was just as implacable as only a very young, pure woman can be when she is disillusioned in her lover. In this hour of his humiliation he remembered Zélie, who had done this thing . . . recalled the time when she had pleaded in agony and tears for his love. And now, perhaps, he understood a little of the torture he had caused her. He was being tortured even more terribly by Madeleine.

'Go,' said that inexorable young voice.

'Won't you believe me?' he stammered. 'Won't you believe that I am terribly, terribly sorry about the wager and that I truly love you, Madeleine?'

'No—I will not believe it.'

'You want me to go—for good?'

'Yes, please.'

He drew a deep breath. So this was the end of his love-dream with Madeleine de l'Orme. Zélie de Chaumet had killed her love. She looked at him with loathing in eyes that had a few minutes ago been soft with passion and love. He felt sick with despair. He remembered Zélie's warning that he could not go through life breaking hearts without paying. Well, he had paid. His own heart was broken, at last. For every woman he had hurt he was going to pay cruelly. He loved Madeleine de l'Orme more than life itself, and she was sending him away from her.

She stood there, like an accusing goddess, terrible in her white wrath and utterly without mercy. Such treatment had never before been meted out to Pierre Boucheron, whom women had forgiven so much. It dazed him. He shrugged his shoulders with a gesture of hopelessness, gave one last look at that stern, beautiful young face which he would never look upon again; took her hand and pressed a long kiss on it which made her shudder; then turned and walked out of the salon. He walked slowly with shoulders bowed . . . like a very old man.

Madeleine had retained her self-control admirably while Pierre faced her. But now that he had gone, the tension snapped. She stumbled to a sofa and sat down on it, the sobs tearing her. She put the hand that he had kissed against her lips. And she said aloud, over and over again:

'Pierre . . . Pierre . . . Pierre . . .'

She had loved him. She would never be able to shut that love out of her life. But Pierre, himself, she had shut out because her pride and her purity would not have allowed her to keep him, to marry him, knowing what she knew now.

'Pierre . . . Pierre . . . Pierre . . .' she spoke his name again and again in a kind of despair. And then: 'Oh, God, I can't bear it . . . I can't bear it, Mary, Virgin of Sorrows . . . help me . . . pray for me . . .'

She fell forward on her face upon the cushions, and lay there, shuddering with her sobs.

CHAPTER ELEVEN

Duval, strolling through the gardens of Château Lernac, idly picking flowers, then stripping them of their petals because he had nothing better to do, was astonished to see the figure of Boucheron emerge from the big carved door of the château and approach his limousine a very few minutes after he had entered the salon.

'*Mon Dieu*!' thought Duval. 'He cannot have had as many kisses as he wanted in so short a time. What has happened? A lovers' tiff?'

He ran towards the limousine, hailing his most admired friend. 'Hi, Boucheron!'

The chauffeur, about to close the door upon his master, respectfully stood back and Duval, dropping a handful of roses as he ran, reached the door and thrust a head inside the car.

'Not going already, are you, my dear fellow?' he panted. (His shoes were much too tight and his corsets too well laced to admit of sprinting!)

Pierre said something inarticulate.

Duval peered closer, and received a shock when he saw the other man's face. Pierre looked ghastly. There was a wild, unnatural light in his eyes. His usually smooth black hair was slightly dishevelled and his whole appearance suggested that he was either physically or mentally ill.

'My dear Boucheron!' exclaimed Duval, who was a kind-hearted little man. 'My poor old chap—are you indisposed?'

'No,' said Boucheron. 'Goodbye, Duval, let the man shut the door, there's a good chap.'

'But, Boucheron—what has happened?'

'Another time, Duval. Goodbye.'

René withdrew his head. The chauffeur banged the door, took his seat, and the car glided away down the avenue of elms.

Duval stared after it, blinked his eyes, and turned back to the château. He felt most concerned. Boucheron looked ghastly ... unnerved ... as though he had seen a ghost or lost a fortune. Surely Madeleine had not turned him down? No—that could not be so! She had been about to announce her engagement when the de Chaumet arrived. Ah ... Zélie de Chaumet! Even Duval's stupid brain saw some connection with Zélie in this affair. Had the woman made mischief between the lovers?

There lived no man in Paris more sentimental than our René, and the idea that Boucheron and Madeleine should be rendered unhappy by a mischief-making woman greatly disturbed him.

'I must see Madeleine,' he thought, scratching his ear. 'Perhaps I can assure her that the beautiful Zélie is a liar and that Boucheron is the most admirable fellow in the world.'

He walked into the château, through the beautiful hall which was hung with great oil-paintings of Madeleine's ancestors and into the salon.

He found the girl on the sofa, sobbing as though her heart were broken. The sight had the immediate effect of reducing Duval to tears. He rushed to her side, slipped on the polished floor and landed on his back beside her. Madeleine gave a gasp, looked up, a handkerchief pressed to her lips, and saw the deplorable spectacle at her feet. An hysterical laugh shook her.

'René, what *are* you doing?'

'Madeleine,' said the poor fool, gulping, raising himself on to his knees. 'I have come to comfort you.'

'Comfort me?'

'No—I don't mean that—to reassure you . . .'

'Reassure me? How?'

'That the de Chaumet woman is as bad as she is fascinating and that Boucheron is . . .'

'Enough, René,' broke in the girl. She was on her feet now . . . laughter breaking on a bitter sob as the full force of her tragedy rushed over her at the mention of Pierre's name. 'You can say nothing that I wish to hear.'

'But Madeleine . . . *mon ange* . . . Boucheron is a most excellent fellow.'

'Do not mention his name!' she interrupted

fiercely. 'And you must pardon me, René, if I do not ask you to remain. I am—not very well. Goodbye.'

She walked quickly out of the room. René stared after her, still on his knees, a dismal expression on his face.

'Heavens! They are all ill. There has been a plague. Or a quarrel. The poor little one . . . my heart bleeds for her.'

He drew a scented handkerchief, painted in the corners with the laughing faces of pretty women . . . and sobbed into the soft and perfumed folds.

A sharp voice behind him made him jump.

'René . . . have you lost your senses? What are you about, weeping like a lunatic on your knees in the middle of my salon?'

He turned and saw the old Comtesse. She had just encountered her daughter; Madeleine, in tears, had rushed through the hall up to her bedroom. She had come to the salon expecting to see Boucheron and hear some explanation. Instead she found René in this undignified position, entirely alone in the centre of the great room, sobbing into his handkerchief.

'Get up, *imbécile*,' she said.

He rose meekly, wiping his eyes.

Your pardon, *ma tante*.'

'What is this all about? Have you all gone mad? Madeleine was in tears and rushed by me, refusing to answer when I questioned her.

Why are you snivelling, fool?'

He cringed and backed from his stern kinswoman. The Dresden-china old lady with her delicate face and snow-white hair possessed a strength of will and a personality which reduced René to pulp.

'I do not know, *ma tante*,' he stammered. 'I have no idea what has taken place.'

'Then why are you weeping?'

'In sympathy with Madeleine.'

The Comtesse gave him a withering look.

'For heaven's sake, pull yourself together, idiot,' she snapped. 'You had better go home if you have nothing better to do than weep over a misfortune of which you are ignorant. Has M. Boucheron come yet?'

'He had been and gone.'

'Ah,' said the Comtesse. 'Then he has seen my poor Madeleine . . . and, presumably, quarrelled with her.'

'Yes, *ma tante*.'

'Lovers have disagreements which come to nothing. I do not worry,' said the Comtesse calmly. 'I must go to my child. You can come another day, René.'

'Yes,' he said meekly.

She swept grandly out of the salon. Duval blinked.

'I do not seem to be needed,' he reflected, tucking his handkerchief into the pocket of his fancy waistcoat. 'This has depressed me. I must find a pair of sparkling eyes to restore my humour.'

He flicked a speck of cigarette ash from his sleeve, put his hands on his slender waist and minced out of the salon. He ran straight into the trim figure of a maid . . . a pretty little thing with sharp black eyes and a saucy red mouth. She drew back from Duval, her hands upraised, and suppressed a laugh.

'Oh, Monsieur . . . *je vous demande pardon*!'

René surveyed her from head to foot, assuming a superior, supercilious expression. Then he drawled:

'I pardon you freely, my child. You have a naughty mouth, but I trust that you are a good girl.'

'Oh, la! la! Monsieur!' she giggled.

He snatched a kiss from her, pressed ten francs into her hand, then walked away, feeling every inch a man.

The girl stifled a laugh and fled to the servants' hall.

'The poor little nincompoop,' she described him to the brawny footman who was her lover. 'If you could have seen him, Georges . . . pirouetting across the hall like a tightly-laced girl. But he gave me ten francs . . . see.'

'For what?' demanded Georges fiercely. '*Dis donc*, Jeanette.'

'For opening the door for him,' said Jeanette glibly.

(Georges was so jealous, and, likely as not, would march upstairs and crush the poor little

Monsieur to powder if he knew he had kissed her!)

René swaggered out of the château, twisting his moustache upward.

'That was not a bad little thing,' he mused. 'She had merry eyes. When I see her again she will expect me to repeat my performance of today. But I shall not kiss her again. No! I must remember Boucheron's advice. She has had the warm embrace. Next time she shall have the cold shoulder. It will be pleasing to me to think that to one woman, at least, I am unattainable!'

Upstairs in Madeleine's bedroom—a truly virginal chamber with white draperies, a delicate powder-blue carpet and a white, hand-painted suite—the girl was crouching at her mother's feet, head on that loving lap, pouring out the whole tragic story.

The Comtesse listened, much agitated. She had not expected so serious a story. She was most indignant when she learned Pierre Boucheron had sailed under false colours all these months, had come to Château Lernac posing as a gentleman by birth and breeding; an aristocrat fit to mate with a de l'Orme; and that he had held the position as under-secretary at the Foreign Office—a low imposter!

'It hardly seems possible, Madeleine,' she exclaimed, staring over the girl's bowed head. 'An apache . . . a creature of the underworld . . .

Boucheron, with his exquisite manner, his Raphael face!'

'No—it seems incredible,' said Madeleine, face hidden, voice hoarse with so much weeping. 'But it is possible that somewhere there is blue blood in his veins . . . that he is not wholly of the peasants.'

'Yes . . . there have been—mistakes—before now,' said the Comtesse, with heightened colour.

'But that would not have mattered . . . that part of it,' said Madeleine. 'I could have forgiven him for being an apache. He has educated himself . . . worked up to his present position and he must be brilliantly clever to have done it. All that is very much to be admired.'

'You are wrong, my child,' said the old Comtesse haughtily. 'No de l'Orme could have mated with a vulgar *gamin*!'

'That did not matter,' repeated Madeleine.

'But his liaison with the de Chaumet woman. That was intolerable!' exclaimed her mother. 'I am furious that the servants admitted her to your presence. Heavens! That such a notorious woman—the *maîtresse* of Mercereau . . . should speak to my daughter . . . insult her! Your mind has been polluted by the interview.'

'That did not matter,' Madeleine reiterated wearily. 'I cannot remain ignorant of life . . . of the darker side of life . . . much longer. I am nearly of age. And I know that men do . . . do these things . . .' She gave a convulsive sigh. 'But Pierre wagered with her to win me. *That* is the thing that matters.'

'Oh!' said the Comtesse, her delicate lips compressed. 'It was insupportable. My poor Madeleine.'

'Such an insult, *maman* . . . to have him make a vulgar bet . . . publicly . . . at the Pré Catalan.'

'And he had the audacity to admit it to you?'

'Yes, he was at least truthful.'

'The nerve that fellow has passes all understanding. Never in my life have I come up against such a case. He has just ridden roughshod over Paris and laughed at us . . . he has been received by us all . . . entertained by us . . . a low creature from a Montmartre cafe!'

Madeleine shuddered.

'That does not matter!' was her incessant cry. 'But the wager about me . . . with that woman . . . that is what has broken my heart.'

The Comtesse lifted her daughter's head, a hand under her chin; looked earnestly down at the poor little face which was not beautiful now . . . distorted with the violence of her grief . . . eyes swollen . . . cheeks ghastly pale.

'Madeleine, my child,' she said in a deeply moved voice, 'your grief, your disillusionment rends my heart. But if you have any pride, . . . and you have, darling, the pride of the de l'Ormes . . . you will put this man right out of your thoughts and cease to grieve for him. You will behave as though the affair never commenced; as though you never came in contact with him or with Madame de Chaumet. You will present a smiling face to the world and let Boucheron, of all people, see that you are above grieving for him . . . for such a vulgar impostor.'

Madeleine shut her eyes. They ached so. Then she gave a dreadful little smile.

'I suppose I can—do that. I can pretend to the world. But I cannot pretend to myself, and my heart is broken.'

'No, *chérie*,' said the Comtesse. 'Only hurt . . . a little bruised, torn, naturally by this shock. But you are very young, dearest, and you will live to know a better love . . . to be the respected and adored wife of a good man whom you can in your turn respect and love.'

Madeleine rose from her knees and walked away from her mother. She stood at her big bay window, overlooking the grounds. The sunlight hurt her swollen eyes, and she turned back again, feeling very sick and weary.

'No, you are wrong there, *maman*,' she said, after a long pause. 'I shall never love any man again. I shall never marry now.'

'*Chut, chut!*' said the Comtesse, with a tender little smile. 'That is hysterical, my dear. You are only twenty. In two years time . . . less . . . you will be laughing at yourself . . . deploring the moment you ever gave Pierre Boucheron a single thought.'

'I deplore that now,' said Madeleine, swallowing hard. 'But I shall never laugh about it. It is too frightful. *Maman*, you make a mistake. I loved him. I am not the type to love twice.'

'All the women say that when they are disappointed in love, *chérie*, but you will ... take my word for it ... Time is a great healer and your wound will heal. Besides, it is lowering your pride to feel such intense grief for an upstart like Boucheron.'

'I loved him!' cried Madeleine. 'And pride ... oh, *mon Dieu*, what is pride ... when one loves? I was proud when I sent him away, but I hope to God I never see him again or I shall not answer for what I will do. Pride will not count ... the next time ... I can scarcely bear this separation from him, now.'

The Comtesse rose and walked to her daughter's side. She was beginning to be seriously alarmed at Madeleine's condition of mind. She had not realised the girl was so desperately attached to Boucheron. This hysteria and drama must be stopped, however. She was not going to allow the regrettable affair to ruin Madeleine's life. Why, she was one of the prettiest, most admired débutantes in Paris. She had already received several offers of marriage from the heirs to big estates, big houses in France.

'Madeleine,' she said, being deliberately

stern, although her maternal heart bled for the girl. 'You must stop this . . . not give way to such unreasoning sorrow. I know you must be greatly distressed and disappointed. Boucheron was a very handsome, attractive fellow. Was I not taken in by his charm like everybody else? But you cannot grieve for him for the rest of your days.'

Madeleine no longer wept. The tears in her eyes seemed to have frozen. She looked at her mother stonily.

'I loved him. When I love, it is for ever,' she said. 'I shall never, never be able to forget Pierre. I sent him away because he offered me an intolerable insult and because I could never give him the satisfaction of possessing me . . . then crowing over it . . . with that woman. He was bitterly sorry. I think for many reasons he must regret what he did. In a way he may have cared for me. But I shall never see him again, otherwise, as I have just told you, I will not be responsible for my actions.'

'You could not give way—even if you did see him!' said the Comtesse, shocked.

'I will not risk it,' said Madeleine under her breath.

Every nerve in her body was quivering. The spell Pierre Boucheron had cast upon her was not yet broken. Through all her pain, her disillusionment, her resentment, she loved him still, and for many long days and nights she was to know the torture of an unsatisfied hunger . . .

The passion he had taught her had sunk very deep.

'You must come away with me,' said the Comtesse. 'We will leave Versailles . . . go to the south.'

'Yes, if you wish.'

The Comtesse put an arm around her daughter.

'Oh, my poor little baby, try to believe this grief is not lasting,' she begged. 'You will regain happiness with some other man, I assure you.'

'Never.'

'Yes, yes, dear, when you have had time to forget.'

Madeleine closed her eyes. She shuddered as her mind leaped back to the memory of last night in the gardens at Château Lisbon . . . to that first, wild kiss Boucheron had laid on her lips . . . to the memory of his handsome head, against the laces on her breast. And now an anguish, so acute that it seemed to tear her to pieces, rent her. She gave a cry.

'Oh, *mon Dieu! mon Dieu!* . . . I shall never forget . . . never cease to love him. Oh, *maman, maman* . . . I wish I could die . . . let me go into a convent . . . let me take the veil . . . anything, anything . . . but I cannot bear this pain!'

She flung herself on the prie-Dieu in the corner of her room, knelt with clasped hands before the statue of the Virgin and stayed there, moaning like a creature in pain.

The Comtesse did not follow. She stared at the kneeling figure, the tears pouring down her own cheeks now. And she felt, with all a mother's fierce desire to protect, to avenge her own flesh and blood, that she would like to have killed Pierre Boucheron . . . watched him die by inches . . . for this thing he had done to her only child.

CHAPTER TWELVE

After he had left Madeleine, Boucheron drove straight back to his flat in the Avenue du Bois. He walked straight past his valet, who stared curiously at his master's dead-white face and brilliant eyes, and shut himself up in his bedroom. Then, like a caged animal, he began to walk up and down . . . restlessly, as though tormented by a physical and mental pain which enraged him and from which he could find no release.

He lit and smoked one cigarette after the other. Hands deep in his trouser pockets, he paced that beautiful, luxurious bedroom, staring in front of him with unseeing eyes.

He tried to collect his thoughts calmly; to review the situation in which he found himself with the cool nerve and nonchalance he would have shown in any critical situation other than this. But the fact that Madeleine had sent him away, had looked at him with scorn, almost with hatred, in those soft eyes of hers, shook his courage, rendered him incapable of calm thought or of analysis of the affair. It had been too great a shock. The wound she had given him had gone too deep. He was like a madman . . . hands shaking; cheeks ghastly; eyes burning in the white mask of his face. Up and down . . . up and down he paced, staring at nothing. And the only clear thought in his head was that the woman he adored had sent him away and refused to believe in his love.

His valet knocked at his door. It was time for him to dress for dinner. But Pierre, in a savage voice, sent the man away. He wanted no dinner. He did not intend to change.

The valet retired, shrugging his shoulders and wondering what had disturbed Monsieur so vastly.

In the bedroom Pierre went on walking, smoking, striving for composure. He was so afraid that he would break down, fling himself on his bed and sob. He did not want to do that; to lose his self-respect by crying like a woman. When, finally, he had smoked his last cigarette he put both hands to his temples. Pain there beat fiercely. He wanted to shut it out. He walked up and down like that, head between his hands.

The twilight deepened into night. The shadows lengthened and, outside, a beautiful starry evening settled upon Paris. In Pierre's bedroom it grew dark. And in Pierre's mind there was a darkness more terrifying than night. It was the blackness of a despair which no ray of hope could penetrate.

Madeleine . . . Madeleine . . . her name reiterated in his brain. He had visions of her . . . beautiful, pure, exquisite . . . in his arms last night in the gardens of the Château Lisbon by the laughing faun. He could feel her lips tremble under his kisses . . . her body tremble in his embrace. A groan broke from his dry lips.

'Madeleine . . . Madeleine . . .!'

The serene sweetness of her face changed . . . became the cold, hard little face which he had just seen . . . with hard eyes in which he had read his doom. There had been no spark of forgiveness, of mercy in those accusing eyes. She had called him despicable; made him feel a beast; a mean thing without honour or decency. She had thrust him out of her life, thinking he had offered her an unpardonable insult. And she had not believed in his love. That hurt Pierre more than anything . . . her refusal to believe that he had loved her. It made him raw. He writhed under the memory of her words. For after all, whatever he had done in his life, he had sincerely loved Madeleine de l'Orme. He loved her still. He would love her until he died.

And he would never see her again.

Up and down . . . up and down that dark

bedroom Pierre walked without ceasing; driven half-mad by the pain of his thoughts. He had bitten his lower lip through. A tiny trickle of blood ran down his chin and dried there. He did not notice it.

'Madeleine . . . Madeleine . . .'

Her name escaped his lips now and then. He shut his eyes and walked blindly . . . knocked into a table . . . a chair . . . bruised an elbow, grazed an ankle . . . but noticed neither. The whole of his past life rose to torment him further . . . to jeer at him. He thought he could hear a dozen voices saying, 'Serve you right!' . . . 'It is what you deserve!' . . . 'Now it is your turn to suffer.' He saw the faces of the women from whom he had taken love, passion, and service to whom he had given only fleeting passion in return. Women whom he had kissed, then forgotten. He saw Rose, America, Mou-Mou, the poor little coquettes of the underworld who had thrown themselves at his feet and served him. He had taken everything from them—given them nothing in return except that passion which in his disgusting vanity he had considered sufficient reward. He had told himself it had been a fair exchange. And today he saw the hideous unfairness of it and knew himself for a rotter and a cad.

He remembered other women he had played with . . . rich Society women, married and single, who had flung themselves at him since his rise of position in Paris. He had considered them fair game and had let them ruin themselves for him. Today he realised that no woman is fair game; that what a woman gives when she loves is something above and beyond anything a man can offer . . . something finer, more unselfish than one man in a thousand can understand.

Zélie de Chaumet . . . ah! Zélie's face rose before him, accusing him more passionately than any of the rest. From her he had taken so much . . . through her he had won the position he held today and which had given him the right to ask Madeleine to marry him last night. Zélie he had loved for a little while, then he had sent her away, abandoned her for Madeleine . . . humiliated her . . . insulted her . . . such had been his ingratitude. Such had been her reward.

He remembered the night, not so long ago, in this flat when she had been on her knees to him, begging for a little tenderness, pity, love. He had only pushed her away or capitulated in a fashion calculated to make her ten times more wretched. What a cad, what a despicable cad he had been! He could see it all now. He admitted every sin, every folly, every act of brutality or meanness he had committed; even magnified them in this hour of his own humiliation and despair.

Now he understood at last what it meant to love . . . to care so much for a human being that death was preferable to life without that person. Now he understood how women in his life had loved him. Now he realised the cruelty he had shown poor Zélie; the magnitude of her grief and her shame.

He ran the gamut of all those emotions while he paced up and down his bedroom tonight. He suffered as he had never believed it possible to suffer. He strove, desperately, to shut out the visions of those women who jeered at him, who could crow over his downfall. But they remained and tortured him. The fierce pain of having loved and lost Madeleine was coupled with sincere remorse for the wrong he had done to others.

And all the pain, the remorse, the despair were futile. He saw that only too plainly. Were he to throw himself out of the window or torture himself with red-hot pincers as outward proof of his penitence, it would be a waste of time. Suicide would be cowardly; self-inflicted physical pain a stupid fanaticism. They could do no good. They could not undo the evil. He had lived a selfish and idle life. He had misused his gifts of beauty and magnetism. He had desecrated the word Love . . . until he had met and cared for Madeleine. Then it had been too late. Nemesis had overtaken him, and from this hour onward he was to pay . . . pay very dreadfully for his sins.

In the first sharpness of agony he asked himself how he could exist without Madeleine; whether life were worth living since she had sent him away and despised his memory? But that wild feeling passed. One must live, even in anguish of body or mind. Death could not wipe out the follies or sins, nor could it give Madeleine back to him.

As thought grew calmer, and reason more sane, Boucheron asked himself what he would do at this culminating point of his career. He realised that with Zélie's vindictiveness at the back of things he might have to fight to retain what he had originally gained through her love. He had already been forced to resign from his job at the Quai d'Orsay. Wounded love and pride were forgotten for a few moments in a sudden anxiety about his social and financial position. It gradually dawned upon this spoiled idol of Paris that any sort of idol . . . social, theatrical, political, literary . . . may be the darling of the crowd one hour and despised or forgotten the next. Nothing is more fickle than the public. The public that petted and fêted Boucheron today might very easily forget him, lay him on one side tomorrow.

Fear flashed across the mind of the harassed man who paced up and down his dark room. The fear that Zélie might indeed have the power, through Mercereau, to ruin him utterly. But this fear was quickly cast aside. A little of the old vanity crept in. He was popular, handsome, attractive . . . he had been under-secretary at the Foreign Office. He would find fresh work.

But . . . the raw, unhappy mind turned to Madeleine again . . . nothing could give *her* back to him. If he became a prince she would not look at him. So what matter if he returned to the gutter? He would not mind. Nothing mattered now that he had forfeited her love and her respect.

He began to feel deadly tired. He must have walked miles in the restless pacing of those hours. At last he switched on the electric light which spilled softly from a huge Chinese orange and blue bowl swinging on gilt chains from the ceiling. He blinked . . . even that soft light hurt his inflamed eyes. He dragged his footsteps to the mirror which stood on a beautiful satin-wood dressing-table by the window. He stared at his reflection and scarcely recognised himself. Where was the spruce, immaculate Boucheron, beloved by all the ladies? This was a haggard wreck of a man with livid face and bloodshot eyes.

He tossed a lock of hair back from his brow and laughed. It was not a very good laugh to hear. Then he walked to his bed . . . an expensive antique four-poster which had been in Marie Antoinette's palace at Versailles, and from which the original satin tapestry curtains hung in rich, graceful folds. An antique spread heavily embroidered with gold thread covered this bed. Boucheron liked luxury, and he had spent a great deal of money on the appointments of his flat.

On either side of this magnificent bed stood an alabaster nymph on an ebon stand, holding up an electric torch which, when the centre light was out, was very effective.

At the foot of the bed was a delicate satin-wood table with curved legs and a surface which shone like polished gold. On it stood a large photograph of Madeleine de l'Orme in evening-dress; beside the photograph a crystal vase filled with cream roses and white lilac. The flowers were the only white things in that exotic, vividly-coloured bedroom. It had pleased Pierre to keep nothing save pure white flowers beside the photograph of his lady . . . emblematical of her purity.

He picked up the photograph in his shaking hands and stared down at it. An almost savage pain convulsed his features as he stared down at the pictured face and form of Madeleine . . . Madeleine in one of her typically simple, charming frocks, with a huge feathery flower on one shoulder, and a little shy, upward smile of the eyes. He had loved that photograph, made a shrine of it with the white flowers, and kept it at the foot of his bed so that he could see it last thing before he slept and first thing when he awoke. The knowledge that he would never see her smile at him like that again, save in this cold, lifeless photograph, smote him like a blast. He thrust the photo away in a drawer of his dressing-table. It would drive him mad to see her smiling at him now . . . with the memory of her scornful face as it had looked a few hours ago fresh in his mind.

He took the roses and the lilac out of the vase, wrung the water from the stems and put them away in the drawer with the photograph . . . like the relics of a saint or of the dead . . . of something very dear, very treasured which had been lost.

That done he sat heavily on the edge of his bed and covered his face with his hands.

The valet knocked at the door again.

'Monsieur . . . dinner is served . . .'

'I do not want any dinner,' answered Pierre.

'But Monsieur . . . your favourite hors d'oeuvre . . .'

'Oh, go to hell!' interrupted Pierre.

The valet retired.

Pierre sat on the edge of his bed without moving, elbows on his knees, head sunk between his hands.

Half an hour elapsed. Then the telephone bell rang, startling Boucheron from his bitter reverie. He looked up. The telephone was beside his bed, covered with an expensive doll which had black hair, and a black velvet crinoline gown, somewhat resembling Doris Keane in 'Romance'. Pierre had bought it last summer because it had borne a faint likeness to a dark-haired woman who had been amusing him at the time. Even the memory of that—an idle flirtation—angered Boucheron now. What had he been in his life but a cheap flirt . . . worse still, at times, a common seducer . . . a creature with no respect for womanhood save in the sad, bygone case of poor little Odile whom he had treated as his sister?

He tore the black velvet doll off the telephone, flung it on the floor, then lifted the receiver from the hook and put it on the table. He did not want to answer the telephone. It might be Zélie. He felt a little humble towards Zélie because of the unkindness of the treatment he had meted out to her, but he was not going to risk hearing her jeer at him, triumph because Madeleine had turned him down. His remorse in Zélie's case was dwarfed by angry resentment because she had dared to go to Madeleine and pollute her mind.

The telephone bell continued to buzz and crackle now that the receiver was off. At length Boucheron picked it up again. A sudden, wild, desperate hope had shot through his mind that it might be Madeleine . . . Madeleine ringing him up to say she would forgive . . . that they might start again. The colour flooded his livid cheeks. He put the receiver to his ear, his fingers shaking.

'Hello . . . hello,' he said.

'Oh, hello, Boucheron,' said the voice of René Duval. 'What a deuce of a time they've been getting you.'

Boucheron could have laughed aloud in his misery. His heart sank like a stone and his flush faded. Fool! Poor fool that he had been to imagine for a single instant that *she* would ring him up. She would not lower herself to speak to a *Rat*. She knew now that he was only a Rat. Well, he did not blame her for her pride, her lack of mercy. He might have felt bitter because she had changed so quickly, but it never entered his head, once, to feel bitter towards Madeleine. It was himself that he blamed for everything.

'Hello, Boucheron, are you there?' came Duval's high-pitched voice.

'Oh, yes, what is it?' asked Pierre wearily.

'Have you seen the evening paper, my dear chap?'

'No . . . why?'

'Well . . . my dear old fellow . . . I mean to say . . . it's a bit thick . . . look here, now . . .'

'Oh, what is it—speak up!' said Boucheron.

'I really can't, my dear fellow. I'm too upset.'

'Damn it, what about?'

'What they say about you in the paper.'

Boucheron grew rigid.

'What do they say?'

'I honestly don't like to say, my dear old chap.'

'For God's sake, don't be hysterical, Duval . . . do they speak of my resignation from the office?'

'Yes . . . but worse than that . . .' Now there came a distinct sob from Duval's end of the wire. '*Mon Dieu*, Boucheron, I've never been so upset in my life as I've been today . . . first of all Madeleine in tears . . .'

'In tears!' Boucheron caught him up sharply.

'Yes, crying her pretty eyes out. I suppose Zélie made mischief and . . .'

'Oh, don't talk of that,' interrupted Boucheron. 'What's in this infernal newspaper?'

'I really can't speak of it on the 'phone,' said Duval with another sniff. But I want to assure you that *I* still admire you tremendously, my dear Boucheron, and I don't care what people say . . .'

Silence. Boucheron stared at the wall. Two questions were burning in his brain . . . what the papers were saying that could have so distressed Duval . . . and why Madeleine had cried. Ah! of course, her pride had been so hurt . . . that was it! . . . She had not cried for *him*. But to think of her in tears . . . his beloved for whom he would have died rather than that she should suffer any grief or pain . . . that hurt him, worried him horribly. Madeleine in tears! It was not to be thought about, otherwise it would really send him out of his mind.

'Boucheron—hello—are you there?' came Duval's anxious voice.

Pierre pulled himself together. He realised vaguely that the poor fop was attempting to be kind; to prove himself a loyal friend, and he was suddenly grateful.

'Thank you, Duval, for what you have said. I will get the paper now.'

'Can I come round, Boucheron?'

'No, thanks. I want to be alone.'

'But, Boucheron—'

'Goodbye, Duval,' said Boucheron.

He hung up the receiver. Then he pressed the bell by his bedside.

The valet, an excellent man who had been in his service for two years and on whose loyalty Pierre would have staked a great deal, entered.

'I want an evening paper—late edition at once—' began Boucheron. Then he stopped. He saw a queer expression on the man's face. And in his hands was—a newspaper.

'I've just been reading this,' said the valet without the habitual suave *politesse*, or 'Monsieur': 'I'd like to give immediate notice.'

Boucheron, slightly dazed, stared up at the man with his bloodshot eyes.

'Notice . . . what do you mean, Varjean?'

The valet held the paper out to him.

'Maybe you haven't seen the article concerning yourself, but I have,' he said with an insolent laugh.

Boucheron sprang to his feet, his cheeks crimson, his eyes burning.

'Speak to me like that again, and I'll knock you down, you impudent dog,' he said between his teeth.

The valet cowered back, but his lips sneered.

'Oh, all right, come to that I'll go right away tonight, and sue you for my wages, too, if you don't give 'em. I am a respectable servant and

I've been with respectable gentlemen for years. I reckon I've damaged my reputation in being with you so long. I'm only a servant, but I'm respectable, and my father was an honest bootmaker. But you . . . living in style like this . . . and only a *gamin* . . . an apache . . . from "The White Coffin" . . . bah!'

He literally spat the last few words at the astonished Boucheron, then rushed from the room, as though fearing retaliation, and slammed the door with such force that the room shook.

Boucheron, whose fingers had automatically closed over the evening paper Varjean had held out, dropped back on to the edge of the bed, his heart thumping so fast that he could scarcely breathe. His throat felt hot and dry . . . his distended eyes searched the columns for the mention of his own name. Fear . . . a strange fear of the unknown was shaking him. What in God's name had been put in this paper to make Duval sob for him . . . to give a servant the right to insult him?

Then he read . . . and understood.

It was all on the front page of the paper—a popular evening edition—and doubtless occupied a prominent position in a good many other Parisian papers. His name stood out in capital letters . . . and his own photograph stared up at him . . . mocking him. Dozens of times he had seen his name, his photo in some pleasant report of a Society gathering, of a ball, of sport. Such articles had been fulsome, flattering, every word written to feed his vanity. But tonight the article was a deliberate insult . . . every word calculated to cover him with shame.

'PIERRE BOUCHERON.—Resignation of under-secretary from the Foreign Office. At the Quai d'Orsay today our correspondent was given to understand that M. Pierre Boucheron was asked to resign his position in the Foreign Office at once, owing to the discovery made by clever Paris detectives that M. Boucheron had no right to the position he occupied and has practised a huge hoax on the entire public. Boucheron, who lives in extravagant style in the Avenue du Bois, and is famous for his good looks and charming personality, has occupied much the same place in Paris that Beaucaire once occupied as the prince of fashion and idol of the women.

'His parties, dances, suppers, both in his flat and in the best-known cafés of the West End of Paris, have been unrivalled for their popularity and extravagance. Of recent weeks he has been constantly in the company of the beautiful daughter of the Comtesse de l'Orme. There was even the rumour of an engagement between the two. Our correspondent understands that all negotiations for the hand of Madeleine de l'Orme have been broken off, however, and that M. Boucheron will shortly be no longer seen or heard of in Paris.

'The hoax he has played upon the unsuspecting members of Society, with whom he has mixed freely and from whom he has accepted much hospitality, is an outrageous one. He is not the gentleman of birth and breeding he made out. He has only existed on money borrowed from the generous Comte Henri de Mercereau, who was, with the rest, deceived in him. He is, in actual fact, an apache from the underworld . . . once famous as a dancer in 'The White Coffin' in Montmartre, and a very dangerous criminal on whom the police kept a vigilant eye when he was not under lock and key.

'He first came before public notice when a girl, named Odile, who was at the time living with him, was arrested for the murder of M. Stets (a well-known financier) in the Rue Vaudray. Boucheron, known in the underworld as THE RAT, pleaded guilty to the charge, but was found not guilty, and the girl was acquitted on the grounds of 'self-defence'. The case aroused much interest at the time. Little has the unsuspecting Society of Paris realised that the young man they have entertained and applauded as Pierre Boucheron, under-secretary . . . is a common apache . . . THE RAT himself.

'Doubtless The Rat will return to his hiding-places and little or nothing will be known of him in the future . . .' Boucheron, with glazed eyes, read this article through to the bitter end.

It filled two or three columns. It breathed contempt . . . righteous indignation on behalf of 'Society' and when Boucheron finished it and every word had soaked into his bemused brain he saw THE END written for himself in flaming letters. The end of his reign in Paris as Boucheron; the end of this life of luxury and ease; the end of everything! Paris would read the article tonight. Already Duval and Varjean had read it. Everybody would be talking. The tongues of scandal would wag merrily far into the night. The families who had received him would hold up their hands in horror. Boucheron . . . The Rat . . . from Montmartre. (He noticed with irony that those words had been printed in capital letters in the paper.) Once he had thought of his nickname with pride. The Rat of Paris. But now it was a shameful title. It would be on everybody's lips . . . to his detriment, to his disgrace.

He crushed the paper between his hands. He felt cold . . . limp . . . lifeless. He no longer had any 'fight' in him; even his indignation against Varjean had vanished. He laughed at the thought of the valet sneering at him and deserting his post. What else could one expect? What decent 'respectable' servant would remain an hour in the service of a Rat? Varjean was only *vox populi*. Tomorrow everybody would sneer at him and abandon him. He would not have a single friend left, except, perhaps, poor Duval . . . who was a fool, but a loyal fool . . . and his old associates in Montmartre.

This then was Zélie de Chaumet's revenge! This was the beginning of the attack she intended to make on him in order to pay him out for loving Madeleine de l'Orme.

Another very bitter laugh escaped the man. Such was the fury of 'a woman scorned'. She had brought about his exposure, in the papers, through Mercereau.

The paper fell from Pierre's hands. His eyes became suffused. His whole body shook. And suddenly he fell on his knees beside his bed and laughed . . . shook and shook and shook with terrible, hysterical laughter.

CHAPTER THIRTEEN

The summer passed. Autumn, like a pale-faced woman of mature age who sees her vivid colour pass and counts the grey hairs in the russet-brown of her hair, grew desperate and in sudden wild storms of weeping passed into dreary old age.

Winter came. Over Paris the leaden skies were like a pall, and finally the surcharged skies let loose the drifting snow which settled on the roofs, streets and parks of the gay city.

Now everything was white . . . aching white. A thin film of ice hardened the face of the lake in the Bois, and the trees stripped of their leaves were like dark, stark sentinels pointing heavenwards. Every sharp gust of wind shook the powdery snow from the boughs.

It can be bitterly cold in Paris in midwinter. The winds can be furious, cutting like a knife, through the thin garments of the poor.

Cars continued to roll up before the Pré Catalan Café and inside it was warm, inviting, bright with artificial light which dispels the winter gloom for the idle rich. The delicate gossamer frocks of the ladies are replaced by warmer velvets and rich furs. Oh, winter can be splendid when one has warm sables and a warm car! It is even pleasant to walk through the snow-covered streets and parks, when one is warmly clad, and the sky is blue, the sun shining and the wind not too boisterous. Still more pleasant to remain indoors before a roaring log fire, or in a house heated by hot-water pipes. Then, one can look through the windows and even enjoy a storm . . . The snow falls so prettily in white, crisp feathery flakes, and Paris is beautiful with her wide river running like a dark serpent under her snow-whitened bridges, by her snow-covered banks.

But for the poor, who shall say the winter is a pleasure? They shiver in their rags and grumble in their cafés and look with eyes of longing towards the spring.

Six months had elapsed since Pierre Boucheron resigned from the Foreign Office and disappeared from the eyes of all who had known him in his glory.

December found him in a lodging house in a poorish part of the city . . . No. 13, Rue Yvetot. There he occupied a top room, almost an attic, containing a skylight, an iron bedstead, a cheap deal chest of drawers with a mirror on it, a chair and a table.

One week before Christmas, Boucheron sat at the table with a newspaper spread out before him and a pencil in his hand. He was running the pencil down a list of 'Situations Vacant', ticking off the most likely ones for which he might apply.

It was a biting cold morning and the temperature of this unheated bedroom was well below freezing. Pierre shivered and coughed incessantly. He was not used to the extreme cold and it affected his chest. He had had a severe cold in the head for the last two weeks and it had left him with a hacking cough.

The alteration in his position was remarkable. Sometimes he allowed himself to look back; to remember recent winters when he had been the most popular man in Paris and lived luxuriously in the Avenue du Bois. How warm, how comfortable he had been in that flat! What excellent food he had eaten! What cheery times he had had, dancing, attending the theatre, staying in the country with friends who hunted, rode, shot.

Pierre had gone down . . . down . . . down

since that night when his identity, his shame had been made public. Once a fire is extinguished nothing is left but ashes. Pierre was tasting the ashes, now that Zélie had very successfully put out the light of his triumph. He had been hounded from pillar to post by a certain formidable detective known as Jules Benoit. Everywhere that Pierre went, Benoit went. So far every job for which Pierre had applied, Benoit had prevented him from getting. Benoit had informed would-be employers that the charming and handsome young man was an apache, a Rat from the underworld, and Boucheron had been turned down.

At first Pierre had laughed ... gone doggedly ahead, trying to find honest work. But he had ceased to laugh as the months went by and his small store of savings vanished. Things were becoming serious. If Zélie with her sleuth-hound continued to prevent him from securing employment, how could he live?

It was an unfortunate fact that at the time of his downfall he had been heavily in debt. Like many young men of fashion in his position, he had been unconcerned; hoping to pay his bills in good time. On the morning following the exposure of his true identity, he had been besieged by creditors who had been terrified of losing their money. He had had to sell everything of value which he possessed in settlement of his debts. He had finally faced a practically empty flat; all the servants had deserted him; he had had nothing left but a few clothes and a diamond ring given him in the past by an infatuated Duchesse.

He had given up the flat, and sold what remained of his expensive clothes . . . dinner jackets, tunics, riding-habits, shooting clothes, hundreds of silk shirts, satin pyjamas, Eastern dressing-gowns; all of which the second-hand clothes shops grabbed at willingly and paid him a fraction of what they cost.

Looking back at those days, at that extensive wardrobe, Pierre was now appalled at his own extravagance. What he had then paid for one article of apparel would keep him for a month or more now.

Having sold everything and with just a few thousand francs at the back of him, Pierre had left the Avenue du Bois for ever. In the turmoil and difficulty of selling out and departing he had scarcely noticed the fact that none of his old 'friends' had called to see him or offer a helping hand. Rats desert a sinking ship. The women who had been so madly in love with his beautiful face in the days of his glory sighed a little, regretted his downfall a little . . . but were much too afraid of their reputations to stand by him in his shame.

The men who had been his 'pals', had eaten with him, enjoyed hundreds of drinks at his expense, borrowed from him, kept away from him once he was exposed as an apache; were indignant to think he had been their associate; never dreamed of showing him a little mercy or charity because he had once been good to them.

Of all that selfish, greedy, insincere crowd which formed Paris 'Society' only one person came to see Boucheron and commiserate with him. That was René Duval. Boucheron often thought with deep gratitude of the poor fop who was the laughing-stock of his friends. A fool he might be; a clown; a joke. But he had the finest heart of them all. Boucheron had been his friend, his pattern. Duval did not consider it a crime that Pierre had once been an apache. With the tears streaming down his face, he had offered him the hand of friendship, against the opinion of Paris. And Boucheron, tears in his own eyes, had refused that hand.

'You will only be boycotted by everybody—and you are *her* cousin,' he had reminded Duval. 'You must forget me, Duval, and not try to see me. I wish to disappear from everybody who has known me. God bless you for coming, all the same.'

That was all months ago. He had not set eyes on poor René since then. But he was the one person of whom Boucheron could think without bitterness. It is a fact that amongst the most despised and stupid folk we know we often find our truest friends.

There remained nothing of Boucheron's

possessions today save the suit of clothes he was wearing . . . a dark grey serge which was a relic of past smartness and had begun to look shabby, greasy about the cuff-rims, baggy in the trousers. This was merely the shadow of the Boucheron who had been the best-dressed man in town. He had sold the last ring he possessed two months ago. The money received for that had gone in rent and food.

And now a fortnight's rent was owing to Madame Plachons, landlady of these dark and dingy lodgings. He had gone without supper last night and had had only a cup of coffee and a roll today. It was now twelve o'clock. During this last month Boucheron had learned the true meaning of poverty . . . It was not as it had once been with him when as The Rat he had found money, or stolen food. Then he had rarely gone hungry; faced the world with a contemptuous smile. This was a changed man . . . a man who had learned to be a gentleman and to appreciate good things . . . His lithe body, once impervious to wind, rain or cold, had grown soft—it had been pampered by the luxurious life he had led in the Avenue du Bois. Lack of good food and the intense cold made him suffer cruelly. And because of Madeleine . . . because he had once held Madeleine in his arms and kissed her virgin lips, he was resolved to keep himself bodily and mentally clean. He suffered through lack of hot water and clean clothes. It was torture to him to go without fresh underlinen; to stand naked in a basin of water (ice-cold, because Madame Plachons could not afford the fuel to heat it). But he did that rather than go unwashed. And he remained hungry rather than go back to his old game and steal.

Hunger, cold, loneliness and misery . . . these are often the wages of virtue, whilst the wicked prosper. One of life's little ironies. But if Boucheron suffered, he did not complain. He had had plenty of leisure to think over facts and to face them honestly. Being sincere with himself he was forced to admit that he deserved the privations to which he was now exposed. He had had his chance and abused it. He had taken everything, given nothing.

What he did feel undeserved was Madeleine's disbelief in his love for her. That had and always would rankle and hurt him.

When he thought of Madeleine in these days it was as of a star—infinitely remote—nevertheless beautiful and shining. It was the image of her in his mind and the memory of her sweetness which guided him in his worst hours of temptation, helped him to resist the evils into which Fate might lead him. It is not difficult for a young and very handsome man to lead an evil life in Paris—or in any great capital of the globe . . . even when he has fallen from great heights. But a life of vice at the expense of some unprincipled woman who might use him as a decoy to lure other, more innocent women into sin scarcely tempted Boucheron. He had been bad, inconsequent, cruel, but never vicious. The memory of Madeleine was a safeguard to him even against evil thought. If he lost his self-respect, if he broke the vows he had made to her in his own mind, when he had first won her love, he could no longer say to himself, 'I truly loved her!' To be untrue to her would be to lose faith with himself. So he kept the star of her memory perpetually before him.

Pierre Boucheron—The Rat—had indeed found his own soul.

Although he took his punishment like a man he was far from being a saint, and many were the hours when he indulged in bitter, gloomy thought, reviling the Destiny that had so altered the course of his existence.

He had lost all his pity for Zélie de Chaumet. He had begun to hate her, as the boycott which was of her machination continued and he was turned away from job after job. That was grossly unfair of her. She had taken Madeleine from him. That had been punishment enough. She had taken away his position, his home; his life as Pierre Boucheron. But she had no right to take away his chances of making an honest living. Of course he saw what she wanted. It was her vindictive desire to send him back to the gutter and turn him into a thieving Rat again. But if she were stubborn, so was he, and he set his chin obstinately against the old evil.

He was cold, he was ill; he was very heartsick and tired. But he was not beaten yet.

On this grey December morning he sat at his table, poring over the list of 'Situations Vacant'. He felt very empty and his hands were so raw with cold that he could scarcely hold the pencil. His face, his figure, had altered during these hard six months of his banishment from Society. He was thin, drawn about the lips, hollow-eyed. There were dark shadows under those fine dark eyes. He slept badly because of the intense cold. The blankets Mère Plachons provided were thin and the icy winds whistled through a broken pane in the skylight and stung his ill-nourished body. He had been reduced to sleeping fully dressed, because had he taken off his things he believed he would have died from pneumonia.

Lack of good food and long tramps through the streets of Paris in all kinds of weather, whilst he searched for work, had told on his vigorous constitution; robbed him of much of his splendid vitality. And he had lost that look of pride, of boredom which had curved his lips in past days when he walked gracefully through an admiring crowd. He looked hungry and very tired.

On the table beside him stood the one treasure which he still owned and from which he would never part. The framed photograph of Madeleine de l'Orme. Once or twice, sublimely stupid, he had denied himself a meal in order to buy a bunch of white flowers to place before that shrine, as in the days of his luxurious flat. But now he no longer had a centime to waste.

He raised his head from the paper which he had been studying, having marked with a cross the ones he considered possible.

'Cutter wanted.'
'Locksmith and ironworker required.'
'Chauffeur for American visitor.'
'Shopwalker . . .'

A motley crowd. The chauffeur seemed the most likely. But little doubt Jules Benoit would leave his card on the Americans and warm them not to engage The Rat, he reflected bitterly. Shopwalker . . . God . . . what a job; to march up and down a ladies' store, meet perhaps several of the women who had known him in his glory . . . what shame, what humiliation! But that, even that, yes, gladly, for the sake of food! Soon he would be applying for employment as a dustman, a bartender, or a crossing-sweeper.

His gaze fell on Madeleine's photograph. A deep sigh broke from him.

'Ah, Madeleine, adored one, if I could see you now!'

If he could but look at her . . . touch her hand . . . lay his head on her lap and weep . . .

lay his head on her breast and die! If he could only know the heaven of her love, her tenderness once again, he could then welcome death. But life without her, this hunger, misery, misfortune, totally cut off from her, was worse than death. It was utter hell. To a man of Boucheron's temperament the hell was slowly becoming insupportable. He had hope still of a job . . . but when that hope died he would want to die sooner than beg.

Never a day passed but he remembered Madeleine . . . the thousand and one little intimate things a lover remembers about the woman of his choice . . . all her beauty, her grace, the curve of her lips, the softness of her breast, the thrill of her hands. Never a day or a night but he prayed to God . . . (he, who had never prayed in his life before!) . . . that she might one day realise he had truly loved her.

Through newspapers he followed her movements . . . as hungrily and hopelessly as Mou-Mou followed his six months ago. He knew that she had been taken abroad by her mother; that she was now in Monte-Carlo in their villa there. He supposed she had been taken out of Paris until the scandal of 'The Rat' had died down. He wondered if she had utterly forgotten him; if soon he would have the agony of reading an announcement of her betrothal to some man of her own aristocratic breeding . . . some Comte or Duc whom the old Comtesse would be proud to welcome into her distinguished family.

Had she forgotten? *Could* she forget . . . that passionate hour in the moonlit gardens of Château Lisbon . . . Pompadour in the arms of her Beaucaire? Ah, he would never forget in a thousand centuries, and surely she too would remember? She was human and she had loved him. But she was also very young and youth soon forgets. And if she remembered, perhaps it was only to despise him and loathe herself for every kiss or caress he had taken.

Time had not healed Pierre's wound. It ached and bled as painfully today when he stared at Madeleine's portrait as when he had said goodbye to her. He pressed the pictured face to his lips, then put it down and returned to his job.

The door was thrust open. Madame Plachons marched into the room. She was fat, blowsy, untidy; wisps of hair hanging over her red face. She was perspiring from her labours and the exertion of climbing the stairs to her top-floor lodger. Arms akimbo, she stood over him.

'*Eh bien*, Monsieur!' she said shrilly. 'You sit here dreaming and I wait for my rent. My babies must go hungry in order that I feed you—*hein*?'

Boucheron gazed at her wearily.

'No, no, Mère, wait a bit. I will make some money and then you shall have double.'

'I have heard that before,' said Madame

Plachons.

'It might even come true if you wait long enough,' he said. Then he added with a smile: 'You do not believe me?'

'No, I do not,' said Mère Plachons. 'You have said it too often. I will not wait any more.'

Fear crept into the eyes of Pierre. This miserable bedroom was wretched enough but it was at least shelter. He gave the woman a supplicating look.

'Come, *ma mère*, you would not turn me into the streets?'

What woman had ever been able to resist Pierre Boucheron's smile or voice when he chose to be charming? Even the over-worked, bad-tempered landlady softened her heart towards him. He was a handsome boy, she thought, and he looked ill.

She drew a bill from her apron pocket and handed it to him.

'Have the goodness to look at that,' she grumbled. 'It is long overdue.'

'I know,' he said. 'But give me a few more days, Mère. My luck is bound to turn.'

She shrugged her shoulders and moved her head from side to side, her face sour but not without pity for him.

'*Nom de Dieu*, I have been without enough money, and kept a husband who drinks, for ten years and my luck has not yet turned.'

Pierre rose and put a hand on her shoulder.

'If I get some money you shall have most of

it, Mère,' he said, good-humouredly.

Her fat, dirty face creased into smiles. She was fifty and she had had sixteen children, but she was woman enough to melt under Pierre Boucheron's smile and touch.

'*Eh bien*, maybe I will wait a day or so, but after that I must turn you out and get a lodger who will pay me. And *voyez-vous*, I will bring you a few boiled potatoes for your lunch when I give *mon homme* his dinner.'

Pierre started to thank her. There is nothing on earth to touch the generosity of the poor towards the poor, and he was moved by the kindness of this blowsy, unsavoury old woman.

She made her way from the room, grumbling and muttering. After she had gone Boucheron sat down in his chair and closed his eyes wearily. But he soon unclosed them again, for the old woman rushed back within two minutes, bearing a letter in her hand.

'For you,' she said excitedly. 'Maybe it is this luck that has turned.'

Boucheron sprang from his chair. He seized the envelope and ripped open the flap. He began to read the letter, which was neatly typed. Madame Plachons, frankly curious, peered over his shoulder. The letter was headed with the name and address of a business firm in the Rue Royale and addressed to M.P. Boucheron.

'Monsieur,

Your application for the vacancy on our staff has been favourably considered. Please, therefore, call upon us immediately.

Yours faithfully,

PIERRE LEMOIRE ET CIE

Boucheron read the letter aloud. His haggard face underwent a transformation. His cheeks flushed, his eyes grew brilliant. He was a boy again . . . on fire with enthusiasm . . . thrilling with hope. He gave a 'whoop' and began to dance around the room, holding the letter above his head.

'I have got the job—I have got it—*Mon Dieu*! But how marvellous . . . how wonderful!'

Madame Plachons almost beamed.

'*Eh bien, mon enfant*, I am pleased,' she said. 'Go and see these people without delay.'

Boucheron rushed to a cupboard which was let into the wall and pulled out a hat . . . He rushed to his chest of drawers and brushed his thick black hair back from his forehead. He put on the hat and then rushed to Madame Plachons.

'Thank God! . . . Thank God!' he said in a state bordering on hysteria. 'I go . . . I go immediately to *Lemoire et Cie*.'

Madame Plachons seized his arm. Panting and flushed she brushed the dust from his coat, then from the brim of his hat.

'You must look fine and smart,' she said, her enormous bosom heaving with emotion.

Pierre seized her round her shapeless waist and danced her about until the good woman panted for mercy. He then dropped a kiss on her cheek and rushed out of the room, down the creaky staircase, three stairs at a time, singing the 'Marseillaise'.

Madame Plachons stood where he had left her, a grimy hand pressed to the cheek he had kissed. Her eyes, half-sunk in folds of fat, bulged.

'*Nom d'un chien*, but the young man is certainly crazy,' she reflected. 'He will be asking me to leave my man and my children for him, next. And I'm not sure I wouldn't . . . the handsome lad!'

CHAPTER FOURTEEN

Boucheron made his way from the Rue Yvetot to the Madeleine and thence to the Rue Royale. He had forgotten hunger, cold, weariness. He was intensely alive . . . his eyes were radiant with hope. *Lemoire et Cie* had considered his application. Benoit had obviously not discovered about this, and not stood in his way.

The way that he might soon be earning a living wage as a respectable office-clerk filled Boucheron's heart with joy. That letter had changed the face of the world for him.

He noticed suddenly that the sun was shining; that the snow on the house-tops and the branches was white and sparkling; that all the shops in the big boulevards were beautifully decorated for Christmas and that it was good to be alive. Soon he would be working, and he would save—he would pinch and scrape in order to save enough to start a little business of his own—run a little garage somewhere, perhaps; become a prosperous business man. He saw his own name "*Boucheron et Cie*" over his garage. He saw himself with a fine house and garden. And he would lead a quiet, rather sober life with just enough to eat and drink and perhaps, sometimes, he would be a little gay.

His thoughts ran away with him. He was lost in imagination . . . in dreams. He nearly got run over crossing by the Madeleine, just opposite 'Cook's'. A taxi-driver pulled up sharply and cursed him. He ran on, laughing. He had found work and it was good to be alive. His Christmas would not altogether be the tragedy he had anticipated.

Panting, flushed, ardent-eyed, he reached the offices in Rue Royale and found the brass plate '*Lemoire et Cie*.' He felt every inch a gentleman of leisure again as the lift attendant saluted him and asked where 'Monsieur wished to go.' He asked for M. Lemoire, and was whirled up in the lift to the offices which were on the third floor.

There he entered the outer office. He found a girl sitting by a switchboard on a swivel chair. She was not attending to her switchboard. She was gazing at her reflection in a small round mirror in her handbag, and outlining the shape of her mouth with a vermilion lipstick.

Boucheron, hat in hand, stood hesitating. He was trembling with nerves; with the eagerness to state his case . . . to interview M. Lemoire. He was pathetically anxious to please—even this girl who was the telephonist of *Lemoire et Cie*. But he wished she would realise his presence in the room and attend to him.

'*Bonjour, Mam'selle*,' at length he said huskily.

The girl was far too engrossed in her occupation to hear him. She finished with the lipstick and began to pat her nose with a powderpuff. In bygone days Pierre Boucheron would have looked at her critically and found her rather pretty in a fluffy, dolly way. She had a lot of flaxen hair 'permanently waved and curled'; a pink and white skin and small, impudent mouth. The figure in the neat blue skirt and white silk jumper, with Eton collar and tie, was trim and quite attractive. But today Boucheron was too anxious about his job to feel the attraction of sex. He shifted from one foot to another.

'Mam'selle,' he repeated.

She dropped her powderpuff into her bag

and swung round.

For an instance she stared at him with round, blue eyes, impudent, in keeping with the mouth and *retroussé* nose. Then she sat upright and became all attention.

'Monsieur!' she said archly. It was a long time since she had seen a gentleman quite so handsome as this one in the office.

'I have come to see M. Lemoire,' said Pierre.

'Your card, please, Monsieur,' she said.

'I—I have no card,' he stammered. 'I am Boucheron. It is in answer to your letter . . . for the job . . .'

'O-oh!' she said, mouth round, eyes big and round. She regarded him in a fresh light. Not a gentleman on business, but a clerk applying for the job. Now the job was of importance to the young woman at the switchboard. The clerk had quite a lot to do with her. She saw a lot of him. The last clerk, Jean Roussent, had been ugly, elderly and a misogynist. He had annoyed Mlle. Yvonne. It had been as impossible to flirt with him as though he were a statue. Mlle. Yvonne was vain and full of coquetry and to flirt was part of her daily routine. Not to flirt meant missing something out . . . something very important in life. Here, now, was a handsome boy who looked an aristocrat and had marvellous eyes. She leaned her elbows on the desk, cupped her chin in her hands and flashed him an inviting look.

'Oh! so you're M. Boucheron, after the job? Well, I hope you get it.'

'I-oh-thanks,' he said.

He could have laughed at himself. He was stammering, flushing, behaving like a schoolboy. Where was The Rat? Where was the bored gallant of the Avenue du Bois? Months of privation and disappointment had made an idiot of him. He looked down at the fluffy, blue-eyed telephonist and realised that she was 'making eyes' at him. The corners of his mouth curved into a smile.

'Thank you, Mam'selle,' he said. 'May I see M. Lemoire?'

'Oh, at once. I'll go and tell him. I *do* hope you get the job,' she repeated, rising, and patting a fair curl into order.

Boucheron thought her very stupid, but he was still masculine enough to be flattered by her obviously sincere desire to have him as her associate.

'What is your name?' he asked.

'Yvonne Lambert. I say, I am glad you're young,' she said frankly, with another coy smile at him. 'It isn't much fun having an old skinflint round you all the while. Wait a minute, I'll go and see if the Boss will talk to you.'

All impatience, Pierre waited. Yvonne returned, hands on her hips. She appeared quite excited.

'The Boss'll see you,' she said.

Boucheron walked through into an office marked 'private'. As he passed the girl who held the door open for him she threw him an inviting glance, but he had forgotten her existence. He was rivetting his attention on the man whom he believed would be his future employer and his heart beat so fast that it seemed to shake his whole body. The excitement made him feel faint, he was sick with hunger. His face was very pale. But he tried not to appear nervous or anxious as he said: '*Bonjour, Monsieur.*'

M. Lemoire, a big, stout man with a cigar in the corner of his mouth, was seated before a large roll-top desk littered with papers. He looked good-natured and gave Boucheron a gracious nod that filled the would-be clerk with hope. The office was thickly-carpeted, well-heated by radiators. It breathed comfort and opulence . . . gave Boucheron a sense of being in another world . . . the old world he had left in such disgrace. He stood before Lemoire, silent, eyes very bright and appealing.

Mlle. Lambert was still in the doorway, her round, blue eyes rivetted on him as though she were lost in admiration and had forgotten where she was. A sharp order of dismissal from M. Lemoire sent her hurrying off. She closed the door behind her.

M. Lemoire looked at Pierre.

'Er—you are the Boucheron to whom we wrote yesterday?'

'*Oui*, Monsieur.'

'I have been considering your application which I picked out of many others because I liked your handwriting and style. It is obvious that you have education, you have known better times . . . *hein*?' Lemoire gave Pierre a shrewd but kindly look.

'*Oui*, Monsieur,' said Pierre, flushing painfully. 'That is so.'

'You have references?'

'I . . . that will be a difficulty,' said Boucheron, twisting his hat in his nervous fingers. 'I—I have never worked before.'

'Quite so. But there is somebody to speak for you, surely? I cannot take you without some kind of character. The work is simple . . . you have only to file my letters, stamp and post the out-going mail . . . takes messages when I am out . . . in fact it is an office-boy's place more than an experienced clerical job.'

'I understand,' said Pierre. 'But I will be glad to take it.'

M. Lemoire chewed his cigar and regarded Pierre's pale, handsome face. It seemed to him too thin, bloodless, almost transparent. The young man looked as though he had suffered badly. But there was something fine and courageous about the dark, bright eyes that pleased Lemoire. He believed a man with such eyes could be trusted. He rather fancied himself as a judge of character.

'I will let you have the post, Boucheron, if

you can give me some sort of reference,' he said.

Pierre considered this. The muscles in his cheeks were working and his heart beat in that hard, thumping way that made him feel faint. But he was determined to secure this post at all costs. It seemed a chance . . . a beginning. What did he care, even if he had to do an office-boy's work? The drudgery of sticking on stamps and running errands would be paid for—and he was hungry, desperate. He suddenly remembered Duval. Poor René had besought him to write if ever he needed help. Well, perhaps this once he would call on his one-time friend, the poor fop. Duval would concoct some sort of reference for him. He could rely on that.

'I—yes—you could get a character for me from a M. Duval who knew me well,' he stammered. 'If that will do.' He gave Duval's address.

'That sounds all right to me,' said Lemoire, jotting it down. 'You may consider yourself engaged pending your reference, Boucheron.'

Pierre's heart leaped.

'Thank you, thank you, Monsieur,' he said.

'Poor brute,' thought Lemoire. 'He is starving. The unemployment is terrible today. If he is honest—a genuine case—I shall be glad I have engaged him.'

There came a knock on the door.

'*Entrez*,' said Lemoire.

Mlle. Yvonne tripped in, holding out a card.

'A gentleman to see you, Monsieur.'

'Who is it?' said Lemoire, and glanced at the card. Then his brows contracted. He said sharply: 'One moment, I will see the gentleman in the outer office.'—To Pierre: 'Wait for me one moment, Boucheron.'

'*Oui*, Monsieur,' said Pierre.

Yvonne caught his gaze, questioning him. He guessed that she was dumbly asking if he had got the job. He nodded eagerly and smiled. She looked pleased. She made her exit with the Boss.

Left alone, Pierre took a deep breath and looked round the warm room wherein his future work would lie. He felt as happy as though he had come into a fortune. He rubbed his cold hands together and began to walk up and down the office, humming under his breath. He had not felt so happy since his downfall.

This was his chance . . . his chance to begin again . . . to show Zélie de Chaumet that it was not possible to bring him to the gutter and stamp him out . . . like a rat is stamped.

He paused by the desk. His gaze fell casually on the card which M. Lemoire had just had brought to him. The effect upon Pierre of that name, printed on the oblong of pasteboard, was extraordinary. He went scarlet; dead white. Bitter disappointment flickered in his eyes, then faded into utter despair.

Jules Benoit.

Benoit—Zélie de Chaumet's detective. So the sleuth-hound had followed him, even here? At this very moment he was acquainting M. Lemoire with facts of his—Boucheron's—past life, telling him that Pierre Boucheron was an ex-apache, ex-criminal . . .

'*Mon Dieu*!' was the anguished cry of Pierre's bursting heart. '*Mon Dieu*! How cruel . . . how cruel!'

The office-door re-opened. M. Lemoire marched in. His genial face had changed. His lips were thin and stern. He put his arms across his chest and gave Pierre a terrible look. Pierre did not speak; did not even attempt to plead or argue his case. He picked up his hat, then with bowed head and drooping shoulders walked out of the office and shut the door behind him. It was very final. Benoit had done his dirty work with the customary success. This office, like all the others, was closed to him. René Duval would not be called upon to supply a character.

Yvonne Lambert, anxiously awaiting Boucheron, stared at him as he came out of the Boss's room. How queer, how pale he looked. What had happened? What had that other silly fellow said to the Boss to alter his point of view about Boucheron?

Pierre, with lagging steps, moved to the door which led out of the offices of *Lemoire et Cie*. Yvonne ran after him.

'*Mon Dieu*! what is it? Haven't you got the job?'

He turned and looked at her. For days and nights the foolish little telephonist was strangely haunted by the sheer despair in those dark, handsome eyes.

'No!' he said hoarsely. 'I—haven't got it.'

He passed out, and shut the door behind him. He was no longer alert. Every movement was slow, unutterably weary.

Mlle. Yvonne flung herself back into her chair and cast a furious look at the closed door between her and the Boss.

'*Imbécile*!' she said.

Boucheron walked out of the building into the street. The sun was still shining and the snow, heaped by crossing-sweepers on to the sides of the pavement, was crisp and sparkling. But for Boucheron the sun had gone, and it was a grey and bitter world which he faced.

He must return to Rue Yvetot without his job; he must tell Madame Plachons that he had failed and that he would not be able to pay her bill. He was ashamed to go back and make such an announcement. The woman had been good to him in her fashion. He had wanted to pay that bill—to give her double. And he was to go hungry again, except for the charity she might offer. Tonight he would go to bed, cold and hungry, with the knowledge that he would wake up tomorrow in the same plight, unemployed, penniless.

An hour ago he had been alive with hope. Now Zélie de Chaumet had crushed every fraction of it. For the first time since misfortune had overtaken him he was without any hope at all. Hunger and cold added to his depression. He felt very nearly beaten; bitter; furiously angry with the woman who was eking out her mean revenge in this fashion.

'What right has she to stop me getting work every time, every time?' he inwardly cried as he walked down the crowded street, staring blindly ahead of him. '*Mon Dieu! Mon Dieu!* what can I do now?'

Hunger gnawed at him. The biting wind brought the tears to his eyes. He brushed them fiercely away and went on trampling down the Rue Royale, not caring where he went. He could not go back to Rue Yvetot just yet . . . could not face Madame Plachons and the fresh humiliation of it all.

It had seemed such a chance at *Lemoire et Cie*. He was cruelly disappointed. Jules Benoit . . . God . . . how he loathed the name of that man . . . more than he had loathed Caillard in the past.

He thought of 'The White Coffin'. He could always go down there and get food and drink at Mère Colline's expense . . . always be certain of welcome from Mou-Mou, for instance. But he shrank from asking for charity from his old friends in 'The White Coffin'. That would be a greater humiliation than any he had yet endured. So he religiously kept away from Montmartre, avoided the old pals there, just as he avoided the rich circle he had known in the days of his success.

Tomorrow he would not even have the shelter of a roof at Rue Yvetot, he reflected grimly. Mère Plachons would turn him out—and rightfully. She had to live, poor devil. She must find a lodger who could pay.

He faced the appalling fact of being without a centime in the world and with nothing to sell but the suit of clothes he was wearing. He had avoided selling that suit because without one decent one how could he apply for a decent job? Now, however, it appeared unlikely that he would ever secure decent employment, with Zélie's sleuth-hound tracking him down. What use to keep the suit and the grey felt hat?

He set his teeth and turned his steps toward the poorer part of the city wherein he might find a second-hand clothes-dealer.

He found a Jew in the Jewish Quarter who bought the grey lounge suit, because it was good cloth and an expensive cut, and the hat. In exchange Pierre was given a threadbare blue serge; frayed, shiny, indescribably shabby; one of the cheap ready-mades which Pierre had never put on before, for as The Rat he had worn more picturesque attire. A cheap tweed cap replaced his grey Homburg. Several five-franc notes found a home in his pocket. Such was the bargain struck between a desperate man and a Jew.

Pierre came out of the second-hand clothes shop laughing . . . a laugh not good to hear. The strange blue suit which fitted so shockingly had a curious mental effect on him; made him feel like his clothes, cheap and shoddy. He wondered if the man who had sold that suit to the Jew had felt as miserable and bitter as the one who bought it now.

He felt colder than ever. The wind cut cruelly through the blue serge, which was much thinner than the grey cloth had been. But at least he had a few francs in his pocket. Half must go to poor Mère Plachons. With a franc or two he could buy something to eat. That was the immediate need. He was sick, rocking on his feet with hunger.

He walked into a small café close to the secondhand clothes shop. It reeked of garlic and cheap tobacco and was full of working men, drinking and eating. Pierre forgot his disappointment, his misery, the hopelessness of his outlook. He licked his lips and found a place at the counter where he could get garlic-sausage and a roll for a few centimes. The man behind the counter served him with filthy hands. But Pierre Boucheron seized the roll and began to eat it wolfishly. It is terrible to be hungry and terrible to watch a starving man attack the first food he has had for many long hours. But nobody in that low café watched the desperate young man in the cheap blue suit.

Everybody who entered was hungry and too busy eating their own food to pay attention to anybody else.

All thought passed from the brain of Pierre. His mind a blank, he sat hunched upon his stool, eating . . . eating . . .

CHAPTER FIFTEEN

As week succeeded week, Boucheron sank lower and lower. He left his room in the Rue Yvetot, Mère Plachons' fat friendly face became a ghost of the past to him. Christmas Eve found him in the lowest possible straits, calling a dirty and sordid garret in Montmartre by the name of 'home'. He was still without employment and without the hope of securing a job. Since his failure with *Lemoire et Cie* through the arrival of Benoit he had applied for job after job and met with the same fate. Each time he was accepted Benoit interfered, and the job was closed to Pierre Boucheron.

He changed his name. He called himself by a dozen different names. But Benoit was swift and sure; a deadly sleuth-hound, well paid by Comte Mercereau and Madame de Chaumet, and the change of name made no difference to him. He was always on the heels of the young man who had earned Zélie de Chaumet's undying resentment, and he never let him escape many yards before he caught him again. Boucheron was reduced to rags and a bench on the banks of the Seine for sleeping accommodation.

The fine courage of Pierre began to fail. He was very thin. His eyes were great dark wells in his gaunt face and the hollows in his cheekbones were pitiful. With the illness and weakness of his body his mind became dull. He began to forget that he had ever been a gentleman of leisure; that he had ever lived a life of ease and luxury; made love to beautiful pampered women; boasted that he was the idol of Paris. He began to forget the books he had studied; the ideals he had set up before himself; even the vow he had made of loyalty to Madeleine's memory. Gradual starvation and the degradation of being hounded by Benoit from pillar to post submerged the finer instincts of the man and reduced him to a lower state than that in which he had lived before his first meeting with Zélie. The personality of Boucheron disappeared with that existence which Boucheron had led. Reaction set it. And when, at long last, he was reduced to selling even the frame of Madeleine's beloved, cherished photograph, the last remnants of his courage, his refinement seemed to go with it. He became The Rat again . . . a slinking, desperate creature with a sullen, bitter mouth and a laugh that echoed despair.

He was being slowly and effectively crushed . . . body and soul. Zélie de Chaumet was keeping her vow to send him back to the gutter.

Christmas Day found him without shelter, food or pride. There was one course left to him and he took it. He made his way to 'The White Coffin'. Till then he had avoided that old, favourite haunt, dreading the jeers of his former associates—men like Otto . . . the pity of Mère Colline and Mou-Mou. But when a man is desperate, nothing matters and pride is forgotten. He wanted to live. There was one road out of all the hunger and misery . . . death. But Pierre Boucheron was afraid of death. He was not a man of faith, of religion. He did not believe in life after death. And he was afraid of death as he regarded it, a total annihilation . . . the snuffing out of a candle . . . the crushing of an ant under one's heel. He was not prepared to die. To live one must work and get food. He could get work in 'The White Coffin'. There, they would not demand a character, and Benoit's news would not be news to them at all. So, at last, to 'The White Coffin' went Boucheron, once more The Rat. Never had his footsteps lagged more terribly and never had his over-burdened heart been more sore.

The blue serge suit had long since been sold. He was in rags today . . . a filthy shirt . . . a red handkerchief about his neck. His hair, long and unkempt, hung in black strands over his eyes. There was a week's growth of beard on his chin.

He slouched along the streets towards 'The White Coffin', hands sunk in his ragged pockets, feeling utterly dejected. He was The Rat without the former vigour or the bravado of The Rat. It was very pitiful. And he loathed himself . . . loathed the thing he had become.

Christmas Day. That made him laugh . . . a laughter that had a raw edge to it. He passed shops gay with silver-paper bells; scarlet streamers; holly and mistletoe; bonbons, fruit, toys; all the Christmas fare. He thought of last Christmas Day and then laughed, that raw, bitter laugh again, at the recollection. He had spent that day merrily with Zélie during Mercereau's absence abroad. They had joined a big party; danced all night . . . danced till breakfast time the next morning. Life then had meant rich food, good wine, music, laughter, lights, the thrill of soft lips, inviting eyes, the intoxication of all that a passionate, infatuated woman could offer. He had been sated with the good things of life . . . and Zélie de Chaumet had been at his feet . . . this day a year ago.

'God, what a frightful difference,' he thought. He shivered in his rags and walked painfully down the street, his feet red and raw in a pair of old, cracked boots. 'And it is to Zélie that I owe my present position . . .'

He stopped outside 'The White Coffin'. He crossed his arms on his chest, coughed and shuddered. His lips writhed in that frightful smile which had been assuredly born in hell. He dreaded going down to his old friends and asking *them* for charity.

Only a week ago he had run into Duval and a friend of his at the corner of the Rue de la Paix, where Pierre had hung about trying to earn a few francs by opening car doors, before Benoit had time to spot him and set a gendarme on to him. He had actually opened the door of a taxi for Duval and his friend, who were coming out of one of the big shops, laden with Christmas parcels. Duval had stared incredulously at the horribly-changed face and figure of his friend, dropped the parcels and gone pale with consternation.

'Boucheron . . . *mon Dieu! mon Dieu!*' he had said.

The meeting had very much distressed Pierre. He had turned and run . . . shutting his ears to the voice of his one-time friend who called after him, 'Boucheron . . . Boucheron . . . fool, come back!' But he had run until he had made sure Duval could not follow him. It was more than he could tolerate . . . such a meeting. Duval would have given him money . . . spoken perhaps of Madeleine. That would have reduced him to a dangerous state of self-pity, of sentimentality. And Boucheron had hardened his heart now, got beyond sentiment;

it was better so, better to be hard; to forget Madeleine and the old days; otherwise he would go mad.

He thought of Duval as he stood outside 'The White Coffin', and a tremor passed through him.

'Boucheron is dead,' he said to himself. 'I am The Rat. I go back to The Haunt of The Rat.'

He stumbled down the stone steps and made his way through the coffin-opening into the café. Mère Colline was there at her desk. It was early and the place was empty except for one or two habituées. Mou-Mou, talking to Mère Colline, was the first to see Boucheron. She stared at him for a moment as though he were an apparition. Then her face lit up; her black eyes gleamed with fierce pleasure. She ran to him, panting.

'Rat . . . *mon* Rat!'

He gave the ghost of a smile, put an arm about her shoulders and tried to appear nonchalant.

'*Eh bien*, Mou-Mou—*comment ça va?* And you, Mère . . . how is life?'

Mère Colline stared at him.

'Is it yourself or a ghost?' she ejaculated. 'Mercy on us, boy, but you are all skin and bones.'

Mou-Mou clung to his arm. She was half laughing, half crying. Her great eyes were swimming in tears.

'But it is he . . . it is our Rat,' she said. 'I had thought he was dead.'

'Better that I were dead, little one,' he said gloomily. 'But I am not fit even to die.'

'Have a drink and a roll,' said Mère Colline, the ever-practical.

The Rat put a hand to his throat.

'I can't pay for it,' he said, 'but I'll work it off. That's what I've come for, to ask for a job, Mère.'

She nodded, her plump face puckered with trouble. She could see that something was very wrong with The Rat; that there had been great changes since he had left the rich friends with whom he had associated. Regretfully she thought of the days when he had come down here, spruce and smiling, ready to give her as many hundred franc notes as she demanded.

But Mou-Mou, who loved The Rat, had no regrets. He had come back. That was all that mattered. He was hungry and he looked ill. That tore her loyal little heart.

'Sit down . . . eat and drink, *mon p'tit chou*,' she said with emotion. 'Afterwards you can talk of work.'

He sank into the chair she offered. His chin fell forward on his chest. Blindly he stared at the girl who fell on her knees before him and put an arm about him, her gaze rivetted on his face. He said hoarsely:

'Of all the friends I have in the world, Mou-Mou, you are the most faithful.'

That was praise indeed. She gave a laugh that ended in a sob and hunched her small, thin shoulders.

'Poof . . . it is easy to be faithful when one loves.'

'How many practise such a doctrine?' he muttered. He put out a hand and touched Mou-Mou's curly mop of hair. 'Poor little one,' he added, 'I do not deserve your kindness. I have done nothing for you.'

'You have come back,' she said, an almost sublime expression transforming her face. 'That is enough for me.'

Mère Colline placed food and drink before the man who had always been the darling of her elastic heart.

'Times have changed, Rat,' she said; 'but the sun may shine again.'

'Not for me,' he said. 'How right you are, Mère. Times *have* changed. Last time I saw you I could have given you money for all. Today I come to beg charity from you.'

'They owe you a great deal—the whole lot of 'em here,' said Mou-Mou with a gesture which embraced everybody in 'The White Coffin'. 'We are in your debt and if we can pay you back—'

'Surely,' finished Mère Colline, 'you can have work here. We need a bartender, Rat.'

He gulped down the wine she had set before him. His eyes closed. His head nodded forward.

'*Mon Dieu!*' said Mere Colline. 'The poor boy is dead tired as well as hungry. Let him sleep. He can work when he wakes.'

Mou-Mou crouched at the feet of The Rat. Her arm went up, encircled him. She stared up at his face . . . so bloodless, so ravaged, so bitter. It was a mask of bitterness . . . of pain. She guessed that Zélie de Chaumet had brought him down to this, and she felt fierce rage, fierce resentment on behalf of The Rat.

'That any woman could do this to you, *mon* Rat,' she whispered. 'Oh, God, may she be cursed . . . may she suffer the agonies of hell . . . because she has thrust *you* into hell . . . *mon pauvre* Rat!'

Her voice broke in a sob. She gathered the man in her arms, and his head fell forward on her breast. He was fast asleep. He had been exhausted, and the sudden warmth and nourishment had sent him into a sort of stupor.

Mou-Mou, savagely glad, let that boyish head lie where it had fallen, stroked the thick dark hair back from his forehead. Now that he slept, the lines were erased from the gaunt face. It became young again and very pitiful.

Mou-Mou did not move. Rigid, with tears pouring down her cheeks, she sat there staring before her. But she was happy. The Rat had come back. The Rat was sleeping in her arms, as he had slept before in days that she had supposed would never come again.

She thought of Madeleine, Comtesse de

l'Orme. She had read about that broken engagement; about Madeleine's retirement to her mother's villa in the south. And while Mou-Mou pillowed The Rat's head on her breast she whispered to him:

'I am bad, *mon* Rat . . . I have always been bad . . . but God Himself knows I am not so bad as that virtuous woman who turned her back upon you in your shame!'

He slept for two hours without waking once, without once moving.

Mou-Mou kept her arms about him and dared not stir lest she should disturb his rest. The head on her breast became a weight that hurt, but to the woman who loved The Rat it was exquisite agony. She grew chilled and numbed after the first hour. Every bone in her body began to ache . . . the sharp shooting pains of cramp seized her, but she did not move. Staring down at him she sat motionless, suffering, and incredibly happy.

Later, Rose and America sauntered into the room; saw The Rat sleeping there, in Mou-Mou's arms, and came up to the couple; stared at them in wonder and amazement.

'So The Rat has come back,' said Rose. 'In tatters . . . and *mon Dieu* . . . how thin and ill he looks.'

'Hush . . . don't wake him,' said Mou-Mou.

'The poor Rat,' said America, with more softness than Rose had shown. 'What a fall from his high estate.'

'I don't know that I am sorry for him—he is rather contemptible,' said Rose.

Mou-Mou's black eyes gleamed up at Rose. She said through her teeth:

'You ... *mon Dieu* ... you are a piece of straw blown by the wind ... you hang on to his arm when he is rich and prosperous ... Now when he is down and out you call him contemptible.'

Rose shrugged her shoulders and lit a cigarette.

'Poof. I won't quarrel with you. We have all quarrelled enough over The Rat ... He is back ... let him remain. I don't want him ... and I don't suppose America does.'

'One might want, but would not get him,' mused America, looking thoughtfully at the pale, haggard face of the man against Mou-Mou's breast. 'No ... I leave him to Mou-Mou. But she will not get him awake. She only has him when he sleeps.'

The two girls moved away, laughing. Mou-Mou shut her eyes because she did not want them to see her tears. She had always wanted this man, and she knew that America was right ... one could want him and never get him ... no woman could get him. But she, alone, of all the women, had never grown tired of waiting and of loving.

A hot tear splashed on to the dark head of The Rat. But he slept on ... the deep, silent sleep of utter exhaustion. The chatter of the girls had not disturbed him. And later when the music started and 'The While Coffin' filled up and grew noisy with voices, laughter, dancing, he did not wake.

The pain of Mou-Mou's cramped limbs became unbearable, but she dreaded moving . . . dreaded the moment when The Rat would wake and go from her. Like this, asleep, he was hers . . . hers.

'Oh, God, my God, You know how I love him!' she cried inarticulately. 'Oh, God, if only you would give him to me when he wakes . . .'

The Rat stirred, flung up an arm and encircled her neck. His fingers felt for her hair and closed over a soft bunch of it. She trembled for fear that he was waking. She was tortured, yet in ecstacy, because of the careless caress which he gave to her in his unconsciousness.

She saw his lips move and bent down to catch what he said. She heard him whisper a name.

'Madeleine . . . Madeleine . . .'

Her heart, beating so pitifully fast, grew cold and hopeless within her. But she held him a little closer and whispered back:

'Pierre . . .'

It was the first time she had ever called him that. To her, to all of them down here, he had been just The Rat.

'Madeleine,' moaned the man in her arms. And now he pulled Mou-Mou's head down to him and drew her lips to his mouth. She shivered and shut her eyes and endured that kiss which had such power to stir her poor, half-starved little body to fierce passion and love. She knew that it was for Madeleine . . . the young Comtesse who had turned her back upon him. But she—Mou-Mou—took it . . . let The Rat's hungry lips cling to hers and cling . . . and was grateful to God because the man she worshipped turned to her, loved her in his dreaming.

Then the shock of returning consciousness sent a long shudder through the body of the man. His arms fell away from Mou-Mou . . . his lips left her mouth. He opened his eyes. For an instant he stared up at her, wondering where he was. Then he shook his head, drew a hand across his eyes and sat upright. He stared about him dazedly. He saw the crowded café; a couple dancing; Mère Colline at her desk . . . the familiar atmosphere, thick with smoke and fast growing hot and foetid. He remembered where he was and why he had come here. All day he had been tramping the streets, starving. Tonight he was here to work . . . to live. Then he remembered a dream . . . he had just dreamed of Madeleine . . . and he had kissed her.

He put his face in his hands and his shoulders shook with ironic laughter. When he looked up again, he saw Mou-Mou sitting back in her chair, white as a sheet, rubbing her arms and legs. Now that she was free to move again the pain in her cramped body was excruciating.

'What is it, Mou-Mou?' he asked.

'Nothing,' she said; 'I am just tired.'

He did not realise that he had kept her in one painful position for over two hours; that hers had been the tender mouth from which he had drawn that long, hungry kiss in the anguish of his dream. He rose to his feet and thrust his hands in his pockets . . . his face sullen; his dark eyes curiously vague and dimmed. He looked as though hunger and privation and misery had stamped out his former intelligence and taken all his vigour from him. He turned and slouched over to Mère Colline's desk, not deliberately ungrateful or unkind to Mou-Mou but just forgetting her existence now that he was awake.

'Give me work, Mère,' he said hoarsely.

'*Oui, mon enfant*,' she said. 'Jean Lupin is sick and has gone away. You can take his job . . . fetch some casks of wine up from the cellar and take this serviette . . . wait on those who want wine.'

He took the white napkin she handed him, unsmiling. With that terrible, dull look in his eyes, he stared round the café. Already in his bemused mind he was a waiter . . . he was ready to do his job; he, a waiter in 'The White Coffin' where he had once been a king; he, who had been Pierre Boucheron, in Jean Lupin's place, ready to receive orders from men who were the scum of the earth and girls who were prostitutes and thieves . . . to take a kick or a tip . . . whichever he might be fortunate or unfortunate enough to receive.

He shuffled forward into the room, the napkin over his arm.

Mou-Mou, still rubbing her limbs, watched him go, in agony of body and of mind.

CHAPTER SIXTEEN

The New Year came.

Paris went mad with festivity . . . with the balls, the supper-parties, the theatres, the seasonable gaiety of the gayest city in Europe. There was enough champagne opened and drunk to form a vast golden river. The débris of streamers, coloured balls, empty crackers swept up every night in all the cafés and restaurants and piled together would have made a futurist hill. Revellers, rich and poor, ushered the New Year in singing and dancing like children. Then the poor settled down to work again, hoping for better times, although sublimely conscious of the fact that the New Year had made no material difference to their position, and the rich went on more soberly to seek for fresh amusement.

It was the year of 1914 . . . and six months before the tearing in two of a 'scrap of paper' plunged Europe into chaos and the stout-hearted *poilus* marched in their thousands to face the thunder of the guns and keep the enemy out of Paris.

In 'The White Coffin', all that January and the month following, The Rat worked as a bar-tender in Jean Lupin's place. He received starvation wages (for much as Mère Colline loved her Rat she could not afford to give him more) and relied on tips to keep body and soul together. He just managed to live . . . but it was an existence, and it crushed all the desire to live right out of him. Every week he grew thinner and more hollow-eyed, and the girls in the café said that he never laughed . . . rarely smiled. He was not the spirited man of former days, whose smiles, whose caresses had been at a premium, eagerly asked for, carelessly given. He was a slave . . . and in those dark eyes of his burned that sullen smouldering fire of resentment which lies in the eyes of slaves, or prisoners. But he was very silent. He never complained. He wanted to be left alone. The girls, the men, who had been his friends in the old days, began by offering him friendship in a half-pitying, half-contemptuous fashion. But he did not want their pity, and he could not bear their contempt. Occasionally, driven by some half-open jibe or insult, he spat out a furious reply and the flicker of resentment burst into hot fire. Then it died down again, and he remained sullen, indifferent, just smouldering. They learned to leave him alone. He was not popular—as he had been years ago—neither was he disliked. He was just accepted by everybody in 'The White Coffin' and not so much the object of derision as pity. But nobody, after the first few weeks, showed their feelings to The Rat.

Mou-Mou continued to love him and want him in her dog-like fashion, but he did not seem to be aware of her pathetic devotion and hardly ever spoke to her. She did not force herself on him. She waited till he addressed her, needed her. She was so used to waiting. But her great mournful eyes followed him incessantly while he slouched round the tables, opening bottles or clearing away the débris, and somehow she was hurt by the sight of him in that degraded position. She suffered for and with him . . . Once, just before the New Year, she dared offer to make his life happier, more comfortable by sharing it with him, looking after him, but he only touched her hair with careless tenderness and shook his head.

'No, my dear . . . I don't want you . . . I don't want anybody. Just leave me alone. But thank you, Mou-Mou.'

She had gone away, bitterly disappointed. She would have worked her fingers to the bone . . . sold her body to the highest bidder . . . in order to make *him* more comfortable . . . to benefit *him*. But he did not want her. She tried to comfort herself with the memory of his thanks. There was a time when The Rat, spoiled and pampered, would not have bothered to thank her for what she had offered him.

No . . . The Rat did not want Mou-Mou . . . or any woman. He had ceased to want even Madeleine de l'Orme. She had gone so far away from him in these days . . . so far away, in his thoughts. When he had come down to work in 'The White Coffin', to accept what he looked upon as the charity of his old associates, he had been broken in body and mind and heart . . . so broken that not even the memory of his real and selfless love for Madeleine could make him whole again. If he thought of her at all, nowadays, it was as of a radiant creature in another world . . . something that had once been precious, infinitely dear . . . but was lost in the dark, remote shadows of his soul. He was too broken-hearted to strive for light in that darkness . . . too tired. And perhaps he found that he suffered less by not thinking or remembering . . . by just existing in that mental stupor of mind.

The Rat had one bitter enemy in 'The White Coffin', however; one not content to pity him or be quietly scornful, or to let him alone.

Otto, the apache, had not forgotten his old hatred and jealousy of The Rat; the blow he had received when The Rat, in his glory, had come down to the café and punished him for bullying Mère Colline. Otto had vowed, then, to be revenged. It seemed now that he had ample opportunity to pay The Rat back for that knockout blow.

He was immensely pleased to see the once handsome, disdainful young man such a complete wreck. It amused him to sit at one of the tables at night and order drinks . . . to make The Rat serve him . . . to snarl at him . . . tell him to make haste . . . treat him like a dog. The Rat did not snarl back now; did not seem to care what happened. He was utterly indifferent to fate.

This went on for several weeks. Then, one cold night in March when Paris was swept by wild gusts of wind and drenched in sleet, the old open warfare between The Rat and Otto the apache was resumed in 'The White Coffin'.

The Rat had been sent down to the cellars to bring up a cask of wine. He was far from strong now; he who had once had a lithe, splendid body, and strong, supple wrists, was thin, gaunt, weakened by poor food and hard work. His face was a sullen mask, with great dark eyes that mirrored a soul in hell.

The cask of wine was much too heavy for him to lift and bring up that winding stone staircase into the café. But nobody offered to help him. The barman was yawning over *Le Rire*, waiting for the café to fill up. He knew that The Rat had gone down to fetch the wine, but he was not going to bother about it.

The bent figure of The Rat, straining under the weight of the cask, appeared at the opening into the café. He dropped his burden for a moment and leaned against the wall, eyes closed. He was panting, livid, and there was a tearing pain in his side.

'Hurry up, there!' bawled the barman.

The Rat drew a hand across his forehead. It was wet. He dripped with perspiration and he felt sick . . . faint . . . incapable of climbing another step with that great, heavy cask on his back. But he picked it up, gasping, straining; and carried it to the bar. The man who was reading the paper jerked a thumb in the direction of a table at which four men had just seated themselves.

'They want drinks . . . go and ask them what they'll have,' he grunted.

The Rat wiped his forehead with the back of his hand again, breathed deeply once or twice, his aching eyes shut, then slouched over to the table, napkin over his arm. Mère Colline, at her desk, glanced up from her account-book and saw him. She shrugged her shoulders. He looked terrible these days . . . like a dying man. It made her heart ache . . . but she could do nothing. She had no money and no time to waste. Pity is cheap, but what was the use of giving it? It did no good, and The Rat snarled when one offered it. Best leave him alone.

Otto's bullet head was close to that of a black-bearded ruffian beside him. They were all talking animatedly, in lowered tones. Some important discussion was in progress.

'It's a pretty little job we ought to do,' the apache was saying in a hoarse whisper. 'I'll force the bars of the basement window and once inside the job's as simple as kiss me 'and. Don't you agree, Murat?'

'M'm,' said Murat, the bearded fellow, 'it seems safe enough.'

'I'll stand on guard at the door,' put in another of the men . . . a tough-looking fellow with a square, brutal face. He was chewing tobacco noisily. 'Anybody comes I'll crack 'em over the head with my jemmy.'

The Rat approached the table. Otto glanced up at him.

'Clear away this mess and give us a bottle o' drink,' he said roughly.

The Rat wiped the surface of the table, which was wet and dirty with nut shells and beer drippings.

'What d'you want?' he asked laconically.

Otto questioned the others. The tough who was chewing tobacco looked up at The Rat, his brutal little eyes sneering.

'Not so much the pretty boy now are you?' he asked, shaking with laughter. 'Lookin' a bit of a skeleton, aren't yer?'

Pierre made no reply. He went on calmly wiping the table.

Suddenly the fellow spat on the clean surface of the table, making a filthy pool of dark brown spittle and tobacco. He looked up at The Rat, his great shoulders shaking with mocking laughter.

The Rat stood motionless. He stared back at the man, then he stared at the foul pool on the table he had just cleaned. Otto sat back in his chair and guffawed. The other two joined in, secretly a little frightened of the look in The Rat's eyes. It was blazing . . . terrible. The Rat had woken to life. His thin body trembled with sheer, unadulterated rage.

For a full minute the two men stared at each other . . . The Rat with jaws set . . . body quivering . . . the tough still chewing his tobacco. Then the tension snapped. The tough's hand felt for his knife. But The Rat with all the agility, the lightning-grace of old days, sprang at him . . . clutched at his neck and forced his head down towards the table. The others stopped laughing and watched intently. The ruffian tried to sit back, to fight against that steely grip, but The Rat in his fury of resentment at the disgusting action of the man was strong . . . as strong as he had ever been. He forced the man's head lower . . . still lower . . . until his face was in the filth which he had himself spat out on the table. Then he began to protest, to swear horribly. But The Rat with a terrible smile rubbed the squirming fellow's face in the disgusting mess until he was satisfied that he had avenged himself. He then let him go.

The man sat up, blinking, swearing, wiping his face. But he did not address The Rat again. Otto looked on rather sulkily. The other two laughed.

The Rat moved away to Mère Colline's desk to order the drinks. He was still very white and his jaw was set, but he smiled at the woman.

'I feel better after that, Mère,' he said.

'I am pleased,' she said. 'That was a flash of your old self, *mon enfant*. Keep it up. It does not do to let these filthy fellows set on you.'

The Rat shrugged his shoulders.

'I don't much care, Mère . . . but that . . . that was too much even for me.'

He returned to Otto's table with the drinks. As he approached, the bearded man, Murat, suddenly hailed him as though he had thought of something exciting to say.

'Hi, Rat . . . listen to me a moment.'

'What is it?' said The Rat. He had known Murat well, years ago; had broken into several houses with him as a confederate; had used him, but never much liked him.

'What is it, Murat?' he repeated.

Mural leaned up to The Rat.

'We're cracking a crib in the Bois Wednesday night. Better join us.'

The Rat stiffened. Then slowly he placed a bottle of wine and four glasses on the table. He shook his head.

'No, thanks, Murat. I'm through with that kind of job—for ever.'

'Aw, get on,' said Murat, pulling his beard and glancing at his companions a trifle uneasily. 'Don't turn saint-like, Rat. Join us.'

'No, thanks,' said The Rat.

He turned and walked away with that weary droop of the shoulders which had once been so erect, so well set back. Otto watched him go suspiciously, then turned to Murat uttering a foul oath.

'What the hell you want to ask him that for, you? . . . He'll split.'

'Aw, no, he won't,' mumbled Murat, pouring out a glass of wine.

'He's gone soft,' said the other man whose nose had suffered from The Rat's treatment. 'Blast his eyes . . . I tell you Otto's right, Murat . . . The Rat'll split on us.'

'I don't think he will,' said Murat, gulping his wine noisily. 'Come on, now, don't waste time wondering what he'll do when he hasn't done it. Let's make our plans.'

Otto shrugged his shoulders. He listened to Murat's scheme. But his wicked little eyes followed The Rat and never left him. He was suspicious. He was not going to lose sight of The Rat from now till Wednesday night.

CHAPTER SEVENTEEN

On the Tuesday Zelie de Chaumet received Jules Benoit, the detective, in her flat in the Rue Alphonse de Neuville.

With the passing of the winter Madame de Chaumet was unaltered . . . beautiful, glittering, magnificent, like the jewels she wore; and as hard and unchangeable.

She had stayed in Paris until the extreme cold had driven her south with Mercereau. After spending a few extravagant months in Monte-Carlo and Nice she had returned here to enjoy life in her usual idle fashion and—to watch the process of Pierre Boucheron's downfall.

She knew exactly, and in detail, what Pierre had done since he had left his flat in the Avenue du Bois. She had watched his descent into the hell she created for him, coldly and pitilessly . . . as an Inquisitor might have watched the dying agonies of a tortured prisoner. Only passion and not the fanaticism of religion lay at the back of her inhuman conduct.

After her humiliation at his hands she took the keenest and most callous pleasure in reading the written reports which Benoit submitted to her at the end of each month. While she continued to lead her own life of luxury she learned how Pierre suffered and starved and how utterly his attempts to procure employment had failed through the machinations of Benoit. She was pleased with M. Benoit. He had served her well. He was an excellent sleuth-hound.

This evening she read the report for the month of February, while she awaited Mercereau who was to take her to the opera. The detective sat at a respectful distance, his hands folded neatly on his lap; a little smirk of self-satisfaction on his lips.

Zélie, on her sofa with all her favourite cushions was smoking a cigarette, while she perused the typewritten report which so interested her. She was a glittering figure . . . in a new, amazing frock of peacock-blue sequins which scintillated at her every movement. She wore a collar of sapphires and diamonds and sapphire bracelets half the way up her arms. Her bright golden head was neatly shingled and brushed off her ears, the lobes of which were tinted, and from which hung two colossal diamonds. Those ear-rings had cost Mercereau all and more than he had won at baccarat and roulette in the south this season.

When Zélie came to the end of the report she crumpled the paper in her hand, rose to her feet and began to walk up and down the salon, her brows knit. Fascinated, Benoit watched the supple, sparkling figure. Every time he saw Zélie de Chaumet she reminded him of a panther or a tigress. Tonight she was a beautiful panther with a jewelled collar.

'You are pleased, Madame?' he murmured.

'Pleased with the first half, but not with the last,' she said. 'The Rat has got work . . . he is back at "The White Coffin", and as long as his friends there shelter him he is unbeaten. I want to see him in the mud.'

Benoit put his tongue in his cheek. Madame was very like the panther tonight . . . little white teeth clenched; red lips curled back in a snarl.

'Is he not sufficiently in the mud, Madame?'

'No,' she said. 'He has work, food, shelter.'

'You can only bring him down to starvation and death now,' said Benoit softly.

Zélie paused before him. Her eyes narrowed. She could picture Pierre . . . as Benoit described him . . . thin, hollow-eyed, crushed, working as a waiter in that low café. A bad come-down from what he had been this time a year ago. And she wished, vindictively, that the Comtesse de l'Orme could see her hero like that . . . a bartender in a Montmartre café . . . a ragged, degraded creature. But it was not enough . . . no, not enough. From that night in the garden at Château Lisbon when he had finally spurned her, chosen Madeleine, she had sworn to bring him to the very gutter. She had succeeded. She was enjoying her success. Not once did remorse seize her. Not once did she regret all the harm she had done him. She was of that passionately-jealous, vindictive nature that thoroughly enjoys a good revenge.

But he was not absolutely beaten yet, and she was determined to achieve his complete downfall.

'You must think of some way to get him sacked from "The White Coffin", Benoit,' she said.

'It won't be easy, Madame. The old woman, Mère Colline, and some of those cocottes there still have for him their old affection. There is honour among thieves, and they will not turn one of themselves into the gutter unless they have good cause.'

'What sort of cause?'

Benoit shrugged his shoulders.

'If he betrayed one of them . . . of course that would finish him in their eyes.'

'Then he must be made to do so,' said Zélie, tapping one foot on the polished parquet floor.

Benoit rose and bowed.

'I have already thought of a plan, Madame,' he said suavely.

Zélie threw away her cigarette-end and lit another. She was nervy, irritable, in spite of her satisfaction. With the passing of the months she had not altogether lost that feeling of intense resentment against Pierre Boucheron for casting her off.

'Well?' she said.

'The ringleader of the present gang in "The White Coffin" is a man called Otto . . . a Russian-Jew,' said Benoit. 'He hates The Rat.'

'Oh . . . and why?'

'For several reasons. The Rat has knocked him down, laughed at him in former days. Otto would like to kick The Rat out of "The White Coffin".'

'Fetch this man Otto to see me,' said Zélie.

'I have forestalled you, Madame, if you will pardon me,' said Benoit, bowing. 'Otto is outside now, awaiting his orders.'

Zélie smiled. Truly, the detective was an intelligent and cunning creature. His oily voice and ferret-like face disgusted her. But his finished work on her behalf won her admiration.

'Bring the fellow in,' she said, sitting down on her sofa again.

Benoit bowed and walked to the door. He opened it and Otto, who had been listening, ear to the keyhole, sprang back.

'Madame will see you,' said Benoit sharply. 'Go in. Take off your cap, fellow.'

Otto took off his cap and shuffled into the beautiful salon. His little pig's eyes gleamed as he looked round and took professional note of the value of every article of furniture, every ornament, in that salon. Then his gaze rested on the golden-haired woman with her wonderful jewels, leaning amongst her cushions. He was not at all stirred by her beauty. He had no interest in sex. He was arrested only by the value of the diamonds and sapphires on her person.

Zélie gazed at him a trifle dubiously. He was

a rough, shambling, brutal-looking creature; an apache of the very lowest order. In his ragged suit, his red scarf, his cracked boots, he looked sadly out of place in the salon. And instinctively her mind leaped back years to the first day when The Rat had come at her invitation to see her. She thought of the grace, the beauty, the extraordinary fascination of that apache from 'The White Coffin' . . . of his hands on her throat . . . of his lips on her mouth . . . and she shuddered . . . she looked at Otto's coarse animal-face. What a difference! . . . But why remember anything pleasant about Boucheron? She only wished to remember that she hated him and that she wanted to hound him down even to his death.

'You know The Rat?' she questioned Otto in a quick, business-like fashion.

'Yes, lady,' said Otto. 'I know him.'

'I believe you have cause to dislike him?'

'I detest him,' said Otto. And a look so ferocious, so bestial, overspread his face that even Zélie shivered and put a tiny perfumed handkerchief to her lips. He repeated hoarsely: 'I detest him. I'd like to see him in his grave.'

'You are not requested to do a murder,' said Zélie coldly; 'merely to find some method of getting The Rat sacked from his job at "The White Coffin".'

Otto jerked a thumb in the direction of Benoit.

'So he told me. Well, lady, I can do it.'

'How?'

'Like he said . . . the 'tec . . . if the gang could be persuaded that The Rat had betrayed them his number would be up. They'd sack him all right. They'd probably kill him.'

Zélie shivered again. Her jewelled hand shook as it carried the cigarette to her lips.

'Well,' she went on, 'how can you persuade them that he is a traitor?'

'There's a big job on tomorrow night,' said Otto, rubbing his hands together. 'If The Rat were seen with the 'tec, and later the police were found surrounding the house . . .'

He finished with an expressive shrug of the shoulders.

Zélie glanced at Benoit.

'Could that be managed?'

'Easily, Madame,' said Benoit. 'I will send a note tomorrow morning asking The Rat to meet me, which he will do, no doubt, as he may think you have decided to withdraw your persecution. I will then see that the police surround the house which Otto and his gang intend to burgle, and the rest will follow . . . the gang will be certain that The Rat has let them down.'

Zélie thought a moment. Then she nodded.

'That sounds all right. Very well. Get on with it, Benoit.'

Otto peered at her with his wicked little eyes. They were inflamed with greed now.

'I ain't going to do it for nothing,' he said.

Zélie gave him a disgusted look, then opened a bag which was on the sofa beside her; a silver evening bag embroidered with jewels. She drew out a bundle of notes. The sight of them set Otto's palm tingling. He thrust out a hand and Zélie tossed the bundle into it.

'There you are,' she said.

He counted the notes and put them in his pocket, well satisfied. It was an easy game, this. He was too stupid, too bestial, to understand or try to understand why this fine lady should bother to have The Rat sacked from 'The White Coffin', but he was satisfied that her conduct materially benefited himself and that was all that mattered. Besides, it gave him an excellent opportunity to tread on his enemy. And he knew another member of the gang who would be glad to bring about The Rat's ruin.

'You can go now,' said Zélie. 'You have your orders and you have been well paid. See that you don't bungle the business.'

'I will see to that, Madame,' said Benoit.

He bowed himself out of the salon, followed by Otto, who leered over his shoulder at Zélie as he went.

Zélie picked up an ermine cloak, wound it round her shoulders and waited for Mercereau to come and take her to dinner and the opera.

And while this woman sought to destroy Pierre Boucheron, The Rat, . . . another strove to forget.

Madeleine de l'Orme had also been away in the south of France, and she, too, was back in Paris now. Her mother had wanted to remain in Monte-Carlo until the spring, but the life the girl was forced to lead at their villa in the south was even more distasteful to her than the one she led at Château Lernac. In the south she had been dragged to a round of parties; to the Casino; on visits to friends in Mentone, or Nice. Her mother tried to fill her every hour so that she might have no time to think about her broken heart or consider taking the veil, the prospect of which horrified the old Comtesse, good Catholic though she was. Madeleine was too lovely, too sweet, too brilliant a flower to be hidden in the cloistered shadows of a nunnery.

Madeleine had grown sick and weary of the existence in Monte-Carlo. She craved for a little peace. She wanted to go home. It is a strange fact that doctors order patients who have received any great mental shock or suffered any grievous loss to be taken abroad . . . to fresh sights . . . fresh surroundings. They believe in that sort of cure. But so many of the patients, the pining and broken-hearted, yearn towards their own homes . . . the rest, the seclusion of their own familiar rooms and haunts. Madeleine was of that disposition. She wanted her home. So early in February, when the first pale snowdrops were pushing their way through the hard crust of the frozen earth in the gardens of Château Lernac, the Comtesse brought her daughter home.

She was sadly disappointed in Madeleine and in all her efforts to cure the girl of her trouble and turn her attention to other men, other things. She had failed. The Madeleine who came home was as quiet, as melancholy as the Madeleine who had left it soon after her rupture with Boucheron.

She never spoke to her mother of Pierre; had not mentioned his name since that terrible afternoon when she had described their farewell scene. But the mother knew that she thought constantly of him and that she suffered. She was very much changed. She had once been an ordinary, happy, charming girl, popular amongst her friends and as fond of life as any young, healthy girl. But now she had withdrawn into a shell of reserve which her own mother could not break through, and she had lost all joy in living. She seemed to exist purely mechanically. Her actions were those of an automaton.

It was a catastrophe for the old Comtesse, who had had great hopes of her daughter making a brilliant and happy marriage. She had thrown Madeleine into contact with several charming, eligible men in Monte-Carlo. Two had proposed. Both were refused. Madeleine declined to marry. The disastrous love affair with Pierre Boucheron seemed to have eliminated all her natural instincts and desires for love or matrimony.

On that very night when Zélie de Chaumet schemed with Benoit and Otto, the apache, to bring about Pierre Boucheron's final ruin, Madeleine sat in the salon of Château Lernac, attempting to play the piano, and haunted all the while by memories of Pierre.

She was very fond of music and played Chopin and Debussy (her favourite composers) charmingly. But she felt none of her old fervour for music now. It was too emotional. She could not bear to come up against emotion in any shape or form. Anything that was beautiful or sentimental hurt . . . reopened the wound that Pierre had made in her heart, her soul. She could not forget him. She made desperate efforts to do so, for her mother's sake as well as for her own; but she found it an impossibility. She remembered Pierre vividly during the long, unhappy days, and she dreamed of him at night . . . slept very badly, dreamed of him, woke herself up by crying . . . then in the bitterness of recollection sobbed herself to sleep again; a rosary pressed to her lips which murmured prayer after prayer for the forgetfulness that never came. She could not forget the man who had loved her and taught her to love so passionately for one mad, rapturous night at the Duchesse de Quintreville's ball. Every kiss, every caress he had given her burnt in her memory . . . had seared her as though with white-hot irons that had left ineffaceable scars. The unhappy part of that brief episode with Pierre, the humiliating scene with the de Chaumet woman, the agonising parting from Pierre, all played very small parts in her memory now after these long months. It was of Pierre as her adorable lover and best beloved that she thought . . . whom she missed . . . hungered for without ceasing.

Tonight while she played, sitting alone with her mother, she found herself thinking . . . remembering . . . and the old Comtesse, who sat working at a piece of silk tapestry, looked up now and then and watched her; watched with something like despair in her eyes. The child was so changed, she thought, so pale and silent. She seemed to have drooped as a lily droops its graceful head before a violent storm. Her face was thinner; her great hazel eyes were so full of shadow, of tragedy, that it hurt the mother to read what lay in them. Madeleine was still grieving for Boucheron . . . visibly pining away. And the man had been a cad, an outsider; they would never see him again. The Comtesse considered it nothing less than catastrophic.

Madeleine's slender fingers, hovering over the keys, suddenly dropped into her lap. She sat staring at her music. The Comtesse glanced up and saw tears on the girl's cheeks . . . tears that glistened in the pale light from the two wax candles burning in old-fashioned silver sticks on either side of the piano. She gave a deep sigh, but when she spoke to Madeleine it was in a brisk voice, and without reference to the cause of those tears which she knew only too well. The old Comtesse believed in taking firm action now and paying no attention to Madeleine's melancholy, even while it caused her considerable anxiety.

'Madeleine, *ma chérie*, don't tire yourself with so much music; come and tell me what you think of this tapestry now that it is nearly finished.'

The girl rose obediently and walked to her mother's side. The old lady watched the slender figure approach and thought how much too fragile she looked in her evening-gown which was of ivory chiffon-velvet with long sleeves of chiffon falling to the hem of the gown. It was cut square at the neck in mediaeval style, showing a throat no less white, and with hollows that had not been there a year ago.

'This grieving for that low fellow who insulted her is going too far,' Madeleine's mother reflected, half-irritated by the thought that her daughter was fading before her very eyes. 'It is ridiculous.'

'What do you think, child ... does the colouring appeal to you?' she asked, trying not to throw down the work, clasp Madeleine to her breast and weep with her.

Madeleine looked at the tapestry; it was a charming pattern—a grey knight on a black horse with a background of brilliant orange. The old Comtesse was famous for her tapestries.

'It is beautiful,' said Madeleine vaguely.

Then suddenly, staring at the needlework, she caught her breath and turned from it and handed it back to her mother. Something in the poise of the knight's head, in the erect, graceful figure which had been so skilfully embroidered, reminded her of Pierre. Everything . . . everything reminded her of him.

She walked to the fireplace and sat down on a highbacked, antique chair with carved arms. She let her own slim pale arms, veiled in the winged chiffon sleeves, rest on the carved arms of the chair, and, with her fair head slightly bent, stared into the fire. For a few moments in silence she watched the red-tongued flames curl about the pine-logs which gave out a fragrant odour. She gripped the chair very tightly as though she were in physical pain, trying not to cry out. She was thinking of Pierre . . . wondering what had happened to him . . . where he had gone . . . how he had fared after his disgraceful exit from Paris Society. She was feeling more than usually depressed and infinitely lonely. In the deep recess of her heart she hungered for Pierre . . . needed him tonight more than she had ever needed him in all the weary months behind her.

Why was it? Why could she not forget him? She did not know. She was only confident of the fact that no other man whom she knew or whom she might meet in the future could take Pierre's place; could make her thrill to passionate love again. She only knew that she would give everything she possessed in the world to see the door of the salon open and Pierre enter. Ah! Then she would run to him . . . be caught to his heart . . . rest there with her wet cheek pressed to his cheek, her arms enfolding him just as his would enfold her. She only knew that she would die gladly after that embrace . . . after just one more hour of perfect happiness . . . united to him again in mind, body, heart and soul.

She shut her eyes tightly and the knuckles of her little hands, gripping the arms of the chair, gleamed white. She wanted him . . . wanted him . . . wanted him . . . the need for him, for his arms, his lips, became intolerable pain. And at the back of it all was the devastating knowledge that she had sent him away; refused to forgive him; that in her pride she had separated herself from him like this, utterly. In moments of cold sanity she believed that she had done the right thing; that no woman bearing the name de l'Orme could tolerate the insult he had offered and pardon it. But in moments like these tonight, when the aching hunger for him became more acute, she felt she could and would forgive everything if she looked upon his face again.

'But I will never see him,' she told herself desolately. 'I can never call him back, and he will never come back. He has gone out of my life, for ever.'

The old Comtesse folded up her work; tapestry, silks, scissors, neatly put away in a little silk bag. She rose.

'It has gone ten, Madeleine, *ma chérie*. I am going to bed. Are you coming, or do you want to nod over the fire, you dreamy girl?'

Madeleine, brought up strictly by a French *dame* of the old school, rose and advanced to her mother politely to bid her goodnight.

'I will say goodnight now, *Maman* . . . I want to stay down a little longer.'

The Comtesse kissed her tenderly, then tapped the pale cheeks with a forefinger.

'No brooding over things that can't be helped, my child. It is a mistake. You must really face the future and not think of the past. It is such a mistake to look back . . . for you . . . for me . . . for anybody, if it comes to that.'

Madeleine did not answer that little speech. She knew so well to what her mother referred; just as the mother knew the reason for her daughter's melancholy. But neither did more than make the most veiled allusions. They both found the subject too painful for candid discussion.

After the old Comtesse had gone and Madeleine was alone in the big salon, she walked back to her chair and sat there staring into the log fire and thinking . . . thinking . . . thinking . . . thinking . . .

At last she found her thoughts too agonising for endurance. She got up and pressed a hand to her eyes.

'God,' she said; 'God, I shall go mad if I can't forget him . . . God, where is he? What is he doing? Is he alive or dead? . . . because if he is dead, I would like to die, too. Oh, God, my God, I want to forget him, or I shall go mad . . .'

She said the words aloud, in a kind of mental panic . . . her slim body shivering from head to foot . . . But there was no answer to that frenzied appeal to her Maker . . . only the silence and the flickering firelight in the big salon.

Then a sort of lassitude came across her; a great weariness which made her crave for her bed and for sleep. She was too numbed with suffering to think any more. She walked to the piano . . . stood an instant between the candles which illuminated her face . . . such a tragic face with the haunted eyes and sorrowful lips. She bent slightly forward, blew out the two candles and then walked slowly out of the room.

CHAPTER EIGHTEEN

A wild day of sleet, snow, and tempestuous wind which had swept the streets and boulevards of Paris like a hurricane had settled down to a sullen night. The temperature had risen a few degrees; the snow had melted into rain. But the damp, muggy atmosphere was more trying than the keen, bright frost. By ten o'clock there were few people to be seen outside. A few shivering wanderers remained, slouching through the mist like grey phantoms of the night, but the outside cafés usually thronged with people even in the winter were deserted; the raw starless night had driven everybody indoors to warmth and light.

In 'The White Coffin' even at this early hour quite a few couples occupied the little tables and drank strong spirits to keep out the cold. One or two little cocottes with haggard faces and bedraggled hats, their cheap finery clinging damply to their thin bodies, hung over the bar, drinking punch or eating sandwiches. The atmosphere of the café was thick with smoke, heavily laden with Latakia which clouded all the glasses and copper utensils behind the bar.

Newspaper sellers; a little Chinese juggler with a yellow sunken face and inscrutable eyes; a demi-mondaine of Polish extraction with a face smothered in rouge, ochre, and kohl; a flower-girl with wet, withered flowers yet unsold on her tray . . . one by one they drifted into 'The White Coffin' for food, for drink, for warmth; a queer, motley crowd, united by a common bond of suffering and tragedy.

Mou-Mou had, for the last half-hour, been sharing a table with a boy whose dead-white face, twitching hands and dark, staring eyes pronounced him a victim of drugs. He was not yet twenty, but his livid face with weakness and vice stamped all over it was the face of an old, old man.

He had singled out Mou-Mou from the other girls to talk to. She listened automatically, but his conversation, dealing entirely with the effects of morphia, bored her. She was not interested in drugs and the young maniac . . . one of dozens who frequented 'The White Coffin' . . . disgusted her. But he was well-dressed and seemed to have money, and it was her profession to pretend an interest in a man with money.

Grateful for the *tisane* and aniseed cake which he had ordered for her, she sat opposite him, elbows on the table, chin sunk in her hands. But her eyes were wandering restlessly round the café. She was looking for The Rat. She was anxious because he had been absent over an hour and she did not know where he had gone.

At one of the tables opposite her a young art-student with black velveteen jacket, wide tie, and long wavy hair sat close to a golden-haired girl with a cigarette in a long holder between her carmined lips. As Mou-Mou looked, the girl put an arm around the young man's neck and with a voluptuous movement drew his face down to hers, took the cigarette from her lips and kissed him, then drew back again. He sighed and expelled through his nostrils the smoke she had breathed into his mouth. Then they kissed again, passionately.

Mou-Mou shrugged her shoulders and turned back to her companion.

'They are fools,' she said.

The drug-taker stared at her with his brilliant, dilated eyes.

'You are a cynic, *petite* . . . as I am . . . you do not believe in this craving of one sex for the other.'

Mou-Mou raised her brows tragically.

'It is not that I don't believe in it. But I find it so futile . . . it is a hunger never appeased . . . it is an elusive demon, leading you on and on to the brink of despair.'

'Ah!' said her companion in his slow, dreamy voice. He had just taken his dose of morphia. The drug was beginning to work; he was serene, at peace with the world. His hands had ceased to twitch. 'Ah! Then you have known love, *ma petite*, and have reached that brink over which you are about to fall.'

'Oh, no,' she said with a hard laugh. 'I shall not fall now. I have been on the edge so long that I have learned to keep my balance.'

'Love,' said the young man drowsily, his head drooping a little forward, 'the desire of man for woman . . . ah, no, my dear, it is most unsatisfactory. Respectable passion moderately indulged in becomes mawkish and dull. Excess of passion becomes a vice, and of all the vices is the most undesirable, because the ecstasy is too fleeting and the satiety too long and sad. Drink too much and you become a hog . . . but you may snore in oblivion for hours and find rest. Take morphia . . . ah! . . . that is the most delicate and delightful of vices . . . you do not make a pig of yourself nor of anybody else . . . you just sleep and dream . . . sleep and dream . . .'

His voice trailed away. His chin fell forward on his chest. He was heavily drugged and quite unconscious.

Mou-Mou, who had scarcely heard his discourse on the passions, gave him a disgusted look and rose. She walked over to Mère Colline's desk.

'Where is The Rat, Mère?' she asked.

'He went out some time ago,' said Mère Colline.

Mou-Mou bit her lip anxiously.

'I am so worried,' she said.

'Why, *mon enfant*, why? The Rat can take care of himself, and you know he dislikes being watched for . . . worried over.'

'Yes, but there is Otto and his gang. They

are cracking a crib tonight, and I'm so afraid The Rat has joined them.'

'*Tiens, tiens,*' said Mère, shrugging her shoulders. 'Leave him to his own affairs, stupid one. But I do not think you need worry. The Rat has given up that kind of thing.'

Mou-Mou stared at the door which led up the stone staircase to the main entrance of the café. She had a cigarette between her fingers, but it burned to long ash, unnoticed. She was wrapped in anxious and gloomy thought. The Rat might have been persuaded to join the others, and if so . . . he was in danger . . . he might get caught . . . thrown into gaol.

She stood there, thinking . . . thinking . . . until the red point of the cigarette burnt her fingers. She dropped it with a little oath, trod on it, began to walk up and down the café, restless, tormented. On the brink of despair . . . she thought of the conversation with the drug-maniac. She could have laughed aloud in the bitterness of her soul. Yes, she despaired as utterly today of winning the love of The Rat as she had despaired years ago. She jeered at the word 'love'; she mocked at the student and his golden-haired girl who alternately drank their cognac and kissed each other. But she envied them . . . with all her heart she envied them. For with all that fierce, hungry little heart of hers she loved . . . and wanted The Rat. Drink, drugs . . . bah! she hated the drunkards and the drug-fiends. But love . . . the love of man for woman, of woman for man, she understood.

Suddenly there was a commotion on the main staircase; the sound of hoarse voices; shuffling feet. Mou-Mou faced the coffin-entrance just as Otto, the apache, and his gang rushed into the café. Otto looked flushed and excited, and there was a wicked look in his little pig's eyes that warned her evil was afoot.

He held up a hand and shouted to the man at the piano and to the couples who were dancing.

'Stop . . . stop, all of you!' he said hoarsely.

The music ceased abruptly. The dancers stood still, arms enclasped, staring at him. Mou-Mou, a hand on her hips, drew nearer the apache.

'What would you say if I told you all that there was a traitor amongst us?' Otto shouted, obviously in a state of wild excitement.

The habitués of the café exchanged glances and murmured to each other. Something serious had occurred. What could it be? Mou-Mou, with her thoughts centred on The Rat, grew suddenly ice-cold with apprehension.

'Well, there is a traitor—a dirty traitor in our midst!' shouted Otto, banging one fist on the other. 'And it's *The Rat*. The Rat has double-crossed us. The police have surrounded that crib which we meant to crack in the Bois.'

'That's a lie!' Mou-Mou shouted back instantly.

'Yes, The Rat wouldn't betray you,'

seconded America, who was in a corner with one of her admirers.

'I tell you it's true,' said Otto, waving his arms wildly about his head, his under-lip protruding in an ugly, menacing fashion. 'He was let into our game and he's gone soft—he's split on us. We know it. When we got to our crib, we found the place guarded by police . . . we managed to slip away, but we might have been caught . . . and all through that sneak . . . him!' he finished with a sinister oath.

'It's a lie!' said Mou-Mou again, raising her clear young voice fiercely above the murmur of the crowd.

'Ah! here he comes!' said Otto, swinging round to the stairs.

The couples who had been at the tables rose and joined in the crowd in the middle of the floor. In hushed expectancy they all stared at the coffin-opening, waiting for The Rat to appear, considering the matter before they passed judgment on him.

The Rat came slowly down the stairs and appeared. His movements were weary and his face might have been carved out of ivory; the features sharpened by suffering; the eyes large and sunken.

He proceeded down to the lower part of the café, glancing to the right and left of him in a bewildered way. He did not know why the crowd had gathered together like this, nor why they stared at him. They fell back and made way for him to walk through the room. He looked at some of the familiar faces in a puzzled, tired way. What were they looking at? Why was Otto standing up on the steps, pointing at him?

The Rat shrugged his shoulders, and with hands dug deep in his trouser pockets, mooched on to the bar to fetch his table-napkin and apron and begin work for the night. Then Otto shouted to him.

'Stop!'

The Rat paused and looked at Otto.

'What the hell is the matter? What's biting you? Why are you all gaping at me like a lot of sheep?' he asked.

'You dirty traitor,' snarled Otto. 'You double-crossed the gang.'

The Rat stood rigid a moment. Then his sunken eyes glittered with sudden fire. He walked up to the apache, hands clenched at his sides. The curious crowd followed, peering over each other's shoulders and whispering.

The Rat reached Otto and looked him straight in the eyes.

'Take that back!' he said.

Otto laughed.

'Take it back, indeed. Oh, no, my fine fellow. You just own up. We let you into our game, and you double-crossed us. We found the crib surrounded by the police.'

'And what has that to do with me?' The Rat's thin body shivered with suppressed rage.

'Everything. You split on us, you hound, and you know it.'

'You're a filthy liar,' said The Rat. 'And I'll break every bone in your filthy body for accusing me of such a thing.'

Otto backed from him, a hand upraised.

'Wait a moment—not so fast. I can prove you betrayed us.' His ferocious face creased into a sly grin. 'Were you with Benoit, the 'tec, just now?'

The Rat fell unconsciously into the trap.

'Yes,' he said.

The apache turned triumphantly to the crowd.

'There you are. He split to Benoit. Benoit and his men were surrounding that house, waiting for us.'

'Shame . . .

'Dirty sneak . . .'

'Chuck him out . . .'

'Slit his throat for a mean traitor.'

These cries, followed by others equally threatening, came from a dozen throats. The crowd surged round The Rat, faces hostile, fists clenched. A traitor in 'The White Coffin'; a sneak who consorted with Benoit and his kind was not to be tolerated for an instant.

The Rat's face was livid. His eyes dilated. For a moment he seemed dazed by the onslaught. Then he said:

'I was with Benoit . . . but I didn't split . . . he sent for me . . .'

'He's trying to get out of it!' shouted Otto. 'He'll try and make excuses. But he was with Benoit half an hour ago and that's enough, isn't it, *mes enfants*?'

'Yes, it is enough . . .'

'He split all right . . .'

'Turn him out . . .'

'Chuck him into the street!'

Invectives, threats, burning words of contempt, of anger were flung at The Rat from all sides. The apache had done his work well. Feeling was dead against The Rat tonight. There is honour among thieves . . . and down there in that hell-hole full of criminals a traitor was not shown much mercy . . . no . . . not if he were the most handsome, the most popular man in the place. And The Rat had lost his popularity long ago; he had been a 'gentleman'; associated with the class of people who trod on the poor and flung rogues into prison. Down here they were ready to be suspicious, to mistrust him. They found him guilty of treachery . . . the one unforgivable crime amongst them.

Mère Colline, who had been listening to the whole scene, her plump face puckered with distress, suddenly pushed her way through the shouting, gesticulating crowd, and came face to face with The Rat. She looked up at him. He was breathing quickly, his deep eyes smouldering with fury, with resentment.

'Rat,' she said in the silence that fell when

she reached him, 'is it true . . . were you with Benoit?'

'Yes, Mère, but not to . . .' he began eagerly.

It was enough for the excited crowd. They shouted down Mère Colline's next question.

'Chuck him out.'

'Go on, Rat, . . . get out . . .'

'Get out, you white-livered sneak, and never show your face in "The White Coffin" again!'

'Out with you, Rat—we've finished with you!'

Mère Colline bowed her head and walked slowly back to her desk. She believed that he was guilty and she was sorry—terribly sorry—because she had always loved The Rat.

The Rat gave one swift look about him . . . then as he saw the sea of white, accusing faces, the eyes which held no sympathy, only scorn and dislike, an expression almost of horror, of shocked amazement, came into his eyes. That his old friends, these good people of 'The White Coffin' should think such a thing of *him* . . . that they should believe the worst, be influenced by a loathsome dog like Otto . . . it was frightful! Of all the blows he had suffered this was the heaviest . . . it stunned him . . . indignation and the desire to defend himself was submerged in the crashing pain of the blow.

'Get out!' shouted Otto. 'And never show your face in here again.

The Rat turned on his heel and began to

stumble towards the door. The crowd fell back and let him pass, but they murmured against him as he went. Then Mou-Mou, who had watched and listened in a sort of stupor, gave a great cry and ran to him. The tears rained down her cheeks.

'Rat, *mon* Rat, say it isn't true!' she moaned.

He turned and looked at her with his tragic eyes.

'No—it is not true, Mou-Mou—I did not split,' he said. 'Goodbye.'

A sullen, menacing sound rose from the crowd.

'Let him go, Mou-Mou . . .'

'Why cry for a mean traitor . . .?'

'Get out, you . . . Rat . . .!'

Mou-Mou stared after the retreating form of the man she loved and who was making such a disgraceful exit from 'The White Coffin', then flung herself into a chair and sobbed aloud.

Otto, thumbs in his waistcoat, swaggered up to the bar. He was satisfied. He had done his work. Tomorrow he would get another roll of notes from the pretty lady in the Rue Alphonse de Neuville.

The music recommenced. Couples began to dance again. The crowd dispersed and the tables filled up. The young man who took drugs slept on in his corner, a beatific smile on his vicious face. Mou-Mou went on sobbing, desolately.

The Rat, turned into the streets, stood outside 'The White Coffin' for several minutes, head sunk on his chest, body still shaking with indignation and rage. Then, as he grew calmer, the trembling ceased. He raised his white face to the starless sky.

'*Mon Dieu*,' he said aloud. '*Mon Dieu*!'

The cry whistled through his clenched teeth. The dazed feeling vanished and clearer thought came. He understood it all now; realised that it was a mean trick . . . had been arranged between Jules Benoit and Otto . . . in order to get him turned out of his job.

When he had received a note from the detective, asking him to meet him in the Bois this evening, he had gone at once, hoping that Zélie had regretted the harm she had done him and might be withdrawing the detective, which would give him, Pierre, the chance to get decent work.

He had gone, and the meeting had resulted in bitter disappointment. Benoit had merely warned him that unless he were careful he would be losing his job at the café. The Rat had laughed at that. The work was uncongenial and the pay poor, but it was work, and meant a living, and his old friends would not turn him out. He could afford to laugh at Benoit.

But now he did not laugh.

He realised how he had been trapped. And, of course, he thought, Zélie de Chaumet was at the back of it; the long arm of her revenge had reached him even in the one place where he had imagined himself safe. It had been cunning . . . oh, very cunning . . . she and Benoit must have known that the one thing his friends would not forgive was treachery.

He was innocent. Torture to the point of death would never have dragged a word of betrayal from his lips. Even to Otto, his enemy, he would have been loyal. Who understood the meaning of honour—that kind of honour—better than he, The Rat?

But Benoit, Zélie and Otto between them had beaten him. It was impossible for him to clear his name, and the doors of 'The White Coffin' were for ever closed to him.

The Rat stared blindly before him. He could hear the faint sounds of music and laughter which drifted on the wings of the wind up from the underground café. And he felt sick . . . sick with misery. For although his life had been wretched there and he had been working until he was only skin and bone, 'The White Coffin' had been home . . . an old haunt . . . and there had been friends there . . . kind Mère Colline and Mou-Mou . . . faithful little Mou-Mou. Mère Colline believed the worst against him with the rest. But Mou-Mou believed in him. Of that he was sure. Loyal Mou-Mou . . . poor Mou-Mou.

The Rat gave a shuddering sigh. He began to move away from 'The White Coffin' up the winding, cobbled Montmartre alley, his footsteps lagging, his heart like a stone within him.

He was an outcast . . . unjustly accused and flung out of 'The White Coffin'. He was henceforth an outcast on the face of the earth. He had been deserted by all his friends . . . he had nothing left now . . . nobody.

Pierre Boucheron had been through hell since Zélie de Chaumet's revenge had commenced. But of all his bitter moments . . . this was the most bitter . . . this undeserved dishonour.

That night Zélie received a brief communication from Jules Benoit which brought her great satisfaction.

'Boucheron turned out of his job at 'The White Coffin'. Now on the streets.'

She folded the slip of paper, brought to her by special messenger at midnight, and lay back on her satin pillows in her luxurious bed. She stretched her white arms and limbs as a lazy panther stretches and yawns. If she had not been quite so civilised she would have licked her lips and purred like a creature of the wilds who has achieved the final defeat of a hated enemy.

'My work is done,' she said to herself. 'Now, my dear Pierre, I wonder if you would still choose Madeleine de l'Orme instead of me?'

CHAPTER NINETEEN

There comes a time in some men's lives when they have gone down so far they can go no further.

Pierre Boucheron—The Rat—had reached that pitch. After his banishment from 'The White Coffin' he went down from a degrading job to the deeper degradation of begging. Once he had been very proud; he had sworn that he would never ask for alms; that he would die before he became a beggar. But one never knows what one will do until one is faced with the actual plight. The Rat could get no employment of any kind. He was shadowed day and night by Benoit. 'The White Coffin' no longer offered food or shelter. He was reduced to begging from passers-by, and he only dared do that at rare intervals when there was no gendarme in sight, because it was against the law to beg.

There was nothing left for The Rat but death.

For days and nights he was on the streets, homeless, wandering, frozen with cold and mad with hunger. A dozen times during the twenty-four hours round he contemplated suicide, toyed with the idea of throwing himself into the Seine. But he had always had a horror of death, of the Unknown. And he was still afraid to die, even when this nadir of misery and shame was reached.

His brain grew dazed, dulled by lack of food. He suffered from the frightful exhaustion of tramping through Paris picking up a few sous here and there where charity offered them, sleeping on the banks of the Seine, until he was roused and sent about his business by a gendarme, or on the doorstep of some empty house in some dark sinister alley.

He ceased to think or to desire anything but food. He became like an animal; a stray cur that searches in garbage heaps for a morsel to eat. He grew filthy and tattered. Of Boucheron the man whom Madeleine had loved, whom Paris had fêted and adored, only a terrible shadow remained, a skeleton-like face and frame with great, haunted eyes and lips screwed up with the constant pain of hunger and cold.

February brought milder weather; the first signs of spring; the feeble stirring of young green things under the earth; buds breaking out over the stark trees; snow and ice melting; that sensation of joyous anticipation, of softness and youth which comes with the birth of spring.

But to The Rat it was a month of horror, of such dreadful suffering that his body and brain became warped. He sank into a mental stupor from which he rarely awakened. He spoke to nobody and nobody spoke to him. He was terribly alone in his hell. Yet he was not lonely, because he had ceased to feel any such emotion as loneliness. He only wanted to appease the excruciating pangs of hunger which often assailed him, or to drink when he was parched with thirst. And although he could not bring himself to end his existence, he was every day becoming more ready for death, would have welcomed it. He was too feeble now, too stupefied by his misfortunes to make any attempt to prolong his life.

It was as though he were in the throes of a nightmare which went on and on . . . from which he could never wake.

Bare, raw feet in boots which showed his ankles and most of his toes, rags clinging soddenly to his bones, The Rat tramped slowly through Paris . . . West End, East End . . . parks, boulevards; everywhere . . . nowhere in particular . . . an animal . . . an outcast . . . a terrible spectacle to testify to a woman's jealousy and revenge.

One night, towards the end of February, he turned his steps towards one of the more fashionable streets of Paris. Chin sunk on his chest, hands in his torn pockets, he slouched along. He had no hat, his dark hair was matted and hung in wisps over his brow. He was cold, for there was a chilly wind blowing, and he was ravenous for food. He had not succeeded in getting any alms for two days. He had eaten nothing for the forty-eight hours, and his head was light; the horrible pains of acute hunger gnawed at his vitals.

At the corner of the street he paused. His sunken eyes, heavy-lidded with exhaustion, tried to focus on the brilliant lights of cafés and restaurant windows. But he saw them as through a mist . . . all the lights were blurred . . . dancing up and down like golden specks before him. The bright headlights of cars gliding up and down the road dazzled him. He stood swaying on his feet, watching them for a moment. There was a traffic-jam and a big limousine pulled up by the kerb quite close to him.

The Rat's heavy eyes turned to this car. There were two ladies seated inside. The electric bulb in the roof of the saloon illuminated them. The Rat, his vision growing clearer, stared at their faces, their fur wraps, sparkling jewels. How pleasant they looked, he thought; how comfortable and warm they must be in their furs, in that warm saloon. Then suddenly he gave a hoarse cry and drew back further into the shadows. The face of the younger woman in the car had grown quite clear to him as the mists dissolved from his addled brain. It was a fair, beautiful face framed in pale gold hair . . . a face he knew only too well, which had once been exquisitely dear to him and poignantly remembered.

It was Madeleine de l'Orme. Madeleine in the car with her mother.

For one pulsating moment The Rat stared at her, hunger and exhaustion forgotten as memory swept across him, and made his heart thud, his pulses race. Madeleine . . . Madeleine, whose memory had faded . . . who in the recent terrible months had been totally separated from his thoughts because she could have no place in the dark and hellish recess that his mind had become.

But now, at this unexpected sight of her, a great cry burst from his broken heart.

'Madeleine . . . Madeleine . . .'

The girl turned her head at that moment and looked out of the window. It was a coincidence, and not because she had heard that cry which could not have reached her in all the hum and noise of an important Paris boulevard at night. But The Rat thought she heard and stumbled towards her, half-mad, not realising what he did.

For an instant her gaze fell on the white, gaunt face and ragged figure of the man, *but she did not recognize him*. Then the gendarme, holding up the traffic, moved to one side, and the car bearing the Comtesse de l'Orme and her daughter to a dinner-party at Claridge's glided past The Rat. There were many starving loafers in the streets of Paris. To Madeleine de l'Orme this one was no more than the others.

The Rat stared after the vanishing car. When it turned the corner out of his sight he relaxed into the old position, shoulders bowed, head bent, and slouched down the road. His heart-beats slowed down. The flush which had stained his thin cheeks at the sight of the woman he had worshipped in days that might have belonged to another existence in another world faded.

Once the momentary excitement of seeing Madeleine had gone he became dull-witted again, heavy-eyed, torn with the pains of famine. His lips twisted into a ghastly smile. Madeleine did not matter now. He could forget her again. Nothing mattered except food and rest . . . and, God! how hungry he was . . . how terribly hungry!

He came to a big restaurant—one of the most expensive cafés in Paris. Leaning up against the glass windows he stared at the crowded tables. Waiters were hurrying hither and thither with bottles and trays of food; the lights, the crimson carpet, the flowers, the electric candles on the tables, the beautiful frocks and jewels of the women, the sleek, well-dressed men, were to The Rat like a vision . . . a dream . . . something he had known and delighted in aeons and aeons ago but which was no longer a reality—merely a mocking shadow that eluded his grasp.

He only knew that he wanted food. His mouth watered and his great sunken eyes gleamed as he saw the joints, the chickens, the big trays piled with *sole à la maison*, duck wonderfully served *en casserole, filet de boeuf*, potatoes in crisp golden chips, a dozen and one rich and tempting dishes. The starving man saw them all and dabbed at his mouth, agonised by the frightful pains of want. One crust . . . one roll from any of those laden tables would have assuaged some of that want. And not a crumb would be given to him.

He moved on, dragging his footsteps along the pavement. He turned into another street and stopped at the corner, on which there was a huge open-air café. Under a striped awning many people were eating their food, regardless of the cold, preferring an out-of-door meal to one inside the over-heated restaurant.

The Rat leaned up against one of the posts which supported the awning, and watched a man who sat alone at a small, round-topped table. He was devouring, rather than eating, a chicken. He was a huge, fat fellow with a bald head, pompous red face, with double chin and a thick greedy mouth, and the eyes of a glutton. Napkin tucked in his waistcoat, he was chewing the wing of a chicken. He sucked in the juicy parts noisily. He tore off the white, sweet flesh, his eyes fixed upon it, then sat back in his chair and gazed about him with a smile of satisfaction while he chewed.

Half hidden in the shadows, The Rat watched him, fascinated. His sunken eyes focussed on the chicken in the fat man's hand and could not leave it. It was a cruel sight to a starving beggar . . . that well-fed, well-satisfied glutton, enjoying his food. With head bent forward The Rat stared and stared, until his own lips began to work up and down, and the saliva formed in his mouth, frothed from it, dribbled down his chin. He licked his lips, and clutched at his throat. His eyes grew frightful in their intensity, their agony of hunger.

The fat, sleek man, unaware of that frightful gaze concentrated upon him, seized knife and fork and hacked off another piece of the chicken in the dish beside him, a leg with the skin nicely roasted to a rich brown, and dripping with fat. With a pleasant smile at this agreeable sight he began to eat the leg, tearing at it with his teeth in a way that sent The Rat mad. If *he* could only have a morsel of that chicken . . . a morsel . . . God, how hungry he was . . . how unbearably hungry. With a ghastly smile he sucked in his lips and chewed at them.

Suddenly the fat man, tired of his chicken-leg, flung it to his dog, a terrier, stretched out on the pavement beside the table. The animal, dozing with his head on his paws, blinked, sniffed at the bone, to which quite a shred of chicken adhered, and went to sleep again. He was a well-fed dog, and the bone did not tempt him.

The Rat's staring eyes left the man and fastened on the bone which the dog had not touched. His mouth slavered, his throat worked, he staggered slightly, famished, half fainting. Then he gave a sly glance from the man at the table to the sleeping dog. He went down on his knees. Licking his lips he crawled towards the bone. Cautiously he put out a hand, gripped the bone, and slunk away. The anguish in his eyes changed to an expression of eager anticipation. He walked quickly away from the open-air café until he reached another big restaurant. Then, leaning up against one of the windows of this place, he watched the lavish and expensive meals which were being served in the luxurious room.

Outside in the cold and the shadows The Rat flung back his head and laughed . . . a dreadful laugh to hear. Let them enjoy themselves in there, he thought . . . let them eat their food, drink their wine. He had something to eat now. He was happy . . . happy. Like a madman with his gleaming eyes and shaking hands he drew out the bone which a dog had refused, and began to gnaw at the flesh which was still upon it. He devoured every morsel wolfishly, laughing as he swallowed it. And when he had gnawed the bone clean, he began to tear at the dry bone with his teeth.

At a table beautifully decorated with hot-house roses and quite close to the window a golden-haired woman sat opposite her escort, barely tasting the variety of rich dishes placed before her. She exchanged a few remarks with the man, who was obviously more interested in her than she was in him. Her gaze wandered incessantly about the room as though she were bored, dissatisfied, seeking some diversion.

It was Zélie de Chaumet with Mercereau.

As lovely as ever in her hard, brilliant way, she was conscious of the fact that she received many admiring looks; that she was the best dressed woman in the room. Her gown, a deep claret-coloured georgette, was exquisitely embroidered with silver thread, and, as usual, she wore many wonderful jewels. A huge bunch of orchids was pinned to the left shoulder by a long bar of diamonds.

Her ermine opera-cloak, flung over the back of the chair, with its ivory-satin lining embroidered with huge claret-hued flowers, to tone with her frock, had just cost Mercereau a small fortune. But Zélie de Chaumet was not happy. She was one of the unhappiest women in that room.

In some queer way, since she had last seen Jules Benoit and had received the report that Pierre Boucheron was starving on the streets, conscience had suddenly awakened and begun to prick her. She could no longer sleep well at night. She was stung by remorse a dozen times a day. She was haunted by the thought of Pierre in some dreadful condition of beggary, brought about through her, and it worried her despite all her efforts to shake off her depression and enjoy her victory.

This evening Mercereau was taking her to the new show at the Casino de Paris. He had just promised her a new set of sables which she had seen yesterday at Revillon's ... and coveted. But she could not enjoy herself; could not banish the thought of Boucheron.

Her restless gaze wandered to the window. She stared through it as she sipped her kümmel which had just been handed to her with some Turkish coffee. Suddenly she stiffened and changed colour. She put down the liqueur glass, leaned forward and stared more closely through the window. Her blue eyes dilated ... her breath quickened ... the room seemed to spin round her. For she had seen the ghastly face of the man whose memory had been causing her so many hours of uneasiness. She could see Pierre Boucheron leaning against the pillar just outside the restaurant, *gnawing a bone*.

'What's the matter, Zélie?' Henri de Mercereau asked her, noticing her sudden pallor.

She did not answer, only stared at the man outside the window, taking in every detail of his appearance ... the ragged clothes ... the ravaged face with its terrible, sunken eyes and despairing mouth ... the twitching fingers that held the bone to his lips.

Pierre, gnawing a bone like that in the streets! ... Oh, God, it was too frightful, thought Zélie. And she had brought him down to that ... she, who had loved him so passionately.

She was horrified. All these months she had

revelled in her revenge . . . laughed when Benoit told her of Boucheron's gradual downfall. But to-night, seeing her frightful handiwork, she was aghast at herself . . . overwhelmed with remorse for having brought Pierre down to *this*.

'Zélie, are you ill?' asked Mercereau anxiously.

'I . . . want fresh air . . . just a little faintness . . . don't follow me . . . I'll come back,' she gasped.

She wrapped her white fur cloak about her and walked out of the restaurant, her cheeks ghastly under the rouge. She reached the entrance and then began to run . . . as though she was afraid of missing Boucheron. Out on the pavement she paused, panting, her golden hair blowing in the night-wind, the air striking chill after the heat of the café. But she did not care. She only wanted to speak to Pierre . . . to tell him she was sorry . . . to do something . . . something to show her remorse.

The Rat had finished his bone and moved away from the restaurant window. When Zélie rushed out it was only in time to see him slouching down the street. But she followed him, calling to him in a frenzied tone.

'Pierre . . . Pierre . . .'

That name which he had not heard for so many long weeks penetrated The Rat's dull brain. He turned and stared at the woman who had called him. She reached his side.

'Pierre,' she said. 'Oh, my God, my God, what have I done to you?'

He did not answer her. His great black eyes gazed down at her vacantly. In a dim way he recognised her . . . the beautiful, hard face, the golden hair, the voluptuous figure in the ermine cloak. As from afar he heard her voice, choked with sobs, was amazed to see tears raining down her cheeks. They were the first genuine tears of grief, of contrition, that Zélie de Chaumet had shed since her long lost childhood.

'Pierre, my poor, poor Pierre, forgive me . . . I was mad with jealousy over Madeleine; I didn't know what I was doing . . . oh, Pierre, Pierre, how terrible, how ill you look!' she moaned.

He rocked slightly on his feet. His eyes still held that vacant, wondering expression. The miserable chicken-bone had assuaged some of the pangs of hunger, but he was still very famished and his mind was clouded.

He gave another look at Zélie, turned from her and began to plod in his weary fashion down the street. She, horrified, shaken with weeping, followed him, clutching at his arm. She forced him to stop and speak to her again; drew him into a quiet, secluded corner of the street where they could not be seen. She felt she must look at him, although it nearly broke her hard, sinful heart to see the frightful ravages of her work, the skeleton-like face and figure which had once been the most handsome in all Paris.

'Pierre,' she said brokenly. 'Speak to me!'

He shook his head vaguely.

'Let me go,' he whispered.

'No, no, tell me you will forgive me,' she said. 'Pierre, let me make amends; come back with me to my flat . . . let me give you food, clothes, warmth . . . let me make up to you for what I have done. Pierre, I must have been mad, but I regret it now. I'll leave Mercereau; I'll help you to get work; anything, anything, only come back with me.'

He shook his head again.

Zélie, in a sort of panic, horrified that she had dragged this boy down to such depths, hung on to him and pleaded again and again. She put her arms around him. He was dirty and unshaven, but she drew his head down on to her breast and wrapped her white fur cloak about him as though to shield him from the cold wind.

Her tears fell thick and fast on to his dark, matted hair. She stroked it, sobbing, crooning over him. All her old wild passion for this man revived now that she saw him, held him in her arms again. She had always wanted him . . . always . . . and she had never been able to possess him . . . never would.

The Rat rested his head on her breast just for a moment without moving. His heavy eyelids closed. Just for a moment he forgot that he had been through hell and felt himself in heaven; the heaven of a soft, fragrant bosom, of tender arms, of the love, the shelter offered him.

Then he remembered who it was who held him and what this woman had done to him . . . remembered that she was responsible for his frightful downfall, for his separation from the girl he had loved.

He gave a hoarse cry and pushed Zélie from him so violently that she nearly fell. He glared down at her, eyes savage in his white face.

'Get away . . . leave me alone . . . you—' he spat a foul word at her.

Zélie shrank back.

'Pierre, Pierre, don't be angry—give me a chance to make amends,' she sobbed.

He put a hand to his forehead . . . shut his eyes . . . then opened them again. The fierceness of anger, of resentment passed. He was too feeble, too broken to bear ill-will to any human being . . . even this woman who had ruined him. His eyes stared down at her tear-drenched face sadly now.

'No . . .' he said. 'It's impossible . . . Goodnight. Goodbye . . .'

He turned and walked away from her. Chin sunk on his chest he stumbled along, out of her sight.

She stood still a moment, staring after him. She heard the voice of Comte Mercereau.

'Zélie, Zélie, *ma chérie* . . .'

She shuddered, pulled herself together and wiped the tears from her eyes with a little lace handkerchief. Mercereau reached her side and took her arm.

'Feeling better, dearest?'

She turned her head so that he could not see her face.

'Yes,' she said, 'I'm all right. Let's get off to the Casino now.'

But all through that brilliant, vivacious revue she sat like a creature of stone beside her companion. She did not see the sparkling scenes before her; she did not hear the music or the words. She only saw Pierre Boucheron, with his frightful sunken eyes and skeleton frame, tramping into the night . . . God alone knew where to . . . or what would become of him. She was obsessed by the vision, the horror of it all; devoured with futile remorse. From that night henceforward Zélie de Chaumet was not to know one moment's peace of mind or happiness. The victory she had won over Boucheron had ended in her own defeat.

CHAPTER TWENTY

In 'The White Coffin', one blustering night in March, a huge black man, with a top-hat of pink-and-white striped paper on his head, was performing a ludicrous dance. The café was full and the audience, in good humour, clapped their hands and urged the black man on to greater buffoonery.

Mou-Mou was standing in her favourite position, her back against the wall, hands on her hips, watching the clown. The little cripple boy whom she had so often defended down here stood leaning on his crutch beside her.

Mou-Mou's face looked pinched and tired. Apathetically she watched the black man, without a smile on her face. It took a lot to make Mou-Mou smile these days.

She missed The Rat—terribly. Ever since he had been turned out by Otto and his gang she had suffered . . . wanted him, endured untold pangs of anxiety, wondering what had become of him. Nobody had heard, nobody ever would hear, she supposed, for of course he would never come back here.

Sometimes she half hoped he were dead. She could bear the thought of The Rat sleeping that last long sleep, rather than alive, tortured by want and misery, on the streets.

The music, blaring out the latest fox-trot, made her head hum and buzz. The black man was performing weird and wonderful steps, eyes rolling, grinning at the crowd.

Otto and some of his friends who were hanging over the bar, drinking and watching, shouted at him, 'Bravo! Bravo!'

The band stopped. The man retired amidst vociferous applause. Then suddenly a girl at one of the tables shouted:

'*Look*!'

Everybody stared at the main entrance to which she pointed. Mou-Mou stared too. And then her amazed and horrified eyes saw the man who had occupied all her thoughts.

'*The Rat*!' she gasped.

Otto, the apache, swung round.

'The Rat? Dared to come back here? *Mon Dieu*! I'll . . .'

He stopped. For The Rat's appearance was so terrible that even Otto was struck dumb by the sight of him. Everybody in the café remained rigid, staring at The Rat. His face was ghastly, his eyes looked twice their normal size. He was swaying from side to side down the staircase. He stumbled down the last step into the café, then suddenly fell . . . crumpled up on the ground.

Mou-Mou rushed forward.

'Rat,' she said in a wailing voice. 'Oh, *mon Dieu*, he's starving . . . *mon pauvre* Rat!'

The couples at the various tables had risen and gathered around the prone figure of the man who had been turned out of this room in disgrace some weeks ago.

'What the hell is he doing here?' shouted Murat from the bar.

'What's he come back for?'

'Shame on him, coming here . . .'

'Turn him out again . . .'

'Poor fellow, he's dying . . .'

'Let him alone . . .'

Remarks poured in from all sides. Otto, the apache, moved nearer The Rat, his ugly face menacing.

'I'll soon turn him out,' he said.

But Mou-Mou crouched on the floor beside her beloved Rat and pillowed his head on her lap. With arms about him, supporting him, she wept over him, aghast at the sight of his ravaged face. His eyes were closed; his body sagged in her embrace. She had a terrible feeling that he was a dying man.

'Rat . . . Rat,' she sobbed his name.

His eyelids lifted. He stared up at Mou-Mou's face. Two words came from hm:

'Food . . . drink . . .'

America had already seized a glass of wine and brought it to him. She had not loved this man as Mou-Mou had loved him, but she had cared, in a way, years ago when he had been her lover, and she felt sick at the dreadful spectacle of him in this starving condition. She knew that he must be at the end of all things to have come back to 'The White Coffin' after what had happened.

She handed Mou-Mou the wine, and Mou-Mou lifted the glass to The Rat's lips. He drank thirstily; drained the glass to the dregs. A tinge of colour came into his livid cheeks.

'Thank you,' he whispered.

Mou-Mou drew his head closer to her breast.

'My God, my God, what have they done to you, Rat?' she cried desolately.

Otto elbowed his way through the gaping crowd and stood beside the man, who was gradually regaining consciousness and some strength after the stimulant.

Otto kicked him brutally.

'I'm not going to have you whining for charity down here and getting it off these girls,' he snarled. 'Get out of it!'

The Rat stumbled on to his feet . . . stood swaying . . . staring at Otto.

'Get out of here, quick,' repeated Otto, doubling his fists.

'He isn't going to be turned out,' cried Mou-Mou, her eyes blazing. 'He's starving . . . and you're a great bully.'

The apache turned to her.

'You're a traitor, too, eh?' he said. 'You want to give shelter to this swine of a sneak . . . you give him wine, eh? Well, I'll show you . . .'

His hand shot out and caught her a stinging slap across the face. She stumbled back and fell on to the ground under the force of the blow. The marks of his cruel fingers left red lines on her pale skin. Dazed by it she crouched there, a hand to her cheek. The others looked on, afraid to move or speak.

The Rat stared at Mou-Mou, then back at the man who had struck her. Just for the moment he was fired by the wine; he was the old Rat, strong, fierce, purposeful. The sight of the girl felled to the ground by that cowardly and brutal blow roused him to frenzy and suddenly, without any warning, he sprang at the apache.

The crowd moved back, excited by the anticipation of a fight. Otto, taken aback by the onslaught, had staggered, but now he was at grips with The Rat. They grappled; for an instant fought silently with livid faces and bared teeth. But The Rat's strength only lasted a minute. He was much too feeble to battle against the brute strength of a man like Otto. It was easy victory for the apache. The Rat went limp in his hold, and Otto drew his knife, forced The Rat down on his knees and brought the glittering blade nearer and nearer his bared chest from which the ragged shirt had been torn in that short contest.

Mou-Mou, watching with frantic anxiety, struggled on to her feet. Rose and America went to her and took her by each arm.

'It's no use, *ma gosse* . . . let him be . . . you can't interfere,' whispered Rose.

But Mou-Mou called frantically to Mère Colline.

'Stop them, Mère . . . stop Otto . . . he will kill The Rat. It isn't fair—The Rat's weak—half dead—it isn't fair!'

'No, it isn't fair,' agreed Mère Colline, rising from her desk and pushing her way through the crowd.

Several of the men and women agreed with

Mou-Mou.

'The Rat is very weak; Otto can fell an ox,' murmured one man.

'Let him alone, Otto,' cried the girl.

'Fair play!' said several others.

Cries in favour of The Rat, and hostile to the apache, came from all sides now.

The Rat was still on his knees, staring up at his enemy, a ghastly smile convulsing his features. He held the hand which gripped the knife by the wrist, trying to force it away from him. He panted, sobbed for breath as he did so. He was pitifully weak and the room was spinning round him. He was on the point of fainting again. As he laboured against Otto he thought dimly of the tragedy of it all. Not so many months ago he could have beaten this bully . . . thrashed him until he whined for mercy. But now he could not have held out against a puny child, he was so enfeebled by starvation.

He made one dreadful effort to force Otto's knife away, but it came nearer and nearer his bared chest. Otto gave an evil chuckle. The point of the knife pierced The Rat's flesh and drew blood. But the sight of the unequal contest was rousing the crowd to anger. They shouted against the apache. Mère Colline rushed forward and pulled at Otto's hand.

'*Canaille*!' she said furiously. 'Would you kill a man who has not the strength to fight you? Let him alone.'

Otto's knife was still pricking The Rat's chest. The red blood trickled down, staining his tattered shirt. His eyes closed . . . too weak to hold on to Otto's wrist any longer, his hand fell to his side. He did not mind now if the apache killed him. He was finished . . . utterly beaten . . . and he would have welcomed death.

But Mère Colline and several others in the café whose sympathies were with The Rat fell upon Otto and dragged him back. Otto shrugged his shoulders, wiped his bloodstained knife and swaggered to the bar.

'He may be a traitor, but let's play the game and give him food and drink and send him on his way,' said Mère Colline, facing the crowd. 'What do you say?'

'Yes, give him food and drink,' they shouted back.

Mou-Mou, who had been standing in between Rose and America, holding one hand to her cheek, on which there was now an ugly purple bruise, suddenly pushed them aside and made her way to The Rat. She drew out a handkerchief and staunched the blood which trickled from the flesh-wound on his chest. He, scarcely able to stand, stood there rocking on his feet, letting her do what she would. She drew his torn shirt together as best she could, and buttoned up his coat, sobbing hysterically.

Mère Colline came up with a bottle of wine, a long loaf and a parcel of food. She placed the food in one of his coat pockets and thrust the bottle of wine in the other.

'There,' she said, her own eyes wet. 'Now go, Rat. You had better go, poor fellow.'

The Rat was too dazed and broken to speak. But he suddenly leaned forward and kissed Mère Colline on the forehead. With that, the good woman broke down and made her way back to her desk, crying like a child. One or two of the women in the crowd began to weep. The men shifted on their feet and look uncomfortable.

The Rat stared dazedly around him. He was grateful for the pity of his old associates, but he could not voice it. He looked at the girls . . . at the cripple boy who was whimpering in a corner; at the huge black, who was blubbering like a baby; at a dozen faces which had been hostile and accusing him when last he had seen them and were now kindly and compassionate.

A long shudder passed through his tormented body. Clasping the loaf to his breast he turned and began to stumble out of the café. In dead silence the crowd watched him go, but the tears of the women fell unrestrainedly and some of the men turned their heads to wipe the moisture in their own eyes.

The Rat reached the first step of the entrance. Then Mou-Mou, who had been standing in the middle of the floor as though transfixed, rushed after him. She flung her arms about his neck.

'Rat, Rat, don't go without me . . . take me with you,' she said wildly. 'Let me come with you . . . I'll work for you . . . live for you . . . anything . . . only I can't bear life without you.'

He looked down at her face which was convulsed with emotion. And emotion which had so long been dead in him stirred at the sight of her tears and the sound of her voice. Tears welled into his own eyes. He put an arm about her quivering shoulders.

'Faithful little Mou-Mou . . . faithful heart,' he said.

She leaned her head against his breast.

'Take me! Take me with you, *mon* Rat,' she moaned.

'No, dear, it's impossible . . . I have nowhere to take you,' he said very gently.

'Come with me, then . . . to my room . . . oh, Rat, don't go alone . . . let me work for you . . . I want to . . . I love you so . . . it will be my happiness to work for you, Rat.'

He gave a deep sigh. He drew her against him tenderly just for a moment. He was touched to the depths of his being by the beautiful fidelity of this little cocotte.

'My dear, it's impossible,' he said again. 'It shall never be said that any woman has kept me. No, dear, go back to the others . . . let me go on my way alone.'

She sobbed with her face hidden against his shoulder.

'I love you so, Rat . . . Can't I come with

you?'

'No. Try and understand that it is impossible.'

She raised her head and looked up at him through her scalding tears.

'I do understand, but oh, Rat, where are you going and what are you going to do?'

'Something . . . somehow . . . somewhere,' he said vaguely. 'I may win through yet. Thank you for everything, *petite*. I shall never forget your kindness—your great heart—one day, God willing, I may be able to repay you.'

'Oh, Rat!' she said desolately.

'Goodbye,' he said.

She lifted her mouth to his.

'If you must go . . . kiss me, Rat . . .'

He bent his head and touched her mouth very tenderly with his lips. He had kissed her before; in fun; in passion; never before in real tenderness, in gratitude, and it broke her heart. She clung to him, sobbing convulsively, straining her thin little body against his. She believed that it was the last time she would ever look upon her Rat . . . the last time she would ever feel his arm about her and his kiss upon her mouth. In agony she held him just for a few more seconds, dreading to let him go. And he smoothed her curly head with one of his thin hands, comforted her, blessed her.

'Don't cry for me, Mou-Mou, hush, *mignonne* . . . hush! I'm not worth your tears. God bless you, little one, for your loyalty. Now please let me go while I have the strength. Goodbye.'

'Oh, Rat,' she moaned. '*Mon* Rat!'

He put her arms gently away from him, kissed one of her hands, then turned and stumbled up the staircase. She watched him go, blind and sick with weeping. Her voice followed him out into the night.

'Rat, *mon* Rat . . . goodbye.'

The little crowd in 'The White Coffin' had not moved. Rogues, criminals, poor rouged creatures of the *demi-monde*, whatever they were, they had hearts . . . and in Paris hearts swing rapidly from laughter to tears . . . from tears to smiles again. There was no laughter now. But tears poured down the cheeks of a dozen faces . . . they wept with Mou-Mou over the tragedy of their Rat.

Then suddenly Mou-Mou swung round and faced them, eyes brilliant, cheeks red, hands upraised.

'Dance!' she said hysterically. 'For God's sake, dance!'

The music started. The men seized their women and began to foxtrot madly . . . to laugh . . . to forget the tragedy . . .

There, where she stood, Mou-Mou kept time with the dancers, her shoulders shaking, feet moving swiftly in the foxtrot . . . the tears raining down her cheeks.

Mère Colline hung over her ledger at her desk . . . but tears fell on to the open pages, blotting the ink, and at length she laid down her pen, and her grey head fell forward on her arm.

At the top of the stairs The Rat paused to take breath. He broke a piece off the loaf which was sticking out of his pocket and began to eat it hungrily. As he chewed he listened to the sound of the music which followed him up . . . and peering down he could just see Mou-Mou, arms stretched out. She looked as though she were crucified by the agony of her grief. She urged them on to dance . . . sobbing as though her heart were broken.

'Mou-Mou,' The Rat whispered her name. 'Brave, faithful little thing!'

Then he stumbled out into the darkness. He did not know where he was going. But he had food and wine to carry him on a little further. He would never have returned to 'The White Coffin' tonight but that he had been driven by the sheer torture of hunger grown unbearable.

When Otto had beaten him to his knees and drawn blood from him with that knife he had wanted to die . . . he had felt that nothing save death could end his misery. But now, after the queer kindness shown him by his old friends and the touching devotion of Mou-Mou, some faint spirit of courage, of the will to live, to fight on, pierced through the thick wall of despair which had encased his soul for long days. He had told Mou-Mou that he would win through somehow . . . somewhere . . . he would like to repay her for her love and her loyalty. Well, he would. And more than that, he would triumph over himself . . . rise in spite of himself . . . wash himself clean, although Zélie de Chaumet had flung him into the mire.

He raised his white face to the sky, where a million stars glittered, and a young moon hung like a pale crescent of ivory light over the house tops of Montmartre. For the first time for long, unspeakable days, he felt his old independent will, his old pride struggling to the fore. The mists in his poor, dulled brain cleared away. He had been beaten . . . broken . . . he had become a Thing without name, without purpose, without hope. But out of the wreckage he would reclaim his own personality, his own soul. Out of the débris, the ashes, the triumphant Phoenix should rise.

A great cry went up from his soul.

'God help me . . . Christ have mercy . . . help me to begin again . . . give me another chance!'

He moved through the mean alleys, the reeking, cobbled slums of Montmartre, like one in a trance . . . eyes fixed on the stars . . . heart and soul bathed in the white splendour of one increasing purpose.

He reached a crowded thoroughfare and began to cross the road oblivious of his surroundings, of the traffic, or the people; his transfigured face upraised to the sky.

A gendarme, directing the traffic, saw the ragged, stumbling figure . . . a strange spectacle of a man clasping a loaf and a bottle of wine to his breast . . . walking blindly in and out of the swift-moving vehicles on the wide road. A taxi turned the corner and bore down upon that reckless figure . . . The gendarme shouted to him.

'*Attention . . . mon Dieu . . . prenez garde!*'

But it was too late. The Rat neither heard the warning nor saw the taxi. The driver pulled up with a harsh grinding of brakes, but the right mudguard had caught The Rat in the side. He went down like a ninepin. The bottle of wine crashed into a thousand pieces, broken glass tinkled on to the road, and the red wine ran out, soaking the tattered coat of The Rat and mixing with the more sinister red of blood which welled out of his body.

He lay there in the muddy road without moving, eyes closed, white face, curiously serene and smiling, upturned to the stars.

CHAPTER TWENTY-ONE

Pierre Boucheron, The Rat, remained for nearly four months in the hospital to which he had been taken after his accident. The injuries he had received were bad, and, in addition, pneumonia and pleurisy set in, brought about by the frightful exposure and starvation which he had suffered for so many weeks.

That he did not die, to the doctors and nurses was nothing short of a miracle. He ought to have died. He was terribly ill, unconscious, raving in delirium for days and nights, and little hope of his recovery was entertained by those in charge of him. He was worn to skin and bone and he had no vitality left to fight fever and sickness. Yet he lived. He had an iron constitution and he pulled through after hovering on the borders of death for weeks.

The doctors visiting the casualty ward to which he had been taken were interested in his case. They had all predicted death for him. It was interesting to discover that he refused to die. The nurses—excellent, capable creatures—believed that it was sheer will-power that saved him. He had the desire, the will to live. Of course they did not understand . . . but he understood, months later, when he was well and strong again, what had been at the back of his mind, keeping the flicker of life alight in his feeble body. The determination to triumph over himself . . . and, in time to come, over those who had tried to destroy him . . .

Even when he reached the convalescent stage, the matron of the big General Hospital, and the doctors and nurses in charge of the case, took more than an ordinary interest in this strange patient. The house surgeon had several private chats with him and saw for himself that although he had been brought to the hospital emaciated and in rags and tatters Boucheron had seen better times. He was a clever and cultured man. The doctor decided to help him. He sent Pierre to a convalescent home in St. Lunaire, and even provided him with a decent suit of clothes. By the end of July Boucheron should be strong enough to work. The kindly doctor wanted to aid him in the search for employment. But Pierre, his old pride renewed, and full of new-born courage, told the good man that he meant to find work without assistance. It was Pierre's desire now to help himself . . . to win through without help from anyone. Zélie, after her meeting with him that night outside the café, had withdrawn Benoit. He was certain of that. He could look for work without fearing the old, frightful persecution.

It was a very altered Pierre who left the convalescent home by the sea in St. Lunaire, at the end of July, and returned to Paris to 'make good'. The skeleton-like Rat had vanished. This in many ways was the old Boucheron, shoulders erect; face thin but healthily bronzed by sunshine and sea air; dark eyes alert, keen, purposeful again. But there was something more in his face than there had been in the face of the old Boucheron whom Madeleine de l'Orme had known and loved; a tightened mouth, which showed a firmer spirit; a rather grim smile, the smile of a man who would not be easily influenced . . . and whose knowledge and experiences of his own weakness had become his strength.

It would not be easy for anybody on earth, man or woman, to bring this new Pierre to his knees.

It was on Sunday, the 2nd of August, 1914, that Pierre Boucheron, The Rat, returned to Paris from St. Lunaire and found that gay capital in chaos . . . men running hither and thither, women standing at their front doors, with grave, anxious faces, bugles sounding, newspaper boys rushing down the streets with glaring posters . . .

GERMANY DECLARES WAR UPON FRANCE . . .

Pierre with that sudden sense of wild excitement which must have gripped the heart of every man in France that day realised that his country had been plunged into a great war. The sons of France were being called upon to help gallant little Belgium stem the vast, destructive tide of human devils that threatened to swamp her out of existence.

Pierre bought a newspaper, gave one look at the headlines, then dropped the paper and turned his steps grimly in the direction of the Quai d'Orsay. Who knew the way there better than he, once under-secretary? And never had he walked there with swifter footsteps, with a more thrilling heart. France was at war, and Pierre Boucheron automatically, like every son of France, became a soldier ready to fight for her to the death.

As he walked along, shoulders erect, head flung back, a little smile of secret exultation curved his lips. To him this meant so much more than it would have meant had he been leading a normal life; been a normal citizen of Paris. But he had been through frightful sorrow . . . frightful despair . . . he was only just reborn . . . he had only just conquered himself . . . and he was prepared to fight for France, fired by wild enthusiasm such as he had not known since his boyhood.

Here was his chance . . . the chance for which he had prayed and hungered. He would go to war. If need be he would shed his blood for France . . . If he were spared he would come back to commence life again and fight his own secret battles. Meanwhile nothing mattered except war. Old griefs, old feuds were temporarily submerged in this white fire of enthusiasm and excitement which burnt him, body and soul.

Outside the doors of the biggest recruiting office in Paris surged a sea of men almost as eager and willing to be led to the slaughter as The Rat. The atmosphere was charged with an excitement which was only slightly tempered by gravity. These were serious and anxious times . . . but on that first day of the declaration of war the thrill dominated . . . famine, heart-break, all the hideous carnage of war were to come later.

When Pierre had finally worked his way into the office and been detailed off to the -th battalion he found himself side by side with an old friend.

René Duval, as exquisitely dressed as ever, white spats, top hat, flower in his buttonhole and monocle in his eye. He had been one of the first to rejoin his old regiment.

When Duval saw the tall, graceful figure of the man in rather shabby clothes, standing, shoulder to shoulder with him, he gave a start, dropped his monocle, and stared harder. That thin, clear-cut face with the dark eyes which were alight with enthusiasm; that wonderful head with the black, smooth hair . . . surely they were very familiar? René gulped, then uttered the name of his old friend, joyfully:

'Boucheron . . . *mon Dieu* . . . it's Boucheron!'

Pierre took the hand Duval offered, his face reddening as he recollected their last painful meeting.

'How are you, Duval?' he said.

'Joining up, old boy,' said Duval. 'And you, too, eh?'

'Yes, thank God,' said Pierre.

'Have you your orders?'

'Yes. I go down to — tonight . . .' he mentioned a big command outside Paris.

'And I return to the Chasseurs Alpins as second-lieutenant.'

Pierre looked at Duval, something of the old

friendly humour in his gaze.

'For the sake of the becoming uniform, eh, *mon cher*? That horizon-blue is what the Americans call "stunning".'

René guffawed.

'Sarcastic as ever, Boucheron . . . sarcastic as ever! . . . Well, my dear fellow, you may be right. That horizon-blue suits me down to the ground. When I'm in my uniform I shall get a few glad eyes from the ladies, what? The "cold shoulder" with a bit of gold braid on it, what, what? That'll fetch 'em!'

He roared with laughter. Pierre regarded him a trifle sadly. The sight of Duval and the sound of that familiar, falsetto laughter recalled days, the memory of which Pierre had buried and which hurt too much to revive. Yet it was good to see the poor fool again. It was impossible for Pierre to forget that Duval had shown him friendship and kindness when everyone else had deserted him. He put an arm through Duval's.

'Shall we have a drink somewhere?'

'Yes—I have a few minutes to spare—then I must get home and say goodbye to all the girls,' said René, stroking his moustache, and his eyes gleamed at the thought of himself in the horizon-blue uniform and becoming képi and belt.

Lieut. René Duval, of the Chasseurs Alpins, was killed in action against the enemy in August, '16 . . . just two years after his chance meeting with Boucheron at the Quai d'Orsay. He died gallantly, the poor fop . . . for Duval for all his imbecilities was at heart a very gallant little gentleman. But no shadow or thought of death troubled him this bright morning of August 2nd.

He accompanied Boucheron to an open-air café and sat talking and smoking with him, in excellent spirits.

'It is good to see you again, Boucheron,' he said, and then, tactfully omitting the mention of their last painful meeting, he added: 'Where in the world have you been all these months?'

Boucheron sat back in his chair and stared at the crowds passing to and fro before them.

'In hell,' he answered briefly.

Duval pursed his lips in thoughtful fashion.

'And you are now about to face another, eh, *mon cher*?'

'War is a pastime compared to the hell through which I have just passed,' said Pierre with a grim smile. 'But don't let us discuss myself. Tell me news of—all the others.'

'Shall I speak of Madeleine?'

'I would like to know how she fares,' said Pierre, his face dark red.

'She is well, but an anxiety to her mother because she has grown so quiet and refuses to marry,' said Duval. 'Candidly, my dear Boucheron, it is my impression that she grieves for you.'

Pierre's hands clenched over the sides of his

chair. The red flush died, leaving his cheeks white under the tan. His eyes half-closed. Then he gave a careless laugh.

'That is your romantic mind at work, *mon cher*. I do not think the Comtesse de l'Orme can grieve for—a Rat.'

Duval looked at him with pity. It was obvious that Boucheron had suffered abominably these months during which Paris Society had neither seen nor heard of him. He thought it might be best to drop the subject of Madeleine.

'Do you remember that little dark-eyed maid at Château Lernac with the saucy mouth?' he asked, his eyes brightening.

Pierre nodded. He did not remember, but for the moment his heart was thudding so painfully with the thought of Madeleine that he could not speak. Madeleine, grown quiet . . . refusing to marry . . . Madeleine grieving for *him* . . . oh, God, if he thought that true . . .

'She was a little devil, that girl,' continued Duval. 'I took your advice, my dear Boucheron, and having once given her the warm embrace I tried the cold shoulder. And it worked . . . beautifully. You were ever a marvel with the girls, Boucheron. I owe it to you that I won a good many kisses from that naughty girl whenever I went to see *Tante* Henriette and Madeleine. You should have seen her sigh for them, too!'

Boucheron finished his drink and rose. The

mention of Madeleine had made him restive. He laid a hand on Duval's shoulder.

'Well, I must be off,' he said. '*Au revoir*, Duval, and good luck to you when you face the guns. We may meet again.'

'*À bientôt*,' said Duval. 'And good luck to you, Boucheron . . . Ah, *ciel*!' he added in a hushed voice.

'What is it?'

'Look,' said Duval, excitedly.

He indicated a pretty girl in a pink summery frock, with bare, sunburned arms, and a pink crinoline hat on her fair head, who was just passing them. She had looked over her shoulder at Boucheron, but Duval had taken the look unto himself.

'I'm off,' he said, sticking his monocle in his eye. 'Consider to yourself, my dear Boucheron, the beauty of those ankles . . . the trimness of that waist.'

He waved a goodbye and hurried after the girl in pink. Boucheron, lighting a cigarette, watched him in some amusement. He saw the golden-haired one toss her head and march on when Duval spoke to her. Duval fell back, crestfallen, shrugging his shoulders. Boucheron, his cigarette alight, turned and walked away, smiling a trifle sadly. The incident was so absurd, yet so reminiscent of old and happier days.

He never saw René Duval again.

Once he had exchanged his mufti for the

blue, baggy trousers and ill-fitting coat of the poilu he had little time to think of Madeleine. He happened to be posted to a battalion which left for Belgium almost at once. He was plunged into the very heart of the inferno. He wrote two cards before he left for the Front—one to *M. le docteur* at the hospital, who had shown him kindness and interest; one to Mou-Mou, poor little Mou-Mou of the faithful and loving heart.

Mou-Mou received that card when her spirits were at lowest ebb. War, to her, to all the girls in 'The White Coffin', was a terror and an anxiety; a greedy monster, devouring all the sons of France. The café was practically empty night after night, from the day that war was declared until the first troops came back on leave.

Mou-Mou hugged The Rat's card of farewell to her breast and sobbed over it passionately. But it brought her untold happiness because it showed that he had not forgotten and it gave her hope . . . the hope that after all she would see her Rat again if he were spared.

Pierre Boucheron, *poilu*, found himself in a crowded troop-train at an important station not far from Versailles, bound for the Front.

He hung out of the window of his carriage, which was crammed with chattering, gesticulating soldiers, and so hot and thick with tobacco smoke that one could scarcely breathe. The August morning was blazing hot, and the perspiration ran down Pierre's cheeks. He pushed his tin helmet on to the back of his head and leaned as far out of the window as he could get without falling, a fag-end between his lips. He was glad that he was going to see some fighting. He wanted it. He was still burning with enthusiasm, and he looked lean and fit after three weeks of military discipline and training. His face was dark brown; his long, lithe body had regained all its old grace and vigour.

The scene at the station on which he looked was a typical one when a troop-train was about to depart for the field of action. Several of the *poilus*, burdened with their field-kit, hung about the platform, smoking and talking to their women-folk. Old women, young matrons, slips of girls in their voluminous skirts and shawls, mothers with babes in their arms and older children beside them, were bidding farewell to fathers, brothers, husbands, sweethearts. Men and women of every type . . . of every class . . . united in this hour by a common bond; the enthusiasm of the soldier about to receive his baptism of fire; the sorrow of the woman dreading lest she should never look upon her man again.

A little to the right of Pierre, a young officer stood beside a beautifully-dressed girl, whose hands were clasped in his. Her eyes were brave and bright, as she tried not to let him see her tears.

They were lovers, thought Pierre . . . and he sighed a little. It was nice to have some girl to see one off; to know that somebody at home would be thinking of one, would care whether one lived or died.

Then suddenly his heart gave a terrific leap, and he gripped the window-ledge so hard that his knuckles shone white. For he saw two women coming slowly down the platform; well-dressed women; one of mature years, one a slender girl in a white linen dress, a white shady hat on her fair head. Pierre stared only at the girl, his dark eyes brilliant with excitement, almost with fear.

It was Madeleine de l'Orme and her mother. They were distributing fruit and chocolate from two baskets to every carriage-full of men.

As he watched Madeleine approach Pierre's heart beat so fast that he thought it would choke him. Hungrily he looked at her . . . taking in every detail of her appearance. How sweet, how lovely she was; as lovely as ever; the pure, exquisite Madeleine of his dreams . . . his poor, broken dreams.

She was two carriages away from him now and had not seen him.

A piercing whistle; a sudden commotion on the platform warned Pierre that the train was about to depart. The soldiers were bidding goodbye to their women-folk and entering their compartments. The wheels of the train began to revolve.

Pierre felt suddenly sick with the longing to speak to Madeleine . . . to look into her eyes once again . . . touch her hand . . . before he went into action. He might be killed. Who knew? It would be good to go into eternity with Madeleine's pardon, Madeleine's blessing.

He gave a hoarse cry.

'Madeleine!'

She looked up, startled, bright-eyed, and saw the young *poilu* leaning out of the carriage window, beckoning to her. For one paralysing instant she stared at his face . . . familiar . . . yet altered; thinner, browner, and in some indescribable way more boyish.

Then she dropped the basket she was carrying and rushed to him, panting, cheeks on fire, eyes beautiful in their brilliance, their joy.

'Pierre!' she said.

He looked into those eyes, all his soul in one long look. He gripped the two slender hands she gave him. The train was moving out very slowly, but she walked along with him like that, hands enclasped, eyes never leaving his. After all the months of separation, of agony, of despair, through which these two had passed, it was heaven to be together . . . yet infinite pain to meet thus, only to part again.

'Pierre, Pierre,' said Madeleine. 'You are a soldier . . . you are going into action!'

'Yes,' he said. 'Give me your blessing before I go, Madeleine . . . tell me you forgive . . .'

'I forgave long ago,' she said, the tears gushing into her eyes and pouring down her cheeks. 'Oh, Pierre, I never forgot . . . never will forget you!'

'You still care?' he asked incredulously.

'Yes, I still love you, Pierre.'

'I adore you,' he said, his eyes rapt, fixed on her face. 'Oh, my beloved . . . I can die gladly now that I know you do not despise me.'

The train was moving out of the station more quickly now. Her hands clung desperately to his. She started to run, to keep up with him; her heart was nearly bursting with the poignant emotion of it all. He caught one of her hands to his lips and pressed a burning kiss upon it.

'Goodbye, goodbye, Madeleine, *mon coeur*,' he said.

'Goodbye . . . and God spare you, Pierre,' she said, sobbing.

'If I only had something of yours . . . to keep . . . to cherish,' he said hoarsely. 'Oh, Madeleine . . .'

Quickly she drew a marquise ring from her right hand . . . a beautiful thing of antique stones, and flung it to him. He caught it . . . his brown face transfigured with happiness. She saw him kiss it and put it in his breast pocket. Then she had to stand back . . . sobbing, panting . . . no longer able to keep up with the fast-moving train. She stood there, half-blinded by tears, waving him out of sight.

Pierre Boucheron took his seat and buried his face in his hands. The good-natured *poilus* around him slapped him on the shoulder and comforted him. They were emotional . . . they loved . . . they had suffered the agonies of parting and they understood.

'*Courage, mon ami*,' said one of them. 'It is not of necessity the end of us.'

Pierre raised his face. His lashes were wet but he gave the smile of one who has caught a glimpse of heaven, and his hand covered his breast pocket wherein he had placed Madeleine's ring.

'No, no, it is not the end,' he said. 'For me, anyhow, it is the beginning! . . .'

We hope you have enjoyed this Large Print book. Other Chivers Press or G.K. Hall & Co. Large Print books are available at your library or directly from the publishers.

For more information about current and forthcoming titles, please call or write, without obligation, to:

Chivers Press Limited
Windsor Bridge Road
Bath BA2 3AX
England
Tel. (01225) 335336

OR

G.K. Hall & Co.
P.O. Box 159
Thorndike, Maine 04986
USA
Tel. (800) 223-2336

All our Large Print titles are designed for easy reading, and all our books are made to last.